CONSPIRACY TO SPY

SCOTT MATTHEWS

BOOKS

By Scott Matthews

The Adam Drake Series

Vinci Books

vinci-books.com

Published by Vinci Books Ltd in 2026

1

A CIP catalogue record for this book is available from the British Library.

Paperback ISBN: 9781036707071

The EU GPSR authorised representative is Logos Europe, 9 rue Nicolas Poussion, 17000 La Rochelle, France
contact@logoseurope.eu

CONSPIRACY /ken-spiŕ a-sē/

noun:

1. An agreement to perform an illegal, wrongful, or subversive act together.
2. A group of conspirators.
3. An agreement between two or more persons to commit a crime or accomplish a legal purpose through illegal action.

To the Founders, who added the Bill of Rights and the Fourth Amendment to the U.S. Constitution to protect citizens from unreasonable searches and seizures that are the cornerstone of a right to privacy.

Chapter One

ADAM DRAKE ENTERED the Signature LAS FBO customer lounge at the Las Vegas McCarran International Airport and saw his contact waving his hand.

Chandler Patterson was a former U.S. Congressman from Nevada and a friend of President Benjamin Ballard. Patterson was the reason Drake had flown to Las Vegas.

Patterson was a practicing lawyer before running for the U.S. Congress and serving five terms. He now owns a string of Ford car dealerships in Nevada and was one of the civic leaders who organized and sponsored the Formula One Grand Prix in Las Vegas.

He was a little under six feet tall, with a full head of wavy gray hair, and wearing a navy blue polo shirt, tan linen pants, and loafers that morning. As he approached, his confident stride and athletic build indicated that Chandler Patterson hadn't settled for a sedentary life of leisure just yet.

"Thank you for coming," Patterson said, holding his hand out.

"Hard to say no to the president when he asks you to help his friend in Las Vegas, and the Formula One Grand Prix circus happens to be in town," Drake admitted. "I understand you were instrumental in getting the Grand Prix to come here."

Patterson smiled and said, "My son was the one who suggested I get involved. He's the racing driver in the family. You'll meet him tonight at dinner. Are you hungry?"

"What do you have in mind?"

"I have lunch at the Nine Fine Irishmen pub every Wednesday," Patterson said. "It's not far. Is that okay?"

"That sounds good," Drake said. "Is Patterson Irish, by any chance?"

"It is, didn't you know," he said with a proper Irish accent.

Drake followed Patterson, pulling his silver rolling luggage out of the terminal facility, and stopped beside a new black Ford F-150 Lightning truck parked at the curb. Patterson unlocked it and tossed the key fob to Drake. "Have you driven an all-electric truck?"

Drake caught the fob and shook his head. "I haven't driven a truck in a long time, let alone an electric-powered one."

"You'll want to drive this one. It does zero to sixty in under four seconds."

"That's as fast as my Porsche Cayman!"

"They're amazing vehicles," Patterson said. "I wish I could sell a few more of them. Since Ford cut production of the Lightning to meet 'consumer demand' for EV trucks, I have fifteen of them parked on the lot at my dealership."

Drake opened the rear door of the Lightning, stowed his luggage, and got behind the wheel for his first EV experience.

Patterson joined him in the cab and said, "Don't worry, you won't have to drive around in this while you're here. I had Chris bring a new Dark Horse Mustang in from my dealership. You can use it this weekend."

"You didn't need to do that," Drake said.

"It's the least I can do to thank you for coming to find out if my son is in danger."

As they left the FBO, Drake concentrated on driving the car and followed Patterson's directions to the New York New York Hotel and Casino, where they were having lunch. He postponed asking Patterson for more information about his son until later.

President Ballard told him Chandler Patterson would give him the details when he asked Drake to take on a special assignment in Las Vegas. Chandler Patterson's son, Chris Patterson, was a President's Intelligence Advisory Board (PIAB) staffer. He'd prepared an updated report on the intelligence communities' domestic surveillance of U.S. citizens, which was scheduled to be presented to the PIAB next week.

Patterson told the president he became concerned when he learned his son was receiving an elaborate and expensive award from the American Karting Foundation, a non-profit corporation he'd never heard of. Chris was a Las Vegas SuperKarts racing hero and later raced in the IndyCar Lights series. Until he crashed at the Road America course doing a hundred and fifty miles an hour, spent six months recovering from his injuries, and quit racing.

The suspicious award was meant to honor his son's influence on local kart racing, according to a letter from the president of the A.K.F. But the award included more than an engraved plaque. There was also an expensive membership in the Bellagio's Fountain Club for the Formula One

Grand Prix that was sold for $11,247.00 a person. The membership included a prime viewing seat in the Fountain grandstand built out over the Bellagio Fountain, several meet and greets with Formula One drivers, and food from celebrity chefs at the club's indoor and rooftop hospitality decks.

Chandler Patterson was proud of his son's racing success but knew there were other national karting champions with more successful and longer racing careers. The award was over the top for someone no longer involved in the sport.

Patterson told the president the whole thing smelled, and he worried it might have something to do with the updated PIAB report. Chandler Patterson had served on the House Permanent Select Committee on Intelligence when he was in the House of Representatives. He knew how sensitive the intelligence community (IC) was about being accused of spying on Americans. A federal court had found a previous NSA surveillance program called PRISM violated the civil rights of Americans by collecting private emails and digital messages.

Two U.S. Senators were currently making noise and claiming that the IC was still spying on Americans. If Chris's report confirmed that, Patterson and the president both knew the IC wasn't above playing dirty when it had a secret it didn't want to be exposed.

When they walked into Patterson's pub, Drake saw why Patterson liked the place. The pub had been built in Ireland and shipped to Las Vegas as an epic-sized monument to Irish tradition to be housed in the hotel.

Patterson explained that the pub was named after nine famous Irish men. Depending on whose side of history you were on, they were remembered as both patriotic heroes and traitorous rebels. The men had fought for Irish independence and lost. After being tried, convicted, and sentenced to death, the British monarchy was afraid they would become martyrs, so it commuted their sentences. The men were exiled to Tasmania, and their tale became a legendary example of Irish heroism.

"It's a nice story," Patterson said, "and I'm proud of my Irish ancestry, but I come here for the food. The Shepherd's Pie is my favorite."

Drake decided to stick with his favorite and ordered Fish and Chips.

Chapter Two

A MILE away in the Premium Penthouse Suite at the Bellagio Casino and Hotel, two men stood at the window looking down at the Bellagio Fountain and the Bellagio Club Grandstand.

Daniel Franklin, CEO and founder of Franklin Analytics, was drinking a GreyGoose vodka martini from a cocktail glass. Marcus Braxton, president and founder of the Braxton Group, drank Woodford Reserve Bourbon from a tumbler. Both men were particular about the alcohol they drank.

"Where is he now?" Franklin asked.

"He's at the family's home at the Summit Club in Summerlin, visiting his mother," Braxton said.

"When will he be at the hotel to meet your man?"

"Williams is meeting him at the Petrosian Bar downstairs at six and giving him his Fountain Club membership card."

"And the girl?"

"She'll be at the Fountain Club. Williams will introduce

her as Patterson's hostess and take him to the meet and greets and events he'll participate in," Braxton said.

"Is there any chance she'll be recognized in Vegas?"

"No, we flew her in from Paris last night. She'll fly back when we have what we need."

Franklin's phone vibrated in his pocket, and he stepped away to take the call.

Braxton walked to the wet bar and refilled his tumbler, watching Franklin out of the corner of his eye. He'd worked for Franklin's company before, but this was the first time he'd spent any time with the man himself.

Franklin became wealthy in the 1990s when he sold his breakthrough cyber security software company for six hundred million dollars. In the early 2000s, when criminal organizations began funding professional hackers to attack corporations and governments to steal data they could use to manipulate and make millions, Franklin recognized that personal data had the potential to be more valuable than gold.

He became a data broker, started Franklin Analytics, and was one of the most successful entrepreneurs selling personal data to corporations and governments. Not surprisingly, his largest clients were the NSA, CIA, and FBI. Although the government was forbidden to collect personal data from American citizens, a loophole in the law allowed it to buy the data from private third parties, like Franklin Analytics.

Braxton was amused by how Franklin dressed, trying to disguise his wealth. Staying alone in the lavish luxury of the Bellagio's Premium Penthouse Suite, Franklin was wearing an old gray long-sleeve Henley shirt, jeans, and a pair of scuffed-up Stan Smith Adidas. The man owned a twenty-million-dollar brownstone in Boston's Back Bay, kept a classic thirty-eight-meter sailing yacht at the Corinthian Yacht Club, and played tennis twice a week at the Tennis & Racquet Club, for heaven's sake.

There was more to Daniel Franklin than he wanted the world to know, and Braxton knew most of it. Franklin sold personal data around the world to anyone willing to pay top dollar for it: foreign governments, people looking for dirt they could use to blackmail someone, and transnational criminal organizations. He knew about Franklin's dark side because his company, the Braxton Group, provided personal close protection for Franklin and security for his company and its offices.

In many ways, he and Franklin were very similar. He started his company after leaving the CIA to provide a similar service, selling business intelligence to other U.S. government agencies, corporations, and countries world-wide as the owner of a private intelligence company.

And like Franklin, he would do whatever was necessary to protect his company and the life it provided him. Most of Franklin Analytics' revenue came from selling personal data to American governmental agencies. The report young Chris Patterson updated for the President's Intelligence Advisory Board, scheduled to be delivered next week, could arouse Congress and pass a bill prohibiting U.S. govern-mental agencies from buying personal data from third parties.

That's why Franklin hired the Braxton Group: to ensure that the report was discredited and ignored by any means Braxton felt necessary. Franklin was protecting his company, and Braxton would do the same.

Franklin ended the call and returned to stand next to Braxton. "That was my CIA friend asking for reassurance they didn't need to worry about Patterson's report."

"What did you tell him?"

"That you assured me they didn't need to worry."

"That's overstating it a little. The report will reach the PIAB. We can't prevent that. Even if we succeed, there's still a chance Congress will do something, even if no one pays attention to Patterson's report. They took a chance when they continued citizen surveillance after PRISM. They can stand a slap on the wrist. They've done it before."

"It's different this time, and I'm not sure why," Franklin said. "They don't trust the president to understand what they're doing is necessary and work with them. Neither do I."

"Maybe they need to find a way to make sure the president understands."

"How?"

"By having evidence of the security risks they'll discover from profiles you put together on Americans from the personal data you collect. They can use them to persuade the president surveillance is necessary."

"They thought of that," Franklin said. "They were successful before with that kind of operation when they discredited General Petraeus with fabricated information about his girlfriend to keep a lid on the Benghazi fiasco. They want to try this way first."

Braxton's phone beeped twice, and he listened to the call without speaking. "Patterson left home and drove to his dad's dealership. They'll let me know when he leaves to come here. I'll make sure the honey for our trap is ready for her night."

Chapter Three

CHANDLER PATTERSON FINISHED his Shepherd's Pie and said, "Congressman Matthew Bridge is a friend of mine. He told me what you did for him when his son was killed last year. The president asked you then to help Matthew, and you did. He's done the same thing for me when I told him I was worried about my son. He could have asked the FBI to investigate this, but he asked you instead. May I ask why?"

"The president encouraged my company last year to branch out and form a private intelligence division," Drake said, "for times when he wants something done outside official channels."

"And this is one of those times?"

"It is."

"Because it involves the intelligence community?"

"By asking us to look into something involving a report on the IC, so he knows he'll get a report he can trust."

"So, what now? Where will you start?" Patterson asked.

"The American Karting Foundation. I have someone

checking out the foundation and its president. Have you met him?"

"No. His name is Walter Williams. Chris is meeting him for a drink at six this evening. I'm going to drop by and introduce myself."

"Where are they meeting?"

"The Petrosian Bar at the Bellagio."

"I'll get there ahead of you. Join me after you've introduced yourself," Drake said. "What does Chris think about this award and the Fountain Club membership?"

"He called me when he got the letter from Williams. He's flattered, of course. He loved karting but was suspicious when he learned the award included a Fountain Club membership."

"Has he been suspicious about anything else that's happened recently?"

"Not that he mentioned. He broke off a relationship with a woman he'd been seeing for six months. But that didn't have anything to do with this report. He works long hours, and she wanted to see him more often than she did."

"Has his report been circulated? Who knows about it?"

"The President's Intelligence Advisory Board and the members of the board, who authorized the report six months ago. But they won't see it until he presents it next week."

"The president appoints the members of the PIAB, and several of them have a background in the intelligence community," Drake said. "So, the IC will know about Chris's report since he was assigned to work on it."

"And they will know he's talked with the two senators who are claiming they have information the CIA is running a domestic surveillance program like PRISM again," Patterson added.

Drake shook his head. "I just can't see the intelligence community getting involved in a phony award like this for your son, Chandler. The president already distrusts the CIA. Finding out they're up to their old tricks won't surprise him. If the IC is involved, there must be more to this."

"You think I overreacted out of concern for my son?" Patterson asked.

"No, I think you acted like any father would, given your experience in Congress," Drake said. "I can't see anyone going to all this trouble over a report that only the president will pay any attention to."

"I hope you're right," Patterson said and signaled to their waiter for the check. "Are you ready to see where you're staying while you're here? It's a condo I own just down the strip from here. When I heard you were coming, I tried to find something close to the Bellagio, but rooms there have been booked for months around here for the Grand Prix. I hope you don't mind sharing it with Chris. We couldn't talk him into staying with us this weekend."

"Not at all," Drake said. "I appreciate your hospitality. Liz couldn't find a room close to the strip for me either."

"How is your wife doing, by the way? The president said you're expecting your first child."

"She's fine, trying to hurry along these last two months."

"Boy or girl?" Patterson asked.

"Her doctor says it's a boy, but we'll wait and see. Liz was supposed to be a boy when she was born."

Patterson laughed and said, "Doc got it wrong with me too. I was supposed to be a girl."

Walking across the self-parking lot at the New York New York Hotel and Casino to the Mustang Dark Horse Patterson was letting him drive while he was there, Drake asked, "Does your son like what he's doing in Washington?"

"He likes the work and hates the city. D.C. wasn't great when I was in Congress, but it's a cesspool now. I'm not sure how long Chris will be there."

"What will he do if he leaves?"

"I hope he'll come here and open a law office," Patterson said. "He talks about it, but he's intrigued with intelligence work. We'll see."

"I look forward to meeting him," Drake said. "Chris might wind up with a career path like mine."

"Did you work in intelligence?"

"No, Special Forces after law school. Then, I worked in the District Attorney's office in Portland before opening my law office. Now I'm the head of the Special Operations at Puget Sound Security and troubleshoot for the president occasionally."

"When we have time," Patterson said, "I'd like to hear more about what that involves."

"If we have time, I'll tell you."

Drake drove down the strip a short way and turned left onto East Aria Place, following Patterson's directions. The condo was in the Veer Towers, twin 37-story luxury condominium towers that tilted at a five-degree angle in opposite directions.

"The condo is on the thirty-second floor," Patterson said. "I bought it as an investment and can't bring myself to sell it. The view of the city is spectacular."

Chapter Four

AFTER SHOWING Drake around his condo, Patterson left him alone and walked the long block to the Petrosian Bar at the Bellagio to meet his son and the president of the American Karting Foundation.

Before Drake unpacked his luggage, he stood before the floor-to-ceiling window, looking down at the Las Vegas strip, and called Liz.

"Hi beautiful, how are you feeling?" he asked.

"Little thumper is kicking up a storm this morning," she said. "I'm fine, wishing you were here."

"I'd like to be, you know that, but I'll be back soon," Drake promised. "I might slip out before the race Saturday night. I think Patterson may have overreacted when he called the president."

"Don't you dare leave before that race. I know how much you've wanted to attend a Formula One race. Make sure there's nothing he and the president need to worry about, and then come home."

"I will," he said. "Wish you could see this view of the

strip from Patterson's condo. It is spectacular."

"Take a picture and send it to me," Liz said. "For now, be safe and enjoy the race."

"Oh, if I must. I'll call you tonight."

"I love you."

"I love you too," he said.

As much as he'd wanted to help President Ballard and fly to Las Vegas, leaving Liz in Seattle had been hard when she was getting so close to having their baby. Not much he could do to help her with that, but he wanted to be there if she needed him. But then she'd stood with her hands on her hips, tapping her foot on the floor, until he said yes, he would go. Now, he hoped he wouldn't regret not being there if she had their son and he wasn't there.

Drake changed out of his travel clothes and put on a white poplin dress shirt open at the neck, black slacks, a dove-gray blazer, and a pair of his favorite black plain-toe Derby dress shoes. Chandler Patterson said there wasn't a dress code at the Petrosian Bar, but he didn't know where the night would take him. Better to be well dressed than not.

He stowed his luggage in the closet of the bedroom Patterson said was his for the night, made sure the key card was in his pocket, and left the luxury modern condo to follow Patterson to the Bellagio.

A quick ride down thirty-two floors in the elevator to the lobby and Drake was out on the sidewalk on a warm November afternoon. He turned left and walked to South Las Vegas Boulevard, past the steps to the Harmon Bridge, and continued walking toward the Bellagio.

The last time he was in Las Vegas, there hadn't been time to walk the strip and look at the hotels and casinos around the layout of the race circuit for the Grand Prix, like the Cosmopolitan Las Vegas ahead on the left, Planet

Hollywood across the boulevard, the Bellagio and ten more like them around the track.

The three-point-eight-mile street circuit with cars speeding past at two hundred miles an hour at night promised to be a Grand Prix race like no other in the world. Chandler and the other organizers had a right to be proud of what they had accomplished in bringing Formula One to Las Vegas.

When he reached Bellagio Drive, he paused to look at the Fountain Club Grandstand built out over a portion of the eight-acre manmade lake alongside the racetrack, with the famous Bellagio Fountains rising in the air behind it.

Drake suddenly sensed that someone nearby was staring at him, and he recognized an old sensation. It was known as morphic resonance or somaesthesia, and he knew to trust it. It had saved his life on more than one occasion when he was walking through tribal villages in Afghanistan where Taliban fighters were hiding.

He pivoted and scanned the faces of the people behind him. Ten feet back, a young couple was walking arm-in-arm and laughing. A man in his twenties with a camera walked around the couple and passed Drake without looking at him. He was wearing a baseball cap, a plain white T-shirt, jeans, and running shoes and moved away quickly.

Drake considered following him when he saw another man stopping to light his cigar. He was older and overweight, wearing black shorts, a cream-colored guayabera shirt, and a Panama hat with a black band. He puffed on the cigar and smiled at Drake before turning and walking away.

He'd been in Las Vegas for two hours and was being followed! Maybe there was something to Patterson's concerns. None of the people who knew why he was in Las

Vegas had any reason to have him followed, and the only places he'd been after leaving the airport were Patterson's Irish pub and his condo. This meant someone wanted to know who he was and why he'd been with Chandler Patterson.

Drake looked around to see if another watcher had replaced the man with the cigar. When he didn't see one, he walked up West Bellagio Drive and into the lobby of the hotel and casino, determined to find out what was happening.

Chapter Five

THE PETROSIAN BAR was directly across from the front desk of the Bellagio, and Drake heard someone playing a version of the Eagles "Hotel California" on a piano inside.

When asked if he wanted to sit at the bar or at a table in the next room, he said a table for two and asked, "Who is that on the piano? It sounds like Peter Osborne, the Pianist to the Presidents."

"It is," the waitress said. "He plays at the Bellagio when he's not on tour. Would you like a table close to his piano?"

"Anywhere will be fine, thank you."

The upscale Petrosian reminded him of a European lounge bar, like the bar at the Monte Carlo casino he'd seen in a movie. It had high sculpted ceilings, gold chandeliers, intricate wall panels, and groupings of high-back uphol-stered dining chairs placed around small round tables.

"Would you like something while you wait for your friend?" his hostess asked, handing him a Petrosian menu.

"Maker's Mark, neat, thank you," Drake said.

He looked at the menu and smiled. It offered a Caviar

Taco and the Bellagio Martini paired with an edible Ossetra Caviar Cigar, whatever that was. A small plate of peanuts would have been fine for him.

The Maker's Mark was a welcome and familiar taste when he took a sip and saw Chandler Patterson entering the bar and nodding at him. Patterson walked to a table across the room where two men were sitting. The younger of the two was Patterson's son, with his father's facial features.

He watched Chris Patterson stand and hug his father, then turn and introduce him to Walter Williams, the president of the American Karting Foundation.

As the two men shook hands, Drake had difficulty imagining Williams behind the wheel of anything racier than a Toyota Prius. The man looked like an accountant in an old movie, weak-eyed with round rimless eyeglasses, bald and pale. Whoever he was, he didn't look like a frontman promoting kart racing in America.

Chandler Patterson stood and talked with Williams and his son for another couple of minutes, before joining Drake at his table.

"I see you're not drinking the famous Bellagio Martini," Patterson said, sitting down.

"I'm not a big fan of caviar," Drake said.

"I'm not a fan of caviar either, but the martini's good."

"What's Williams like?"

"A phony. I'll bet he doesn't know a 50cc Kid Kart from a 250cc shifter Kart. I asked him who funds the American Karting Foundation, and he said all the karting associations. That's nonsense. Each association has its own program to promote karting. I didn't want to embarrass Chris, so I didn't challenge him."

"Did Chris pick up on it?"

"I couldn't tell. I'll ask him when he joins us for dinner after Williams shows him around the Fountain Club."

"Chandler, if Williams and his foundation are phonies, what's this about?" Drake asked. "How does getting Chris here for this award have anything to do with the report he's presenting to the PIAB?"

"The only thing I can think of is that someone wants to discredit Chris somehow and thereby discredit his report. There's an entire sleazy industry built to take down public figures, as it did with General Petraeus. But they could pull whatever dirty trick they were planning in D.C. without bringing Chris to Las Vegas."

"It has to be something to do with Las Vegas, then," Drake said. "What will Chris be doing while he's here?"

"After being shown around the Fountain Club tonight, I only know about the award ceremony. I gave him a pass to all the Grand Prix venues and he can use it whenever he wants. There's the opening ceremony he'll probably want to attend, some of the practice sessions, qualifying, and then the race on Saturday night. As far as I know, he's on his own here except for this award ceremony that I can't find anything about."

"I'll see what I can find out."

Patterson raised his hand to get the attention of a hostess just as Williams and Chris got up to leave. Drake watched them walk past the bar and saw Williams nod ever so slightly toward a man sitting at it.

The man sitting at the bar was someone Drake recognized. His name was Marcus Braxton, a Special Forces Green Beret Drake met in Afghanistan. Braxton had been disciplined for participating in an interrogation of an Afghan commando, who died after being beaten by his interrogators. Braxton had left the army and joined the CIA as a Paramilitary Operations Officer. That was the last thing he'd heard about the man.

He waited until Patterson's hostess left after bringing his martini and asked, "Have you seen that man sitting at the bar before?"

"Which one?"

"The one sitting in the middle of the bar in the blue suit, getting up to leave."

"I don't think so, why?"

"He was still CIA the last I heard."

"He's probably not the only spook in town this weekend, with all the foreign visitors here for the race. Could be a coincidence that he's here at the Petrosian."

"I don't think so," Drake said. "Walter Williams knows him."

Chapter Six

CHANDLER PATTERSON TALKED Drake into sharing a plate of smoked salmon and trying a Petrosian Worldly Old Fashion while David Osborne finished a set on the Steinway grand piano.

They were waiting for Chris Patterson to return from touring the Fountain Club with Walter Williams when Drake asked Patterson about his relationship with President Ballard.

"Congressman Bridge is a good friend and golfing buddy," Patterson said. "I got to know the president when Matthew asked me to join them for a round at the National Golf Club. We played a lot of golf together after that and I chaired his Nevada presidential campaign."

"You mentioned the sleazy industry that exists to take down public figures," Drake said. "Have you ever heard the name Marcus Braxton mentioned as someone involved in that industry?"

"No, I haven't. But you said he's CIA, and they've used dirty tricks against public figures in other countries."

"We need to know more about Marcus Braxton because this smells like a dirty trick someone might be playing on your son."

"Why did you ask about my relationship with the president?" Patterson asked.

"Just curious about all the angles here," Drake said. "If there is a 'they' involved, you could be the public figure they're trying to take down?"

"I don't see why they would waste time or money on me. I'm no longer the party chairman in Nevada, and President Ballard can't run again."

"All right, so it must be about Chris. Is Chris vulnerable in some way?"

"Not that I know about," Patterson said. "He doesn't do drugs. Despite growing up in Las Vegas, he's not a heavy drinker and doesn't gamble."

"What's true and what's made to look like the truth are two different things. Does Chris know why I'm here?" Drake asked.

"I told him I'm considering using you for IT security for my dealerships and offered to let you stay at the condo while you're here. And he knows you're a Formula One fan."

"Okay, that will give us something to talk about."

When the music stopped, and a new pianist took David Osborne's place, Drake excused himself and left for the men's room. Out in the Bellagio lobby, he saw Marcus Braxton walking past the open entrance to the Petrosian Bar, and he went out to follow him.

Braxton moved quickly around people standing and staring at the famous lobby ceiling, the "Fiori Di Como" hand-blown sculpture of brightly colored glass flowers. Braxton stopped beside a man standing in front of an eight-foot-tall silver and gold mosaic horse made from thousands of tiny, mirrored tiles.

The two men were standing shoulder-to-shoulder, talking softly, when Drake walked by on the other side of the Bellagio Horse and stopped to admire it.

He knew Braxton, and while the other man looked familiar, Drake couldn't remember his name. He moved along the side of the tall artwork until he had a clear view of both men's faces. Taking a step back with his smartphone in front of his face, Drake kept the button pressed as they turned and walked toward the bank of elevators together.

Drake slipped his phone in his pocket and returned to the Petrosian Bar where Chris Chandler sat with his father.

"Chris, I'd like you to meet Adam Drake," Patterson said.

Chris Patterson stood and held out his hand. "Mr. Drake."

"Call me Adam, Chris," Drake said and shook his hand. "Are you here for the Grand Prix?"

"That's the real reason I'm here. The foundation that flew me here thinks I'm here because they're giving me an award."

Drake sat down and asked, "Why is this foundation giving you an award?"

"I won several karting championships here and in Europe when I was young," Chris said. "The American Karting Foundation wants to use my success to promote karting in the U.S."

"I see. Are you still racing?"

"Only when he's home and out on the strip, getting tickets in his old Mustang," Chandler Patterson laughed.

"Like the speeding ticket I could get driving that

Mustang Dark Horse you loaned me?" Drake asked Chandler Patterson.

"What do you usually drive?" Chris Patterson asked.

"A Porsche 718 Cayman GTS."

"So, you're a Porsche guy."

"It's my company car," Drake said with a grin. "But my real love is my old '98 993, the last of the air-cooled 911s."

"Then you should measure your old '98 against my old '98 Saleen Mustang S351 before you leave," Chris said. "Get a feel for what a supercharged V8 with 495 horsepower and a 6-speed transmission drives like."

Drake smiled and said, "Sure, if I have time."

"Chris, do you want anything before we go to dinner?" Patterson interrupted and asked his son.

"No, thanks. I had a beer at the Fountain Club."

"Well, I'll leave you two to talk cars and go see if our table's ready at the Prime."

"What's the Prime?" Drake asked.

"It's his favorite steakhouse," Chris said. "Whenever I'm in town, he insists we share a Porterhouse. It's a tradition."

"How long will you be in town, Chris?" Drake asked when his father left.

"I fly out Sunday with the rest of the race fans. How long are you here?"

"As long as it takes to answer your father's questions."

"Good luck with that. He's a stickler with the details."

"What will you be doing while you're here?"

"According to my guide, I'm going to be busy. She's taking me to the opening ceremony tonight to meet some drivers. Then a paddock tour during Free Practice One tomorrow and visiting several of the teams' hospitality rooms. My award ceremony is tomorrow night. Saturday night, I'm watching the race from the Fountain Club grandstand."

"You do have a full dance card. Who's your guide?"

Chris smiled sheepishly. "She's beautiful, has a French accent, and probably a showgirl here in Vegas. But I'm not complaining."

Drake smiled. "Sounds like you don't have a reason to."

Chapter Seven

CHANDLER PATTERSON RETURNED to the Petrosian Bar and said their table at the Prime Steakhouse was waiting for them.

Drake followed the Pattersons to the lobby and saw Marcus Braxton again across the way, stepping out of an elevator.

"Chandler, you two go ahead to the steakhouse. I'll catch up with you," Drake said. "There's something I need to do."

"Do you know how to get to the restaurant?" Chandler asked.

"No, but I'll find it."

Chandler Patterson motioned with his right hand and said, "Go past Hermes to the entrance to Via Bellagio. On the right-hand side, pass Harry Winston, and take the elevator down toward Terrazza di Sogno. Prime is on the right."

"Got it, thanks," he said, turning away to follow Braxton.

Braxton had changed his clothes from khakis and a black polo shirt to a cream-colored linen jacket and brown slacks. He was shorter than Drake by a couple of inches, still looked fit, but he was walking with a limp. If the limp was a permanent impairment, it could mean Braxton was no longer a CIA Paramilitary Operations Officer.

Drake followed Braxton out of the hotel and stayed behind a guided tour group as they walked down West Bellagio Drive. When Braxton reached West Las Vegas Boulevard, he crossed over and turned left.

The Eiffel Tower was ahead on the right, and Braxton continued for a tenth of a mile before stopping at the Paris Las Vegas Hotel and Casino. Braxton was waving to a beautiful young woman sitting at a table on the terrace of the Mon Ami Gabi French restaurant.

When Braxton walked into the Paris Las Vegas Hotel, Drake stepped to the sidewalk's edge and took out his iPhone 16 Pro Max to take a picture of the Bellagio on the other side of the boulevard.

He continued with his phone raised and pointed toward the musical fountain show at the Bellagio playing across the boulevard until, out of the corner of his eye, he saw Braxton coming out onto the terrace.

When Braxton pulled out a chair across the table from the young woman and sat down, Drake turned and started taking pictures of the hotel and its French bistro with the two of them in view.

Braxton's back was to the strip, but the woman who reminded him of Scarlett Johansson was facing him so she could watch the Bellagio fountains show. She wore a simple white blouse and gold hoop earrings. Her year-round tan was like one you might see on a young woman sunning herself on the deck of a mega yacht in Monte Carlo. Or on the arm of a billionaire at a celebrity gala in New York City. Or the tan you might see on a high-end Las Vegas escort.

Drake had what he needed and returned to the Bellagio to meet Chandler Patterson and his son for dinner. On the way, he sent the pictures of Braxton and the man he met in the Bellagio lobby, as well as the pictures of the woman at the French bistro, to the head of the company's IT division to see if he could identify them.

When he asked the hostess where Chandler Patterson and his son were sitting, he was escorted to a table on the outdoor garden patio with a view of the lake and the fountains.

"I wasn't sure how long you would be, so I went ahead and ordered a couple of appetizers to get us started," Chandler Patterson said.

"Sorry to keep you waiting," Drake said. "Are you on a tight schedule tonight, Chris?"

"No, I'm okay."

"Are you free this evening?" Drake asked.

"I thought I might stop by and check out the Bellagio's Poker Room, but that's all I planned on doing tonight. It's supposed to be the biggest poker room in Las Vegas."

"I didn't know you were interested in poker," Chandler Patterson said.

Chris smiled and said, "After Sandy gave my ring back, I started playing a little poker online to pass the time."

"I played a little poker in the army," Drake injected. "Are you any good?"

"I do okay. I don't play to win big, but I win often enough to keep playing."

Chandler Patterson looked worried when he asked his son, "Are you putting your security clearance at risk, son?"

"No, it's just a hobby, Dad."

"What time will you stop by the poker room?" Drake asked Chris. "I liked to see how the big boys play myself."

"I have no idea; my hostess is taking me there. It might be late, with the performers and the introduction of the drivers and their teams they have planned for the opening ceremony," Chris said.

"That's not a problem. Call me when you leave the opening ceremony. I'll meet you at the Bellagio Poker Room."

After father and son finished off their Porterhouse steaks, Drake was still working on his New York strip steak when Chris Chandler excused himself and left.

"I didn't know he was gambling," Patterson said. "Will that put his security clearance at risk?"

"I don't know," Drake said. "If he's addicted to it or losing a lot of money that could make him vulnerable to blackmail, it could," Drake said.

"It doesn't sound like his online poker is that big a deal."

"It doesn't have to be for someone to claim it is. Remember the man I asked you about sitting at the bar in the Petrosian? I followed him across the street, where he met with a beautiful young woman. If he's still working for the CIA and she happens to be the hostess Chris is talking about, they could make it look like his gambling is a big deal."

"So, this is about Chris's report."

"I'm beginning to think it is," Drake said.

Chapter Eight

CHANDLER PATTERSON LEFT to drive home and bring his wife back for a party the race organizers hosted during the opening ceremony at another location.

Thirty thousand people were expected to attend the opening ceremony and listen to a slate of international artists perform before the ten race teams and their twenty drivers were introduced. Drake wasn't a fan of pop concerts, or any kind of concerts, for that matter, and declined Patterson's offer of a ticket to the event.

Chandler Patterson was a Las Vegas Grand Prix Foundation board member and gave him a Paddock Club ticket and invitations to the teams' hospitality rooms, which was all he needed. Besides, the opening ceremony was televised.

Drake left the Bellagio, and just before turning right onto West Aria Place from South Las Vegas Boulevard to get back to the Veer Towers, he sensed he was being followed again. So many people were walking with him that it was unlikely he would be able to pick out whoever was following him, so he continued walking without looking back.

When he got back to the condo at Veer Towers, he saw on his Omega Seamaster that it was early enough on a Wednesday evening for Kevin McRoberts to still be in his office.

When the condo's door clicked behind him to signal it was locked, he called their young IT guru and walked to the floor-to-ceiling window to stand and look down on the Las Vegas strip.

Tomorrow, the sound of twenty hybrid racing engines racing at fifteen thousand revolutions per minute would shake windows all along the strip. He hoped Las Vegas was ready for the noisy nights ahead.

"Mr. Drake, how's Sin City?" Kevin asked.

"Crowded and expensive," Drake said. "Were you able to identify the man and woman from the pictures I sent you?"

"The man's name is Marcus Braxton, age 41, who lives in McLean, Virginia. He's the founder and CEO of Braxton Group, a business intelligence company headquartered in Bethesda, Maryland.

"The woman's name is Celeste Lemaire, and she is 29 years old. She lives in Paris, France. She was born in Lebanon. Her father was a French diplomat, and her mother was a Lebanese national. They met while he was serving there. Lemaire is a high-end escort in Paris, Mr. Drake."

"Could she be living in Las Vegas now?"

"I didn't find a Las Vegas address for her."

"See if you can find out how long she's been in Las Vegas," Drake said. "Check passenger lists for recent flights from Paris. I have a hunch she's just flown here. Send me everything you have on Braxton and the woman. What about the other man I sent you a picture of meeting with Braxton in the Bellagio lobby?"

"His name is Daniel Franklin, the CEO of Franklin Analytics."

"I've never heard of Franklin or Franklin Analytics," Drake admitted.

"Franklin Analytics is a data broker. It sells personal data to government agencies, corporations, and foreign countries. I'll see what I can find on Daniel Franklin."

"I thought U.S. agencies were forbidden to collect personal data on American citizens," Drake said.

"They are, but they're not forbidden from buying it from private third parties like Franklin Analytics."

"Find out everything you can about Daniel Franklin and his company."

"When I find something, do you want me to call tonight or wait until tomorrow?" Kevin asked.

"Call me as soon as you have something."

"Will do, Mr. Drake."

"Thanks, Kevin."

That was interesting. If his suspicions were correct, Braxton was working on behalf of the intelligence community, which bought personal data from data brokers to use for its surveillance programs. Whatever Braxton was doing in Las Vegas must involve Chris Patterson's report and what it could mean to the IC's surveillance programs.

Drake needed to know more about Marcus Braxton and knew someone who might know something. He called President Benjamin Ballard using the Signal app on his phone.

"Mr. President, do you have a minute?"

"As many minutes as you need, Adam," the president said. 'I'm in the Oval Office Study waiting for the Secretary of State to brief me on a new African crisis. How's Las Vegas?"

"They rolled out the red carpet for Formula One and the race," Drake said. "Every celebrity in the country is here wanting a moment in the spotlight. It's worse than New Hampshire before a presidential primary when all the candidates show up."

"What have you learned?"

"I believe Chandler Patterson has a reason to worry about his son. What do you know about Marcus Braxton and the Braxton Group?"

"I don't know Marcus Braxton, but I've heard of the Braxton Group," President Ballard said. "It's a business intelligence firm that supplies opposition research to the other party, for the most part. I'm not sure what else it does or who its other clients are."

"Marcus Braxton is in Las Vegas. I think it has something to do with Chris Patterson and his PIAB report."

"What makes you think that?"

"Braxton met with Daniel Franklin, the CEO of Franklin Analytics, in the lobby of the Bellagio this afternoon," Drake said. "Franklin is a data broker who sells personal data to our intelligence agencies. Chris Patterson's report is about surveillance programs being conducted by the intelligence community. Those surveillance programs may use the personal data Franklin sells for their surveillance programs. If Congress ends those programs, the IC won't be happy, and Franklin Analytics will lose some big clients.

"Marcus Braxton is a former Special Forces Green Beret. He worked for the CIA after he left the army. I know the man. He's the kind of person Franklin and his company would use."

"Use for what purpose?" President Ballard asked.

"To discredit Chris and his report."

"By doing what?"

"I'm not sure, but I have an idea. I saw Marcus Braxton meeting with a young woman today. She's a high-end escort from Paris."

"A honeypot seduction?"

"That's what I'm thinking," Drake said.

Chapter Nine

CHRIS PATTERSON CALLED on his way to the Bellagio poker room that evening to ask if Drake would join them. By the time Drake got to the seven-thousand-square-foot room with its forty poker tables, it was midnight.

The largest poker room in Las Vegas was fully occupied, with eight serious-looking players sitting around each kidney bean-shaped poker table. Hand-blown glass chandeliers were overhead, helping the players try to read the faces and mannerisms of their opponents at the table.

Drake stood at the room's marble-floored entrance and looked for Chris Patterson. He checked the tables closest to the entrance before moving his eyes to the tables in the middle of the room.

Chris was sitting at a table on the right side of the room next to the woman he saw Marcus Braxton with at the French Bistro. She was leaning in close to him with her hand on his shoulder, whispering in his ear.

Celeste Lemaire was sitting across the table facing Drake, and when she moved away from Chris and sat upright in her red swivel chair, the white satin lapel jacket she was wearing opened. It looked to him like she was topless underneath. He'd seen other women that day in Las Vegas dressed the same way and wondered how Chris could pay attention to play poker with her sitting beside him.

But then, Chris wasn't supposed to. That was the way a honeypot seduction worked; targets were enticed with something irresistible into romantic or sexual relationships that would compromise them in some way.

Drake approached the poker room host station and asked, "Can you tell me what my friend is playing? I'm trying to decide if I should wait for him here or meet him later?"

The man turned away from his computer screen and asked, "Who's your friend?"

"Chris Patterson."

The room host typed in the name and looked toward the middle of the large room. "Table 22 is a 2/5 cash game table. He could leave anytime, but I wouldn't count on it being soon."

"Why is that?"

"Did you see the lady he came in with?"

"Where's Table 22?"

"Middle of the room," the host said. "Blonde hair, wearing a white jacket."

Drake nodded and asked, "I see what you mean. Do you know her?"

"Never seen her before."

"All right, thanks," he said, stepping away from the host's station and sending Chris Patterson a text message on his phone. "How long will you be? I didn't know you were going to play."

"Angeline talked me into it," Chris replied. "Don't wait for me. Not sure how long I'll be."

"Right, later then."

Cute, Drake thought. Angeline was no angel, and Chris was being played. He crossed the corridor leading to the Bellagio Sports Book and Snacks, an all-day eatery, and ordered an espresso. He sat at a small table near the window, with a view of the entrance to the poker room, where he could see Chris and Angeline when they left.

When they did, whenever that was, he would have to decide what to do. Braxton and the escort from Paris weren't interested in getting information from Chris. If he was right, Braxton didn't care what the PIAD report revealed about the domestic surveillance of Americans.

Braxton's goal was to ensure no one paid attention to the PIAD report. To do that, he needed to create a scandal involving the author of the report that was so salacious, the noise the media could create would drown out any uproar about domestic spying programs.

Compromising pictures would do that, perhaps, with drug paraphernalia visible on a dresser next to the bed. A police report and pictures of a bruised and battered prostitute would also do that. Or evidence the author of the report was acting on behalf of a foreign power, say Russia or Iran. Evidence of a meeting with a foreign national and French prostitute, would prove it.

One thing was clear. He wouldn't let Chris Patterson be alone with Celeste Lemaire, aka Angeline, any time that night.

After having a second espresso and eating a croissant, Drake saw Chris leave with Celeste Lemaire clinging onto him. He left a tip on the table and followed them.

He got to within forty feet of the two, heard Celeste's

laughing, and saw that she was swaying a little as if she'd had too much to drink in the poker room. Drake knew it was an act to tell Chris she was available tonight.

When he saw her take out a key card from her jacket pocket and wave it in front of Chris, he was sure of it.

It was time to break up the party and get Chris away from his seductress. He walked faster to close the gap when someone brushed past and cut in front of him.

The man was taller than Drake, broader through his shoulders, and fifty pounds heavier. His bald head and thick neck made him think of a nightclub bouncer or a former NFL lineman working security in the casino.

He dropped back a step to see what the man intended to do by cutting him off. When Chris and his escort were out of sight around a bend in the corridor, he found out.

The bouncer pivoted around instead of following them and swung a looping right-hand roundhouse at Drake's head.

Drake dropped into a defensive crouch, slipped under the man's massive fist, and shot a right-hand body punch into his left ribs. When his assailant dropped his left elbow to protect his ribs from another blow, Drake connected a left roundhouse of his own to the man's right jaw that stunned the bouncer.

With the man's eyes still wide in surprise at the turn of events, Drake finished with a palm-heel strike to his nose that buckled his knees and dropped him to the floor.

Chapter Ten

DRAKE TURNED the corner and walked casually away. Chris and the escort were fifty yards ahead of him on the corridor leading back to the Bellagio lobby. Looking over his shoulder, he saw no one chasing after him and quickened his pace.

He needed to be able to follow Chris wherever Celeste was taking him, and he needed to be in a position to extricate Chris from the trap set for him.

When they reached the Bellagio lobby, Celeste walked with Chris toward the private elevators for floors twenty-nine to thirty-six, the penthouse levels. Drake raised his hand, waved to get Chris's attention, and jogged there to catch up.

The elevator door they were waiting for began to open just as Drake reached them and said, "Celeste, Marcus told me to take over from here on out. There's been a change of plan. You're to fly home tonight to Paris. I'll make sure Chris gets where he's going."

Celeste turned and smiled. "I'm sorry, you must be thinking of someone else. My name is Angeline."

She's good, Drake thought. *Her mind must be racing, wondering how I know about Braxton and Paris.*

He looked at his watch and said, "Celeste, you don't have much time to check out and get to the airport. Marcus said you'd understand."

"What's going on, Adam?" Chris asked and stepped away from her.

"I'll explain later," Drake said.

Celeste stared at Drake, blinked twice, and, shaking her head, said, "Fine!" She spun on the heel of her red stiletto spike dress boot and walked away.

"What just happened?"

"I butted in and spoiled what I'm sure would have been a very enjoyable and costly night for you," Drake said.

"Why would it have been costly?"

"Let's go somewhere, and I'll tell you."

"Let's walk to Dad's condo," Chris said. "You can tell me there."

The ten-minute walk to Veer Towers from the Bellagio gave Drake time to think about how much he needed to tell Chris about Braxton and Celeste. Braxton was a hired gun, working for someone. The CIA? Daniel Franklin? Certainly not Walter Williams, unless he had grossly underestimated the man.

President Ballard would want to know who was responsible for this charade and for what purpose.

Exposing a young PIAB staffer with scandalous pictures of him in bed with a prostitute in Las Vegas would embarrass the president indirectly, but not enough to justify the effort.

There had to be more to it than that. Maybe Chris

found something in his investigation and didn't realize its significance—something tangential to domestic surveillance and important enough to try to keep anyone from looking at the PIAD report too closely.

If that were the case, they would have to play along until they knew what it was.

Drake followed Chris into his dad's condo and tossed his blazer over the back of a white leather sofa facing the floor-to-ceiling windows. The Las Vegas strip below, with its towering hotels and casinos, was a dazzling display of light and color, illuminating the night.

"Would you like a beer or something from the bar?" Chris asked. "Dad keeps it well stocked."

"Maybe a whiskey," Drake said, walking over to the wet bar, which was backlit with a hundred pinpoints of blue light from behind decorative glass.

Chandler Patterson did indeed keep his bar well-stocked, with a bottle of Jack Daniel's 12-Year-Old Tennessee Whisky, a bottle of Old Forester President's Choice Kentucky Straight Bourbon Whisky, and a bottle of Binder's Stash Straight Bourbon Whiskey. Drake had never seen any of the bottles displayed in any liquor store he'd ever been in.

"I don't recognize any of these whiskeys," Drake said. "Your dad must be a whiskey connoisseur."

"Those are mostly for show," Chris said. "A customer of his owns a liquor store and orders them for him. The only whiskey I ever see him drink is Knob Creek."

The bottle of Knob Creek at the end of the row of bourbon whiskeys was the only bottle that had been opened. Drake helped himself to a tumbler with one ice cube from the countertop ice maker.

Chris stood at the window with a bottle of Coors Light in his hand when Drake returned and sat on the sofa.

"Do you stay here when you're in town?" Drake asked.

"Once in a while."

"So, this isn't your bachelor pad when you're in town."

Chris sat across from Drake on the other sofa and grinned. "It would have been tonight."

"Sorry about that."

"Somehow, I don't think you are. How did you find out her name wasn't Angeline?"

Chapter Eleven

DRAKE LOOKED over the rim of his whiskey tumbler at Chris after taking a sip and said, "I saw her with someone I know and had her checked out. Her name is Celeste Lemaire. She's a high-end escort from Paris. Not the hotel and casino across the Las Vegas Boulevard, but Paris, France."

"Why did you have her checked out?"

Drake sat his tumbler down on the glass coffee table and leaned forward with his elbows resting on his knees. "Chris, I'm not here to pitch your dad about cyber security services for his dealerships. I'm here because the president asked me to determine if your dad has a reason to worry about your safety. I'm with Sound Security and Information Services, a private intelligence contractor."

"You're talking about the president, President Ballard?"

Drake nodded.

"I don't understand. Why is he or my dad worried about my safety?"

"You're presenting a report about domestic surveillance

in America to the President's Intelligence Advisory Board next week. The intelligence community or someone seems to be concerned about that."

"My report to the PIAB isn't a reason for anyone to be concerned," Chris said. "It's the same stuff two senators are talking about."

"Chris, I don't know if you're in danger, physical danger, or not," Drake admitted. "But something's going on, and you're at the center of it. The man I saw Celeste with is a former CIA operative and the CEO of the Braxton Group, a private business intelligence company. I saw him with Daniel Franklin, the CEO of Franklin Analytics, which sells personal data to the CIA and other government agencies. I believe Braxton wanted to use Celeste to compromise you and discredit you and your report."

"You think it was a honeypot operation?"

"I do," Drake said. "That's why there must be something in your report that someone doesn't want exposed. How broad was the scope of the research you did for your report?"

"I covered a lot of ground and talked to a lot of people," Chris said. "What exactly do you want to know?"

"Were there people outside the intelligence community that you researched? Maybe you found connections you weren't supposed to."

"I talked with the two senators worried about domestic surveillance and their staff. I interviewed people in the CIA and NSA. I wanted to know how they use the personal data they buy from data brokers. They didn't tell me much. I talked with staff at the FISA court about the government's warrantless access to phone calls, texts, and emails. I also talked with several investigative journalists who are reporting on domestic surveillance. That's about it."

"Did your research include what Franklin Analytics sells to the government?" Drake asked.

"I mapped out the sources data brokers use to collect the data they sell, sure. But I didn't include any of that in the report."

"Then there might be a connection in your report to Daniel Franklin. How about the Braxton Group? Anything in your report about them?"

"No," Chris said and stood up. "I'm on my way to the restroom. Can I get you anything else?"

"Are you coming back? I want to ask you about a couple of things."

"Sure, I'll be right back."

Drake refilled his whiskey tumbler, added an ice cube, and went to the window to look over the city. There were other ways than a honeypot seduction someone could use to discredit Chris and his report.

His father had been surprised to learn that Chris played poker online. That alone wouldn't be a reason to revoke his security clearance unless they found evidence that he was addicted to gambling, heavily in debt, and subject to blackmail because of it.

And the information Kevin McRoberts found about Celeste Lemaire provided another. She was half French and half Lebanese. With all the factions involved in the Lebanese Civil War, the various clans and militias, the PLO, and Israel's support of several of the Christian militias, Celeste was a foreign contact and could be considered a national security concern who might make Chris vulnerable to pressure or coercion by a foreign government.

Chris wasn't with Celeste long enough to produce the results a honeypot seduction was designed to provide, but he was seen with her. Pictures of them together would be enough to prove a foreign contact, albeit a brief one. They were also seen together in the Bellagio poker room, proving that he gambled while playing poker.

Drake didn't need to ask Chris about the time he spent with Celeste, and he didn't expect to see her in Las Vegas again, especially if she told Marcus Braxton that he was with Chris now and had broken up their evening.

He did need, however, to ask Chris if he had a gambling addiction or was in debt because of it.

Chapter Twelve

CHRIS RETURNED and stood next to Drake with another beer in his hand. "What else do you want to know?"

"The work you do requires a security clearance," Drake began. "Losing it would be one way to discredit your work for the PIAB. A honeypot seduction wasn't successful, but you were seen with Celeste in the Bellagio poker room gambling. You told your dad that playing poker online was just a hobby and that you weren't risking your security clearance."

"Correct. I'm not."

"Even a hobby can be expensive, Chris. Like tonight, did you win or lose money?"

"I lost, but it wasn't my money. Celeste made the reservation for the table and staked me with her money."

"How much did you lose?" Drake asked.

"Ten thousand. I went all in twice when I shouldn't have. But she said she was having fun and encouraged me to do it, that it was just money."

"Chris, this whole thing has been planned and in the

works for a while. Celeste wouldn't have reserved a table and staked you with her money if your poker playing wasn't something they thought they could use against you. So, let me ask, are you in debt from playing online poker?"

Chris turned to face Drake and said, "Not that it's any of your business, but no. I'm not in debt from playing online poker. I limit myself to five hundred dollars a month, less than what I used to spend taking Sandy out to dinner when we were engaged. When that's gone, that's it for the month."

"All right, thanks."

"Do you think they, whoever they are, will keep trying to come at me?" Chris asked.

"Yes, I think they will."

"What am I supposed to do?" Chris asked, holding his hands palms up. "Just let them?"

"Yes, for now. We play along, go to what Williams has planned for you, and watch the practice sessions and the race. Give them time to show themselves," Drake said. "I'll have my company do a deep dive on Braxton, Franklin, and Walter Williams. Let's find out who 'they' are and why they're doing this."

"The award ceremony isn't until tomorrow night. What do you want to do until then?"

"Get a good night's sleep. We'll figure it out when we get up. You said you'd let me drive your old Mustang. Maybe we should take it out tomorrow and have some fun."

"You're on," Chris said and held out his hand. "Thank you for doing this."

"You're welcome," Drake said and looked at his watch. "It's one thirty. When do you get up?"

"Seven normally, maybe a little later today. Why?"

"I'm going to check out the fitness center before then and take you to breakfast."

"Sure, see you then," Chris said, leaving Drake at the window.

Drake finished his drink and went to his bedroom to take a shower and get some sleep. In the morning, he'd tell Kevin McRoberts at PSS to start investigating the people they knew about, who were probably involved in a honeypot seduction of young Chris Chandler.

———

AT TWO O'CLOCK THAT MORNING, the man following Drake dressed as a clownish imitation of a Las Vegas tourist called Marcus Braxton at the Bellagio.

"We have a problem," he said. "Your pretty little bird has flown the coop."

"Explain," Braxton said.

"She just boarded a red-eye for New York."

"What happened?"

"A man following Celeste and your target took out my bouncer, said something to her, and she left. One of my men followed her across the street and waited to see if she was meeting Patterson there. She wasn't. She checked out, took a cab to the airport, and left Las Vegas."

"Was Patterson ever alone with her?"

"No."

"Did you get pictures of them in the poker room?"

"Yes."

"At least we have that," Braxton said.

"What do you want me to do?"

"Get those pictures on social media. Use her real name.

We'll let a day go by before we'll identify her as a foreign contact with ties to Hezbollah in Lebanon."

"What about his gambling?"

"His online poker account has been altered to show he's losing big. When the time is right, we'll make sure his security clearance is revoked."

"What about the guy who took out my bouncer?"

"Find out who he is," Braxton said.

"Why do you think he followed the girl and the target?"

"I don't know. He could be here for the race and just got in the way."

"You don't believe that, and neither do I. He was following the kid for a reason."

"Put a team on him," Braxton said. "Let's find out who he is and why he's here in Las Vegas."

"Will the social media stuff be enough? You said you needed this taken care of before he returned to D.C. Do we need a backup plan with the girl out of it?"

"Like what?"

"Something more direct. This isn't like our other projects. You don't have the time to ruin him in the long term. You just want to make him look dirty in the short term. What if he doesn't make it back to D.C. to deliver his report? If he's not there, the report could be tabled and rescheduled. That would give our clients the time they need."

"No, our brief was specific," Braxton said. "Do nothing that involves criminal activity. The last thing they want are subpoenas to testify before a grand jury."

"Accidents happen."

"Finish this the way we planned. If we need to make changes, Franklin will have to order them. I'm not going to risk losing everything I've worked for to keep someone in the CIA from getting their hands slapped."

Chapter Thirteen

DRAKE WAITED until he returned from working out in the Veer Towers fitness center and took a shower before calling Liz Thursday morning.

"Good morning, beautiful. How are you feeling?"

"I'm feeling fine, just tired and not so beautiful," she said. "I never sleep well when you're away."

"I'll be back this weekend," Drake said. "I'm sorry you didn't sleep well."

"Did at least one of us get a good night's sleep?"

"Yes, short but good. I just got back from a good work-out, and then I'm taking Chris to breakfast when he gets up."

"Have you found out why his father is worried?"

"I'm working on it," Drake said. "Someone flew a high-end escort in from Paris to keep him company."

"Honeypot?"

"I think so."

"Were they successful?"

"No, I got in their way."

"Do they know that?"

"If they don't, they will."

"Please be careful," Liz said.

"I will, don't worry. I'll call you tonight. I'll know more then."

"Don't worry about what time it is. I'll be awake."

"Try not to be," Drake said. "You need to rest."

"Come home, and I will."

Drake was loading a Keurig coffee maker for his first cup of the day when Chris Patterson came out of his bedroom wearing a T-shirt and boxers.

"How was your workout?" he asked.

"Good, nice fitness center. Do you have a favorite breakfast place?"

"I do, but it's in Summerlin," Chris said. "The Omelet House is the best breakfast place around here, with over thirty omelets on the menu if you like omelets. Then we could stop by my folks' place and get my old Mustang so you can drive it if you want."

"Now you're talking. I need to make one call, and I'll be ready to go," Drake said, moving to the window. He called Kevin McRoberts at PSS headquarters with a cup of coffee in one hand and his phone in the other.

"Good morning, Kevin."

"Hi, Mr. Drake."

"I need you to do a deeper dive on the people I told you about. I want to know everything, and I mean everything, about their businesses, their backgrounds and educations, their associates, their memberships in clubs and organizations, everything."

"You mean Daniel Franklin, Marcus Braxton, and Walter Williams?"

"And the woman from Paris, Celeste Lemaire. Find out as much as possible about her and her family in Lebanon."

"Anything else?"

"There are two U.S. Senators making news about the intelligence community spying on Americans again," Drake added. "See if they have evidence to support their claims about current domestic surveillance programs."

"Got it."

"Call me as soon as you have something. I'll be here for a couple more days."

"Will do, Mr. Drake."

"One more thing, Kevin. Add Chris Patterson to the list. See if he has any skeletons I need to know about in his closet."

Drake slipped the phone into the pocket of his jeans, finished his coffee, and waited for Chris to get dressed and join him. His focus had been on Chris, the author of a report that someone was trying to discredit. To do it, they'd brought in a prostitute to seduce him. He hadn't considered the possibility there might be something else about Chris they could expose to get the job done.

He hoped he was wrong to consider the possibility.

Chris came out of his bedroom wearing jeans and a black sweatshirt with UNLV in red letters splashed across the front. "Ready, if you are," he said.

Drake handed him the keys to the new Ford Mustang Dark Horse and said, "You drive, you know the way."

"Maybe not now, with all the detours and streets blocked for the race, but I'll get us there."

Chris pulled out his phone and called Veer Towers' parking valet to bring the Mustang up from the underground parking garage. On the way down in the floor's private elevator, he asked, "Would you mind if I ask you a personal question?"

"I don't mind," Drake said, "Depending on what it is, I may or may not answer it."

"You said the president asked you to start a private intelligence company. Why?"

"Why do you think he did?"

"Because he doesn't trust the CIA or the NSA?"

"That's part of it," Drake said.

"What's the rest of it?"

"Sometimes it's more efficient to use a small private company if you want something done quickly and discreetly."

"You mean off the books?"

Drake had to laugh. "Usually, it's the other way around. I get involved in something and then ask the government for help. This time, you could say the president is doing this 'off the books' because your father asked for his help. Asking the CIA or the NSA to get involved when they might be responsible would be counterproductive."

"I think there's plenty more you're not telling me about why the president asked you to come here," Chris said. "I hope I'll find out someday."

"Now it's my turn to ask why. Why do you want to know?"

"Because I think I might like to do what you're doing."

When the elevator door opened, Drake thought, *After you make it through this week, you might want to reconsider that thought.*

Chapter Fourteen

WITH CHRIS PATTERSON at the wheel, it took twenty minutes to travel on US-95 and the Summerlin Parkway to Summerlin, Nevada, west of Las Vegas, for breakfast at the Omelet House.

When they finished eating what Drake conceded to be the best omelet he'd eaten, next to the ones he made for his wife, they continued to drive on to the Patterson home in the Summit Club.

"This isn't where I lived growing up," Chris said as he stopped at the guard house at the private golf resort community entrance. "Dad built Mom her dream house long before Mark Walhberg moved his family here from California and made the place famous. When you tell someone where your parents live, they only want to know whether you met Walhberg."

"Living with the rich and famous must be tough," Drake teased.

"Walhberg's a car guy," Chris said when they drove into the resort community. "He stopped me once to ask about my Mustang, and I found out he owns some Chevrolet deal-erships and knows Dad. You're a car guy. You'd like him."

Drake was also a native of the Pacific Northwest and liked forests and mountains, but he was surprised to find that he also liked the beauty of the desert surrounding the luxury homes and estates of the Summit Club.

"I'll see if Mom's home and grab the keys to the Mustang," Chris said as he turned off the lane lined with palm trees and stopped before a security gate with six-foot tall rock walls extending out on both sides.

Chris punched numbers in the keypad to roll back the security gate and drove into the compound. He stopped at the front of a dazzling white contemporary desert-design two-story house with a red tile roof and a three-car garage and went inside to see his mother.

Drake got out of the Dark Horse and took a deep breath. The desert air was scented with a rich fragrance from pink flowers in the flower beds along the rock walls.

A minute or two later, the third garage door rolled up, and he saw Chris taking the car cover off his rare 1998 Ford Mustang Saleen S351 Speedster. Drake joined him in the garage and walked around admiring the car.

With its custom Saleen bodywork, rollbar, and rear spoiler, the black beauty looked fast sitting still. Drake leaned in, ran his hand along the top of a black leather Recaro passenger seat, looked down at the Saleen short shifter lever, and asked, "Six-speed transmission?"

"Yes," Chris said. "Mated to a supercharged 5.8-liter 351 V8 that does 0-60 in 4.7 seconds and has a top 150 miles per hour. It's a beast. I'll pull it out and let it warm up, then you can take it out and see how it compares to your 911."

Drake followed the Mustang and waited for Chris to get

out and stand beside him. "Do you have a road around here that's fun to drive?"

"Sure, the Red Rock Canyon Scenic Drive. It isn't far. Thirteen miles of one-way road that circles the canyon with great corners and scenery you won't believe. Climb in, you'll see."

They left the Pattersons' home, with Drake careful not to use more than a quarter of the throttle to keep from spinning the rear wheels. The Mustang rode rougher than his 911, but its handling was quick and responsive, and the brakes were great. He couldn't wait to get out on a road out of the city.

Leaving Summerlin, Chris directed Drake to Highway 159 and then to the Red Rock Visitor Center, where he paid the entrance fee for the scenic drive.

While they stopped, Drake said, "Chris, that red Ford F-150 with the lift kit and big offroad tires has been behind us since we left Summerlin. Are there turnouts or parking areas up ahead?"

"Plenty of them. Why?"

"Find one on the map they gave you where I can get far enough ahead and pull off to surprise them. I want to know who's following us."

Chris studied the scenic drive map and said, "The Petrograph Wall would be a good place. The road makes a tight U-turn at the parking area. There's a short trail to the Wall. We can get far enough down it to be out of sight or stay in the car and wait for them to pull in."

"That will work. How far is it?"

"A little over halfway around the canyon. From here to the Sandstone Quarry, you have enough open road to get ahead of them."

"Then I need to get going."

Chris had booked a timed entry reservation for the scenic drive that morning and told Drake that unless the guys following them had done the same thing, they might not be allowed on the scenic drive that hour.

But as they pulled away from the fee station, Drake saw in the rearview mirror the red pickup was leaving the station behind them.

He ignored the posted speed limit of thirty-five miles an hour and accelerated to catch up with a white SUV ahead of them. The SUV was driving slowly to enjoy the view of the red sandstone rocks, but fortunately, it turned into a parking area. A mother and two children got out and headed toward the restrooms.

Drake accelerated past the parking area and drove north, passing the Sandstone Quarry and the High Point Overlook at the northern top of the scenic drive, then south toward their destination, the Petrograph Wall Trail.

When they approached the parking area for the Petrograph Wall, the red pickup was a quarter of a mile back with a car between them.

Entering the parking area faster than he should have and sliding to a stop, he told Chris, "Let's get out of sight around the bend of the trail. If they come after us, we'll have a chance to step out and ask them what they want and who sent them."

Chapter Fifteen

DRAKE JUMPED out of the Mustang and sprinted down the rocky trail ahead of Chris Patterson. When he reached a turn in the trail, he stepped off and ducked behind a large bush tall enough to provide cover for the two of them.

The driver of the red pickup jumped on the brakes when he saw Chris's black Mustang in the parking area and fishtailed off the road. He drove slowly forward and stopped, facing the trailhead with two men visible inside the truck.

Both men wore sunglasses and black baseball hats. The driver was the larger of the two, sitting tall behind the steering wheel with shoulders wider than the bucket seat he was sitting in. The other man was shorter and heavier, with a stubby cigar in his mouth wafting smoke out his open window.

Drake was sure it was the same man he'd seen when he sensed he was being followed the other day.

The men stayed in the pickup with the engine idling, looking for them.

Drake waited for the men to make a move. After two long minutes, he stepped out from behind the bush and walked toward them. "Stay back, Chris. I'll handle this."

He was halfway across the parking area when the F-150 backed up, its passenger side door facing Drake. The older man smiled and pointed a finger gun gesture at Drake as the pickup rolled out onto the road and drove away.

Drake quickly took his phone out and took a picture of the red pickup's license plate. If the men didn't want to stay around to introduce themselves, he would find out who they were and give them another chance when he found them.

Chris jogged up the trail and stood next to Drake. "Should we go after them?"

"We'll see them again. Right now, let's go see the ancient carvings while we're here."

The Petrograph Wall site was enormous, and walking around to see the twenty-five separate panels of petroglyphs took most of an hour. According to the information posted on signs at the site, they were made by the Southern Paiute tribe of Native Americans or by the Ancient Puebloans, also known as the "Desert People."

The ancient carvings were deeply embedded in stone, and some pictographs were made using red paint and wetted charcoal, telling stories about the culture and the land. Drake had seen similar ancient Native American art scraped into boulders at the Picture Rock Pass site in Oregon when he was a boy that was thought to be between 7,500 and 12,000 years old. No one knew the meanings of the old petroglyph designs that had always fascinated him.

Chris insisted Drake continue driving his Mustang around the scenic drive and asked who he thought the two men in the pickup were.

"They probably work for Marcus Braxton, the man I told you about."

"Why were they following us?"

"I think they were following me. They'll know where your parents live. They'll know you will be at the award ceremony tonight and probably know you're staying at your dad's condo. But they don't know who I am and why I'm here. Braxton will want to know who interfered in his plan."

"How did you do that?"

"By following you when you left the poker room. They had someone following you as well. He didn't want me tagging along, so I convinced him to sit this one out."

"How?"

Drake kept looking straight ahead and grinned. "He missed. I didn't."

When they returned to Patterson's parents' home, Drake stayed outside by the garage and sent the photo of the red pickup's license plate to Kevin McRoberts at PSS headquarters. Chris was inside saying goodbye to his mother when Drake's phone vibrated in his pocket.

"I thought you would want to know there's a photo of Chris Patterson playing poker at the Bellagio on social media," Kevin said.

"What's the commentary?"

"Local racing celebrity enjoying a night on the town."

"Does it show him with the woman from Paris?"

"She's draped all over him," Kevin said.

"His poker playing must be the issue they want to use to challenge his security clearance. See if there's anything else on social media about Chris and poker or Chris and gambling. With AI, they can plaster social media with him playing poker in casinos everywhere."

"I'm on it, Mr. Drake, and I'll find out who the pickup is registered to."

"Thanks, Kevin."

Chris returned, handed Drake the keys to the Mustang Dark Horse, and said, "Dad and Mom want to drive me to the award ceremony, so you'll have to drive yourself back to the condo."

"Sure, no problem. Will I see you there?"

"Sure, if you're there when I stop by to change my clothes. Are you coming to the award ceremony?"

"I'd like to," Drake said. "Do I need an invitation to get in?"

"Not sure, just show up. I'll make sure they let you in."

"Chris, before I leave, you should know there's a photo of you playing poker last night at the Bellagio. You might be asked about that."

"Why would someone do something like that?"

"It could be how they'll try to discredit your report by exposing a gambling problem they'll say you have."

"I told you I don't have a gambling problem."

"I know, and I believe you," Drake reassured him. "That won't stop them from trying to make it look like you do."

"How can they do that?"

"By planting evidence that you're in debt or losing a lot of money."

"But I have my bank account records to prove I'm not."

"What about your account where you play online?"

"It will show the same thing."

"Unless they hack into it and change the numbers."

"Can we keep them from doing that?"

"If they can do it, we can, too. Tell me your account

username and password. We'll make sure it's corrected if they tampered with it."

Chapter Sixteen

DRAKE CALLED Liz on the drive back to Chandler Patterson's condo in the late afternoon sun.

"Enjoying the weather?" she asked.

"Yes, ma'am, I am. Thought I'd check in again and ask how you're doing?"

"Ready to burst and wishing you were here."

"Do I need to come home?" Drake asked.

"We're not that close. Stay for the race."

"Really, how are you?"

"I'm fine. Mike stopped by on his way home last evening, and Megan brought me lunch today. They're taking good care of me. What's happening on your end? Is the president's staffer really in danger?"

"I don't think so, but something is going on," Drake said. "We drove to the Red Rock Canyon this afternoon, and someone followed us. Kevin is running the license plate for me. I think I know who they were."

"Are you in danger?"

"No, don't worry."

"I always worry when I'm not there with you. I'm not sleeping well, so call before you go to bed, whenever that is."

"Will that stop you from worrying?"

"It will tonight."

"The award ceremony for Chris is at seven o'clock tonight, and the first practice session for the race is from eight-thirty to nine-thirty. I should be back at the condo by ten. I'll call you then."

"Until then."

"Until then."

Liz was the most self-confident and independent woman he knew, but he was noticing something new: worrying about his safety and wanting to know when he'd be home. She probably always worried a little, just as he did for her safety when they were in the field together, and there were real risks to worry about. He wasn't sure what was causing it now, but he knew it wasn't something he could ignore.

He checked his rearview mirror and saw the red Ford F-150 behind him, three cars back, as it had been since he left Summerlin. They wanted him to know he was being followed.

Or that Chris was being followed. With the tinted windows in the Dark Horse, they had no way of knowing who was behind the wheel. He decided to keep it that way. If he was wrong about Chris being in danger and they tried something, he wanted to be the one who confronted them when they did, not Chris.

When he turned off South Las Vegas Boulevard onto West Aria Place, he watched to see if they followed him. They didn't. They knew where he was going.

Drake left the Dark Horse with the parking valet and looked around to see if anyone was watching or waiting for him. No one was, and he took the elevator to Chandler Patterson's condo alone.

It was four o'clock in the afternoon, and he had three hours until the award ceremony at the Bellagio. That was plenty of time to check out the Formula One course and get something to eat.

Chandler Patterson had given him tickets for the race, the Paddock Club, and the Red Bull Racing Paddock Club suite. Ford was partnering with Red Bull Racing to develop the powertrain for the 2026 Red Bull Formula One car, and Patterson's pass to the team's suite was in recognition of his work to bring Formula One to Las Vegas and the Ford dealerships he owned.

Drake changed out of his jeans and a polo shirt to dress for his venture into the sport's inner sanctum. Celebrities, VIPs, and team sponsors would be there to enjoy gourmet dining and the best viewing opportunity of the race that Formula One and the teams could provide. For the occasion, he slipped into a pair of black slacks and put on a lightweight black Merino wool crewneck sweater to wear under the dove-gray blazer he brought. And almost forgot to exchange his trainers for his black Derby shoes.

It was a short walk from Veer Towers down the Strip and up Harmon Avenue to the Paddock Building at the start-finish line of the street circuit. The building was three stories tall, with the first floor housing the garages for the ten Formula One teams, and the second and third floors providing space for the Paddock Club and the individual team hospitality suites.

He went directly to the Red Bull Racing Paddock Club suite and ordered a gourmet burger and fries from the chef at the grill. When his order was handed to him, he went to a window looking down at the starting grid. He was directly above the Red Bull Racing garage, and from there, you could watch the lightning-fast Red Bull pit crew, during a race, change all four tires on their car in as little as two seconds or less.

Formula One called itself the pinnacle of open-wheel motor racing, and he thought it probably was, although IndyCar racing fans he knew would disagree. It was an extraordinarily expensive sport, with each racing car costing between twelve and fifteen million dollars to build and maintain. Racing on four continents each year, he imagined that it had to cost Red Bull Racing a hundred million dollars or more a year.

Drake finished his burger and fries, sitting alone at a small table near the window, enjoying the scene, watching people, and trying to remember the names of the ones he recognized. Several were actors, and several were wearing outlandish attire and draped with jewelry or gold, probably singers or rappers

Before he left the Paddock Club to attend Chris Patterson's dubious award ceremony, Drake waited in a short line for a chilled mug of OttakringerHelles Austrian bier that was offered to the guests in the Paddock Club before going downstairs for the scheduled pit lane walk that his ticket allowed him to take.

Chapter Seventeen

DANIEL FRANKLIN SUMMONED Marcus Braxton to his penthouse suite at the Bellagio at six o'clock that evening. His plan wasn't working, and he blamed Braxton.

He poured his second glass of Grey Goose vodka and sat in the armchair near the window to wait for Braxton. As soon as they finished talking about how to finish what they'd started, he was flying home to Boston. If the report to the President's Intelligence Advisory Board caused the problem it potentially could, there was work to do. His contracts with the government were too valuable to let slip away without a fight. It was time to remind a few politicians he knew there were skeletons in their closets.

Braxton knocked once and let himself in. Franklin didn't get up to greet him or tell him to pour himself a drink.

"I just got a call informing me his online poker account hasn't been altered," Franklin said tightly. "How is that?"

Braxton crossed his arms across his chest and stared at

Franklin. "That's not possible. I saw it myself. Who told you his account wasn't altered?"

"Did you think I wouldn't have someone check?"

"I'm telling you the account was hacked and shows he's been losing badly."

"When did you check his account?"

"Just before noon."

"Then someone changed it back after that."

"Assuming that's true, what…?"

Franklin stood so quickly that he spilled his drink. "Never question what I tell you! His poker account doesn't show he's been losing. Find a way to fix this! Your plan to bring in a hooker from Paris didn't work. Your plan to hack his poker account to prove he has a gambling problem hasn't worked.

"Now the reporters are going to show up at the award ceremony in an hour to report on the rumor we started of a scandal they've heard about, only to find out there isn't one. So, I was forced to cancel the award ceremony."

"We can go back and change the numbers again," Braxton offered. "We have time."

"I can't take a chance the numbers won't be changed back again," Franklin said. "Do we have any idea who's doing this?"

"I have an idea. My team identified the guy who spooked the hooker. He's a former Special Forces operator. His name is Adam Drake. He was practicing law in Oregon the last time I heard. Now he's special counsel for a security company in Seattle and the director of its intelligence contractor division."

"Why am I just now hearing about him?"

"I just found out. We have a picture of him driving

around with the kid today and were able to identify him from it."

Franklin shook his head and went to the wet bar to refill his glass. "That's just wonderful, Marcus. Is he the one who changed the numbers on Patterson's poker account?"

"I think so. His company will have the ability to do it."

"How did he find out what you were doing?"

"I don't know that he has," Braxton said. "I saw him yesterday afternoon at the Petrosian bar with Chandler Patterson, the kid's father. Maybe he's here for some other reason."

"Does the father know you?"

"No, there's no reason for him to know who I am."

"But this Drake fellow does."

"Yes."

Franklin returned to his armchair and motioned for Braxton to pour himself a drink. "Is there anything we can do to salvage this?"

Braxton took time pouring his drink before sitting in the other armchair. "We planned to get Chris Patterson caught with his pants down in bed with a Paris hooker. Her family is Lebanese, with connections to terrorists there. We can still expose his being seen with a foreign agent.

"The only other thing we thought of was to get him caught with drugs in his possession. We found an old medical record when he was at Stanford that mentions a possible drug overdose. He was taking pain pills while he was recovering from a racing injury, had a drink at a party, and fell down the stairs at his apartment. The ER medical record mentions a possible overdose."

"That's pretty thin," Franklin said. "How are you going to get him caught using drugs?"

"We don't have to get him caught using drugs, just

caught with drugs," Braxton said. "He can have an accident driving and the police can find the drugs in the car. That's all we'd need to put his security clearance at risk and have his credibility questioned."

"Do you have someone to plant the drugs and cause this accident?"

"Yes, we've done it successfully before."

Franklin set his drink down and looked around the room before nodding. "Do it. What about this man who keeps interfering? Can you make sure he doesn't mess this up as well?"

"I can take care of him as well."

"I don't want to know how," Franklin said. "I'm flying home to Boston and checking out as soon as you leave. Wait until I leave town to do it."

"That will be an addition to the bill," Braxton said. "He is alone, as far as we can tell, but he's a former Special Forces operator. It won't be as easy as dealing with the kid."

"With what's at stake here, the size of the bill isn't an issue. Making sure you're successful this time is the issue. Don't fail me, Braxton."

Chapter Eighteen

THE PIT LANE walk was delayed for some unannounced reason, and Drake only had time to briefly watch the activity in the Red Bull garage. He wanted to arrive early enough at the award ceremony to speak with Walter Williams or Marcus Braxton if he was there.

Kevin McRoberts called him before he left the Red Bull Racing Paddock Club suite. He couldn't find out who owned the red pickup because the pickup's license plate was reported stolen in Henderson, Nevada.

Drake wasn't surprised with the information. Braxton and his men weren't going to make it easy to prove they were responsible for what was going on.

It was the second piece of information Kevin discovered that worried him. Someone hacked into Chris's online poker platform and altered his account to show he'd lost over seventy thousand dollars last year. The account had been kept current each month with deposits Chris would have trouble explaining on his PIAB salary.

Kevin deleted the false information in the online poker

account, but it could be hacked again to make it look like Chris had a gambling problem.

Braxton needed to hear that his dirty tricks were not going to work and that he should pack his bags and leave Las Vegas. Drake was going to deliver the message.

When he entered the Bellagio lobby, he went straight to the reception desk and asked where the American Karting Foundation award ceremony was being held.

"The Da Vinci 1, across the lobby to the Ballrooms and Convention area, sir," the attendant said, pointing to her left without looking up.

Drake walked the length of the lobby and by the Promenade Shops to the Convention area. Da Vinci 1 was across the hall from the Tower Ballroom, and when he opened the door, he saw it was empty—except for a bartender taking down a tower of champagne glasses at his station.

"It's been canceled," the man said. "Been nice if someone had told me before I set things up."

Drake walked over and asked, "Why was it canceled?"

"I heard one of the reporters here earlier say it was because of something the foundation learned about the guy getting the award."

"Did the reporter say what that was?"

"Didn't ask and don't care."

Drake looked around the room and saw that the only sign of an award ceremony being held there, other than the champagne station, was a dozen tall cocktail tables along the walls.

He left the room and called Chris when he was out in the hall.

"Chris, where are you?"

"Driving in from Summerlin with my parents."

"Go to the condo," Drake said. "The award ceremony

has been canceled. Wait for me there. If reporters call and want a statement, don't talk with them."

"What's going on?" Chris asked.

"More of the same, another attempt to discredit you. They hacked your online poker account and made it look like you've been losing a lot of money. We took care of it, but that may not be the end of it."

"Dad, the award ceremony is canceled. Adam wants us to go to the condo and meet him there," Drake heard Chris say.

"Chris, I'll meet you there," Drake said

He left the convention area and headed back to the lobby. Braxton had the press attend the award ceremony to hear that the karting foundation had learned something about Chris and knew they wouldn't stop digging until they knew what it was. He would have to find a way to set the record straight before it was too late.

He left the Bellagio and walked along, thinking of a way to satisfy the curiosity of a press that was too quick to quote anonymous sources and not do the work good journalists were supposed to do.

When he turned to walk along West Aria Place toward Veer Towers and Patterson's condo, he didn't pay any attention to a man walking behind him and getting closer with each step he took.

Drake felt arms wrap around him in a bear hug, pinning his arms to his side. Then he saw a white delivery van stopping at the curb with its sliding door open.

Drake dropped down and hooked the crook of his left ankle back around the man's left ankle to avoid being lifted off his feet. At the same time, he shot his hands up to loosen his attacker's grip and counterattacked with a vicious left horizontal elbow strike to the man's ribs and then another elbow strike to his ribs on the other side.

When the man swayed to his right with the second elbow strike, Drake twisted and delivered a left elbow strike to the side of his head, dropping him down onto one knee.

Another man jumped out of the van in front of Drake and got a quick knee to the groin for doing so. It doubled him over enough for Drake to land a blow to the side of the man's head and make him stagger back a couple of steps.

Drake started to turn to his left to confront a third man coming out of the van when something hard and heavy struck the back of his head, knocking him down onto the sidewalk.

He was on the cement when the man leaned down to hit him again. Drake lifted his left arm to block the blow, dug his heels in to push back, and got out of the way.

The sound of a siren approaching turned the heads of the men and ended the attack. As they scrambled to get back in the van, Drake heard a woman far away asking if he was okay before he lost consciousness.

Chapter Nineteen

DRAKE KNEW where he was before he opened his eyes. The antiseptic smell of bleach and the scent of an air freshener told him he was in a hospital.

He turned his head to the left at the sound of someone humming when a sharp, searing pain hit him in the back of his head, making him flinch, confirming the reason he was there: he was injured.

"Just rest, love," a middle-aged black nurse with a British accent said. "The doctor will be back to talk with you in a minute."

"How long have I been here?"

"You were here when my shift started at eight."

"What time is it now?"

"Nine thirty."

"I need my phone."

A young woman wearing blue surgical scrubs came into the room, reading a chart, and asked, "How are you feeling, Mr. Drake?"

"My head hurts, and I have a headache," he said. "Is there anything else I should know?"

"You have fourteen stitches in the back of your head," Dr. Patel said. "You have a concussion. Your CT scan didn't show your brain bleeding, fortunately for you. Someone hit you with a steel baton, I understand."

"I didn't see what it was," Drake said. "When can I leave?"

"We need to keep an eye on you overnight," she said. "Maybe tomorrow."

"I have to leave, sorry."

"You are in no condition to be discharged, Mr. Drake."

"Doctor, I've had a concussion before. A young man and his family may be in danger. If you have something for me to sign that confirms I'm being discharged against medical advice, please go get it."

Drake sat up and dropped his legs over the side of the bed, closing his eyes for a second when his headache throbbed.

"Mr. Drake, please don't get out of that bed!"

"Doctor, get the release for me to sign. I'll take a cab. I'll be fine. If I start slurring my speech, losing coordination, or any of the other symptoms you're dying to tell me about, I promise I'll be back."

Dr. Patel stared at him, shook her head, and left.

"Nurse, will you bring me my phone and my clothes?" Drake said.

"Where'd you get your other concussion?" she asked.

"Playing football in college."

"Is that the only one you've had?"

Drake turned to look at her and asked, "Do I look like I've had several concussions?"

"No, but you told her about the symptoms to look out for if your concussion worsens. Either you have a great memory, or you've been told what to watch for more than once."

"You're right on both counts. I have a good memory and heard that advice from medics in Afghanistan more than once."

"Did you listen to them?"

"Yes, ma'am, I did."

"Uh-huh," she huffed. "Just make sure you remember what you've been told. I'll get your things and call you a cab."

"Thank you."

When the nurse came back with his phone and his clothes, Drake called Mike Casey in Seattle.

"Mike, I could use some help here," Drake said. "This assignment for the president just got a little rougher than I thought it would."

"What happened?"

"Three guys tried to take me for a one-way ride I didn't want to go on."

"Are you okay?"

"Nothing major, a concussion and some stitches. Don't say anything to Liz. I'll call her later."

"What do you need?"

"A three-man protection team for Congressman Chandler Patterson's son. Have Dan Norris come too."

"Anything else?"

"Whatever Dan's carrying."

"I'll let you know when they're on their way," Casey said. "Do you know who the opposition is?"

"Pretty sure it's someone we know, Marcus Braxton."

"The former Special Forces guy they drummed out of the army?"

"That's the guy."

"What's he doing in Las Vegas?"

"Just a second, Mike," Drake said when the nurse came in and told him his cab was there. "Mike, I need to go, my cab's here. I'll call you in an hour."

"Don't worry about the time," Casey said. "It will take me a while to get things organized."

Drake dressed and followed the exit signs to the emergency room waiting room. His cab was idling at the curb outside the Valley Hospital Medical Center when he walked out into the night.

"Veer Towers," Drake told the driver as the cab pulled away and called Chandler Patterson to let him know he was on his way to the condo.

He sat back, fastened his seat belt, and realized he had no idea what contingencies he needed to plan for. If Braxton was willing to come after him, would he be willing to come after Chris Patterson?

Sending three thugs to take him out didn't make any sense. Braxton had to know he'd figured out what he was up to. Coming for him just proved it.

It also meant Braxton wasn't finished. He had to be desperate to finish what he started, though, if he was willing to try something that could get the police involved. Nothing he'd attempted so far involved criminal activity.

Now that line had been crossed, he had to be prepared to protect Chris.

Or go on the offensive and not wait for Braxton to try something else.

A plan was beginning to take shape in his mind.

Chapter Twenty

CHANDLER PATTERSON HEARD Drake entering the condo and met him at the door with a glass of whisky in his hand. "Why was the award ceremony canceled?"

"Pour me a glass of what you're having," Drake said, walking toward the living area. "I'll explain, but Chris will want to hear it too."

Chris was sitting with his mother on the white leather sofa near the window. He stood when he saw Drake and said, "Mom, this is Mr. Drake."

Mrs. Patterson held out her hand. "Please call me Cheryl, Mr. Drake. Chris has been telling me about you."

"Cheryl," Drake said and shook her hand.

Chandler came up behind him with a glass of whisky and saw the bandage covering the stitches on the back of Drake's head. "You're hurt. When did that happen?"

Drake accepted the glass of whisky and sat next to Chris. "Tonight on my way here from the Bellagio. I'm okay, but that's why I wanted you to come here. Three men tried to pull me into a van. I'd like to say, 'You should see the other guys,' but I was the one who woke up in the emergency room."

"Who were they?" Chris asked.

"My guess is they're the ones behind this whole charade; the award, the escort from Paris, and hacking into your online poker account."

"What? Why?" Chandler asked.

"They tried to make it look like Chris is losing a lot of money and has a gambling problem," Drake said.

"I don't understand," Mrs. Patterson said.

"We think they're trying to discredit the report Chris put together for the President's Intelligence Advisory Board, Cheryl," Drake told her. "They tried to lure Chris into bed with a French escort who has a connection to terrorists in Lebanon. Contact with a possible foreign agent must be investigated when someone reports it and challenges his security clearance.

"The same applies if someone exposes a gambling debt or gambling addiction that makes someone vulnerable to blackmail."

"Is this why you called the president?" she asked her husband. "Is that why Mr. Drake is here? Why didn't you tell me?"

"I didn't want to worry you, honey," Chandler said. "I thought there was something fishy about this karting award."

"Well, how do we stop this? If they attacked Mr. Drake, is Chris in danger?" she asked.

"He might be," Drake said. "That's why I have a protection team flying here from Seattle. I want to make sure all of you are safe until we put an end to this."

"How do we do that?" Chandler asked.

"By going on offense. We're going after the man I

believe is responsible, Marcus Braxton. His company does opposition research used to take down public figures or anyone some client wants to be discredited."

"Do you know who the client is that's trying to discredit Chris?" Cheryl asked.

"I think it's a member of the intelligence community who hired a private contractor they hired, Marcus Braxton and his company," Drake said.

"Why do you think it's Braxton?" she asked.

"Because he's here in Las Vegas and it's the kind of work he does. I saw him talking with the escort from Paris."

"What happens when the protection team gets here?" Chris asked.

"I'd like them to go with you and your parents to your home in Summerlin and stay there, out of sight," Drake said.

"If Braxton tries something, won't he be coming for me? Wouldn't my staying here be better, so Mom and Dad won't be involved?"

Chandler walked over to Drake and held out his hand for his glass. "Want a refresher?"

"No, I'm fine. I would take some Tylenol or Advil if you have any. Whatever they gave me at the ER is wearing off."

"Sure," Chandler said and left.

"Chris, we're going to draw Braxton out, give him a chance to come after you again," Drake said. "Except it's not going to be you when he does.

"When the team from Seattle gets here, I want you to go to the airport with me and trade places with one of the men on the protection team. The team will take you to Summerlin with your parents.

"The man who will be your double is a former FBI HRT commander. We've worked together and we both have training for this kind of thing. We'll be able and ready to respond to whatever Braxton tries."

"What do you think that will involve?" Chandler asked when he returned from behind Drake and handed him two Tylenol tablets.

"I don't have any idea," Drake admitted. "This was planned to take place here in Las Vegas, and there are two days left before Chris is scheduled to return to Washington. If Braxton has a backup plan, it will have to be something he thinks he can set up to control the time and place. And be flexible enough to allow him to react if something changes. We won't know what he'll try, Chandler, but we will be ready for whatever it is."

"Is there anything I can do to help?" Chandler asked.

"Between now and the time your protection team arrives, you're safe here," Drake said. "Braxton won't know where Chris might be going, so he'll be watching the condo when we leave. Is there a way to get to the airport he won't expect us to take?"

"Which airport are you asking about?" Chandler asked. "Las Vegas International, where I picked you up, or the North Las Vegas Airport? Northtown is the primary airport for general aviation. You flew the PSS Gulfstream into Las Vegas International, so that's where he would expect you to go. He might not think about you going to the North Las Vegas Airport instead."

"Then that's where the Gulfstream will land," Drake said.

Chapter Twenty-One

BEFORE SUNRISE FRIDAY MORNING, the Tri-tone alert on Drake's phone signaled it was time to leave for the airport. The PSS Gulfstream G280, the newest business jet in the company's growing fleet of aircraft, was landing in half an hour. Drake wanted to be waiting for the executive protection team at the FBO terminal building when they arrived.

He was sitting on the white leather sofa near the window, drinking his second cup of coffee. He volunteered to sleep on the sofa to allow Chandler and his wife to sleep in one of the condo's two bedrooms. Chris had offered to share the king-size bed in the other bedroom, but Drake declined the offer.

His persistent headache and a fierce determination to keep Marcus Braxton from ruining the reputation of Chris Patterson weren't going to let him sleep anyway, so there was no use trying.

Liz had known that something wasn't quite right when he called, but he convinced her that he was fine with a lie of omission he regretted immediately. She was afraid of the risks he continued to take and wanted him to leave the "heavy lifting," as she called it, to the younger and single men in the company. And someday he would. But not before he finished his assignment in Las Vegas.

So, he promised that he'd be home in a day or so and wouldn't leave her alone again before their baby was born. It wasn't everything she wanted him to promise, but right now it was all he could.

Chandler and Cheryl Patterson came out of their bedroom ready to leave and called to Chris to get a move on.

"When we get there, do you want us to be out in the parking lot or waiting in front of the terminal building for your guys?" Chandler asked.

"Wait in front of the terminal," Drake said. "In case Braxton has someone following you, Chris will stay inside with me. I asked Dan Norris to come along because he's about the same size and build as Chris. They're going to exchange clothes in the restroom and Chris will come out wearing Dan's clothes. If you're waiting out front, no one will get a good look at him when he comes out with the protection team and gets in your Expedition."

"What will you be doing while we're home in Summerlin?" Cheryl Patterson wanted to know.

"Looking for Marcus Braxton."

Chris came out of his bedroom wearing a red UNLV Rebels hat, sunglasses, jeans, and a tan windbreaker and said, "Let's get this party started."

"Good choice," Drake nodded, approving of his attire. "Chandler, give us a five-minute head start and then drive to the airport. I won't see you there, but I'll be in touch."

Chandler reached out to shake Drake's hand and said, "Good luck finding Braxton."

"I think I might know where he is, but thanks."

Chris called the parking valet to bring the Mustang Dark Horse up to the valet stand and hugged his mother before leaving the condo.

"She doesn't show it, but she's scared," he said when they were in the elevator.

"She has a reason to be—someone's trying to harm her son," Drake said, patting Chris's shoulder. "She'll feel better when she gets home and has you and the protection team in place."

The morning commute hadn't begun, and the traffic was light on the way to the North Las Vegas Airport. Twenty minutes after leaving Veer Towers, they were walking toward the terminal building from the parking lot where Chris had parked the Dark Horse.

Up ahead, a black limousine was parked in front of the terminal building with its engine idling, but its driver wasn't paying any attention to them.

"Coming here was a good idea," he told Chris. "Braxton may guess you're in Summerlin with your parents at some point, but he won't know for sure. It won't make a difference if he does know. The team will be ready for whatever he might try."

"You think he's that crazy?"

"I don't know the man that well, Chris. He might be. That's why we're not taking a chance."

When they entered the modern terminal building, no one was on the main lobby floor and the Enterprise and Hertz car rental offices weren't open yet. Muffled noise coming from the mezzanine level above was the only sound in the high-ceiling lobby, other than the echo of their foot-steps walking toward the stairs to the second level.

"Let's go up to the observation deck," Drake said after checking his phone for messages. "They just touched down."

From the observation deck, they were able to watch the white and blue PSS Gulfstream G280 taxiing to the tie-down area. A line service representative was waiting to help tie down the aircraft, and a van was waiting to transport passengers to the terminal building.

The G280 rolled to the last row of parking and stopped at the end of the row beside a Bombardier Challenger 350 with red and black striping.

When the G280's door opened and the airstairs came down, Drake saw that Dan Norris was the first man down, walking quickly to the transportation van with three men carrying duffle bags behind him. Norris was wearing a blue Seattle Seahawks hat above his aviator sunglasses and had a smaller duffel bag than the others who were dressed alike, khaki pants, blue blazers, white dress shirts, and red ties.

"What's in the duffel bags?" Chris asked.

"Tools of the trade," Drake smiled. "Let's go down and meet them."

When Dan Norris came through the door and entered the arrival lounge, Drake looked to his left toward the men's restroom and nodded. Norris nodded back and walked that way.

Chris Patterson was waiting there for him and came out minutes later, wearing a blue Seattle Seahawks hat, sunglasses, and a blue windbreaker.

Drake was standing with the protection team. "Chris, these are the guys who will be with you and your parents in Summerlin. Say hello to Pat, Luis, and Anthony."

After each of the men shook hands with their new principal, Drake led them outside where Chandler Patterson's Ford Expedition people-hauler was waiting.

Chapter Twenty-Two

DAN NORRIS WAS WAITING for him at the information kiosk when Drake returned and asked him, "Did you guys have breakfast on the plane?"

"Coffee and bagels," Norris said.

"Let's go upstairs and have breakfast, I'm hungry."

"How's the head?"

"It's fine," Drake said. "I need to stop somewhere and get a hat to cover the bandage over the stitches."

"You can have this one if you want."

"Keep it, you're supposed to be Chris Patterson, remember."

"I didn't forget. I just never liked UNLV."

The Sunshine and Tailwinds Café was open, but there was only one customer inside, sitting alone by the window.

"Can I bring you gentlemen coffee?" an older man behind the counter asked as they walked in.

"Coffee with cream for me," Norris said.

"None for me, thanks," Drake said.

They sat at a table with a model of a World War Two Navy Corsair fighter hanging from the ceiling above it.

"Kevin has the information you wanted," Norris said. "The Braxton Group is a subcontractor that does a lot of work for the CIA. Braxton worked for the agency until four years ago as a Paramilitary Operations Officer in the Special Activities Center. Kevin couldn't find out where he got the money when he left to start his company. His office is in Bethesda, Maryland, he has a Bombardier Challenger 350, and drives a new Range Rover."

"A Bombardier like the one you parked next to when you landed?"

"I didn't notice it. You want me to find out?"

"Let's see if anyone can tell us who it belongs to. What else did Kevin dig up?"

Dan's coffee arrived and they were asked if they wanted to order anything for breakfast.

"The answer is yes," Drake said. "Give us a minute, okay?"

"Sure, no problem," the man said and left.

"You asked Kevin to do a deep dive on Chris and he found something he thought you'd be interested in," Norris said, adding cream to his coffee. "When he was a first-year law student at Stanford, he fell down a flight of stairs leaving a party. He'd been drinking and was taken to the emergency room. At the time, he was recovering from a racing accident, taking oxycontin, and shouldn't have been drinking. The ER medical report called it a 'possible overdose.'"

"If Kevin found it, Braxton will have it," Drake said and shook his head. "Opposition research, unfortunately, is something his company does."

"Is Chris using drugs?"

"I don't think so, and he doesn't use hookers or have a gambling problem. But that hasn't stopped Braxton from trying to make it look like he does. What did Kevin find about Daniel Franklin and Franklin Analytics?"

Norris shook his head and said, "Daniel Franklin, now there's a piece of work. He was a Berkeley radical in the 1970s and one of the early Silicon Valley billionaires. He has a big sailing yacht in San Franciso he uses to host a retreat each year like the Bohemian Grove men's club does, except these guys are all big tech elites and media moguls. They sail down the Pacific coast to Cabo San Lucas and back, partying and thinking of ways to transform America.

"Franklin has a foundation that funnels money to radical groups like George Soros does with his Open Society Foundations. In socialist circles, or whatever they call themselves these days, he's a celebrity.

"You have to laugh, really, at these guys," Norris said. "They make it big in America, then want to change everything as soon as they get to the top of the food chain."

Drake sat back and chuckled. "You don't sound like you adopted the government's party line when you were in Washington working for the FBI."

"Don't get me started."

A young man wearing a black polo shirt with the Flying V logo of the Civil Air Patrol came to their table and announced he was their server. "Would you like to order something for breakfast?"

"What do you recommend?" Drake asked.

"You can't beat our steak and eggs, sir."

"Dan?"

"Sounds good."

"Two orders of steak and eggs, then," Drake said with a

smile. "How long have you been a volunteer in the Civil Air Patrol?"

"This is my second year, sir. When I finish high school, I'm joining the Air Force."

"Good for you and good luck," Drake said.

"Thank you, sir. I'll tell our cook to put a rush on your orders."

"There's still hope for this country," Norris said, "With more of them like him, anyway, volunteering and working a job before school."

"Yeah, impressive. I like this kid."

"Do you have a plan you want to share?" Norris asked. "Mike told me what happened and why you wanted the protection team here, but not much else."

"Braxton hasn't been successful, so he'll try again. That's where you come in. As Chris's lookalike, you're going to be the bait he'll come for."

"Do you think he'll try something like he did with you?"

"I think he wanted me out of the way," Drake said. "It will be something directed at Chris, not like it was with me. Unless I'm in the way again, which I intend to be. Did you bring the equipment I asked for?"

"Two 19s, two of the Byrna pistols, and three real-time GPS trackers," Norris said. "I threw in a couple of other toys I thought we might need as well."

"Like what?"

"Duct tape, flex cuffs, tactical flashlights, and two of the new SOCP tactical folding knives Benchmade's asking us to use and review."

"Just like old times, getting a kit together for a mission," Drake said.

"Yep, nothing's new under the sun except new enemies who keep showing up."

The young CAP volunteer arrived carrying two plates and set them on the table in front of them. "Enjoy."

"I'm sure we will," Drake said. "Before you leave, do you know who owns the Bombardier Challenger 350 tied down outside? It's next to our G280. I'd like to ask the owner how he likes it if he's around."

"When I have a minute, I'll go downstairs and ask. Don't leave before I find out, okay?"

"That's a promise," Drake said.

"This kid's tip is getting bigger by the minute," Norris asked.

"Yes, it is."

Chapter Twenty-Three

BY THE TIME they left the Sunshine and Tailwinds Café, they knew two things: the steak and eggs were as good as promised, and the Bombardier Challenger 350 was registered to the Braxton Group of Bethesda, Maryland.

The protection team reported that the Patterson family was safe in their Summerlin home and had insisted their protectors eat a traditional "Full Irish Breakfast" to start the day. Mike Chadwell, the team leader, told Drake the breakfast included rashers, sausages, fried eggs, hash browns, baked beans, soda bread, and that they were skipping lunch.

While Norris drove the Mustang Dark Horse back to the condo at Veer Towers, Drake called Kevin McRoberts at PSS headquarters and asked him to find out where Marcus Braxton was staying.

"Start with the Paris Las Vegas Hotel and Casino," he said. "That's where I saw him at the hotel's Mon Ami Gabi bistro with the escort from Paris."

"I'm on it, Mr. Drake."

"Thanks, Kevin."

"What do we do if he's there?" Norris asked.

Drake removed the Sunshine and Tailwinds hat he bought to cover his stitches and laid it on his knee. "First, we find the men he sent after me. He'll use them again if he tries something else. We make sure they're not available to do his dirty work. Then we find Braxton."

"Then what?"

"We find out who he's working for and why the report Chris put together for the President's Intelligence Advisory Board is so important to whoever he's working for."

When they stopped at the valet stand, Drake said, "Toss the key fob to the valet and follow me in without saying anything. Let's keep them thinking you're Chris for as long as possible."

"Got it," Norris said.

Drake got out and retrieved the duffel bag from the back seat, while Norris walked around the front of the Mustang and tossed the fob to the valet.

"Will you need the car again this morning?" the valet asked.

Norris shrugged his shoulders as he walked past and didn't answer.

"You handled that nicely," Drake said, as they waited for the elevator to arrive.

"I don't know Chris, so I acted like I thought a rich kid with a condo in a place like this might act."

"Chris isn't like that," Drake said when the elevator door opened, "But don't worry, I won't tell him you think he was."

When the elevator opened again on the thirty-second floor, Drake got out and walked ahead of Norris to the door of Patterson's condo. Leaning forward to enter the code in the electronic keypad lock, he caught a whiff of cheap cigar smoke in the air and stepped back. Chandler and Chris Patteson didn't smoke as far as he knew.

"Someone's inside," Drake whispered.

Norris set his duffel bag down to open it and stood up with an orange Byrna Sd nonlethal pistol in one hand and a Glock 19 in the other.

Drake held out his hand for the Byrna. "If it's one of Braxton's guys, I want him alive and able to talk."

"If you use the Byrna, we may have to wait a while."

The Byrna SD Launcher was a newly developed polymer and aluminum pistol that used compressed CO_2 gas to fire a projectile loaded with a mix of pepper spray and tear gas. With a range of sixty feet, it delivered a strong kinetic punch from the projectile to the body of an attacker and then exploded in a mist of pepper spray and tear gas that would incapacitate a person for as much as thirty minutes. It wasn't lethal, but it would stop a lethal attacker effectively and painfully.

Norris looked up and down the hallway and moved to the other side of the door with the Glock held at eye level and ready. He touched Drake's shoulder, telling him to enter the code on the keylock pad.

Drake pushed the door slowly open with his left hand and searched to the left of the entry vestibule for an intruder, while Norris did the same to the right of it.

"Clear," Drake whispered.

"Clear," Norris answered.

Norris entered and moved to the right. Drake followed him in and moved to the left.

Beyond the vestibule, a long hallway led past two bedrooms, a guest bathroom, and on to the main living area and kitchen. The first bedroom was where Chris slept the night before and the second bedroom was where his parents had slept.

Drake could still smell cigar smoke, a little stronger now, and then the sound of a closet door closing in the first bedroom.

He pointed to the first bedroom and moved forward with the Byrna pistol raised and ready. Norris followed silently behind him.

When Drake reached the bedroom door, he stopped and listened. Then he raised his left hand and held up one finger, two fingers, then the third and poked his head around the door.

The man smoking a cigar was the man wearing black shorts, guayabera shirt, and a Panama hat who followed him the other day. He was leaning over a small shopping bag on the bed and was dressed like a wealthy tourist, wearing a light blue blazer and dark blue pants.

Drake stood in the open doorway with the Bryna pistol pointed at the man's back and said, "I hoped we would meet again. Turn around slowly with your hands where I can see them."

The man stood still but did not turn around. "Or what, you'll shoot me?"

"Something like that," Drake said.

The man's left hand was hanging at his side, but Drake saw his right hand move slowly in front of his right leg. When he spun to the left with a small pistol in his right hand, Drake fired two shots that hit him in the chest.

He fell back onto the bed in a mist of pepper spray and tear gas. They stepped back into the hallway to avoid the tear gas that was making the man yell and then roll off the bed onto the floor, wiping at his eyes and coughing violently.

Norris waited a minute before walking in with a wet hand towel from the guest bathroom held to his face to get the gun the man dropped to the floor.

Norris returned with the gun, a nice little Kimber R7 Mako, and handed it to Drake. "I'll get the duct tape and flex cuffs. He needs to quiet down to appreciate his situation. There are three more rounds in the Byrna to help him understand the consequences if he doesn't want to talk."

Chapter Twenty-Four

WHEN THEY HAD the man restrained and duct taped to a chair, Drake took a headshot with his phone and left to send it to Kevin at PSS headquarters.

"Kevin, see if you can find out who this guy is," Drake said. "He broke into the condo where I'm staying and brought a shopping bag full of counterfeit oxycontin and cocaine with him. I think he wanted to plant it here to frame Chris Patterson for something. See if you can find a connection to Braxton or the CIA."

He returned and stood with Norris in the hallway, watching the man in the chair.

"I think he's smiling at me," Norris said.

"Or trying to squeeze the pepper spray and tear gas out of his eyes. Hard to tell."

"Do you want to see if he's ready to talk to us?"

"Sure, go ahead. Let's see how smart he is."

Norris walked in and pulled the duct tape off the man's mouth.

"Who are you?" Norris asked.

The only answer was the man's steely glare.

"Okay, let's try something else. What did Marcus Braxton send you here to do, make it look like Chris Patterson has a drug problem?"

Still no answer, but the man blinked twice.

Drake went into the bedroom and stood next to Norris. "Dan, he's not ready to talk yet. Let's give him time to think about how he wants this to go. I used two rounds. Three more might help him decide to cooperate."

Norris nodded and walked out of the bedroom. Drake backed up to stand in the open doorway and fire the nonlethal rounds when his phone alerted him that someone was calling.

"Don't go anywhere. I'll be right back," he told the man.

It was Kevin McRoberts at PSS.

"I know who the man is," Kevin said. "His name is Arnold Peter Shelton. He's a former Baltimore narcotics officer in the Baltimore Police Department. He left the department shortly after eight of his colleagues in the BPD elite Gun Trace Task Force were indicted for corruption in 2017. He wasn't indicted but named in the 2016 Department of Justice investigation report. He lives in Virginia and works for the Braxton Group."

"Thank you, Kevin."

"Is there anything else you need to know about him? Should I keep digging?"

"No, that's all I need. I'll have Mr. Shelton tell me the rest."

Drake put his phone in his pocket and stepped back into the bedroom.

"So, you're a dirty cop," Drake began. "You left the Baltimore PD when your friends in the Gun Trace Task

Force were indicted and went to work for Marcus Braxton. He isn't going to be pleased when he finds out you were caught red-handed planting drugs in the condo of a former congressman and respected city leader in Las Vegas. I suspect you were also working with the men who tried to throw me in a van.

"I'm tired of the games you and Braxton are playing, Arnie. I'm willing to give you a chance to tell me what he's planning and who he's working for. I'll let you leave without calling the police if you tell me what I want to know. If you're not willing to do that, I will use the rest of the rounds in this wonderful nonlethal invention and then call the police. Your choice."

"You think I'm stupid enough to believe you'll let me walk out of here?" Shelton asked.

"Your being here proves you're stupid, Arnie. I'm not letting you and Braxton hurt my young friend. If letting you walk is the cost of preventing that, so be it," Drake said.

"You know what he's tried so far. Why do you think he'll try something else?"

"Because whoever is behind this has spent too much time and money to walk away. That's not how they operate."

Dan Norris came in and held out his hand for the Byrna pistol. "He's not going to talk. I was in Washington with the FBI when he and his crew were running wild in Baltimore, stealing drugs from dealers, using illegal GPS trackers to track down people to rob, planting evidence, you name it. He's a disgrace! You leave. I'll finish the rest of the rounds and then call the police. We'll find Braxton and finish this."

Drake looked at Norris, then Shelton. He nodded and handed Norris the pistol.

"You two are a riot," Shelton said. "How are you going to explain using that thing on me?"

Norris shrugged. "We caught a burglar and defended ourselves," he said and shot Shelton three more times.

Thirty minutes later, when they lifted Shelton and his chair off the vintage porcelain tile floor, they learned what the counterfeit oxycontin and cocaine were for. When it was found in Chris Patterson's bedroom, it would confirm that he had a drug problem. Shelton claimed he didn't know what else Braxton was planning because he wasn't in charge of the operation. Braxton was. Yes, he worked for the Braxton Group, but he was only one of Braxton's four-man team in Las Vegas. They were staying at the Palms Casino and Resort on Flamingo Road, a mile off the Las Vegas Strip.

Drake and Norris moved Shelton to the large soaking tub in the bedroom and left him lying there on his back, still duct taped to the chair with tape over his mouth. They told him he would be allowed to walk away, just not now.

Chapter Twenty-Five

DRAKE TOSSED Norris a green bottle of Pellegrino from the refrigerator and sat on the leather couch by the windows across from Norris, sitting on the other one.

"Do you believe him?" Norris asked.

"Maybe, but he's not telling us everything."

"What now?"

Drake watched a tour helicopter fly down the Las Vegas strip and said, "Chris and his parents are safe from Braxton, but Braxton isn't finished. He'll try something else here or in Washington when Chris returns there. We need to make sure it ends here."

Norris chuckled and said, "What happens in Las Vegas stays in Las Vegas, you mean."

"Exactly."

"How do we accomplish that?"

"Braxton has four men doing his dirty work," Drake said. "If we put them on the sidelines, Braxton's finished here."

"Okay, take them out of the game. How?"

"Something Shelton said gave me an idea. He said that when the drugs are found here, it would confirm his drug problem. That means something else will happen first, something that would provide a reason for the police to search the condo for drugs."

"Like what?"

"Where do the police usually find drugs without a search warrant?"

Norris looked pensively out the window with his bottle of Pellegrino held to his lips and turned to Drake. "When they have probable cause to search a vehicle."

"After there's been an accident, especially if someone's injured and a driver might have been under the influence of drugs or alcohol."

"So, they stage an accident and make sure it looks like the driver was under the influence of an illegal substance."

"Let's make it an accident that happens where and when we want it to, somewhere out of the city where no one else gets hurt. Any idea where that might be?"

"Okay," Norris said. "I visited a place not far from here when we had an HRT training exercise with local law enforcement. We were training to prepare for a terrorist attack on Hoover Dam. Lake Las Vegas is a little resort area built to look like an old town in Italy or the French Riviera. The Kansas City Chiefs and the San Franciso 49ers stayed there before Super Bowl LVlll. It's an hour's drive out of Las Vegas. That could work."

"Let's make sure it does," Drake said. "I'll say something about you taking me there, so Shelton hears it."

"What about Braxton?"

"I think I know where Braxton's staying. We can decide what to do with him when he doesn't have his men to help him."

"What do you want to do with Shelton?" Norris asked.

"Let him go. We'll follow him and see if he told us the truth about his mates staying at the Palms Casino and Hotel."

"We don't have to follow him. I brought a couple of our GPS tracking discs. I'll slip one in his blazer. We'll know where he's going."

"While you're doing that," Drake said, "I'll call Kevin and ask him to try to access Braxton Group's IT system and find out who he's working for."

Norris returned as Drake ended his call and hooked a thumb over his shoulder down the hallway toward the bedroom where Shelton was lying in the soaking tub. "You sure you want to let the dirty cop go?"

"We promised we'd let him go," Drake said and grinned. "It doesn't mean we won't see him again."

When they were halfway down the hall to the bedroom, Drake said loudly enough to be heard, "Thanks, Chris. A sightseeing drive to Lake Las Vegas to shop for a gift for my wife is a great idea."

It took both men to set Shelton's chair up and pull it over the side of the soaking tub. When Norris took his Benchmade folding knife and used the thumb disc to flick the blade open, Shelton's eyes opened wide.

"Relax," Norris said. "I'm cutting the duct tape so you can get out of here."

Drake reached in and pulled the tape off Shelton's mouth. "Be smart and leave town, Arnie. Tell Braxton I'm coming for him."

"Can I have my gun back?"

"Now you're thinking that we're stupid," Norris said. "Your Kimber Mako will make a nice little addition to my collection."

Drake picked up Shelton's blazer from the bed and said, "Working for Braxton is a dangerous choice, Arnie. Make sure our paths don't cross again. If they do, you may not like the way it ends."

Shelton took his blazer from Drake and sneered. "You might not like the way it ends either. You don't know who you're dealing with."

"I've got a pretty good idea, Arnie. Get out of here before I change my mind."

Norris blocked his way out of the room and moved into Shelton's personal space. "I hope we do cross paths again, Arnie. There's nothing I hate more than a dirty cop."

Shelton stepped back to slip on his blazer and turned sideways to walk around Norris, who followed him and opened the condo's door for him. "Be sure and tell your boss how you screwed up here, Arnie. I'm sure he's waiting to hear all about it."

When Norris turned around, Drake was looking at him with eyebrows raised. "What was that all about?"

Norris smiled and said, "I do hate dirty cops, but I wanted to wind him up. If he leaves town without going back to see the others, he won't tell them about us going sightseeing. And if he's angry, he'll want to make sure Braxton tells them to finish the job. When I fish for steelhead, I use a lure designed to make the fish angry enough to strike it. If we're going to be the bait on the drive to Lake Las Vegas, I want them mad enough to try something."

Chapter Twenty-Six

NORRIS WATCHED his phone as the GPS tracking disc he slipped into the pocket of Shelton's blazer moved to a location on Flamingo Road.

"He didn't leave town," he told Drake. "He went to the Palms."

"We'll give them an hour to get organized before we call valet parking for the Mustang. I brought my laptop. Let's see what that road to Lake Las Vegas looks like."

Drake pulled up a Google Map of the I-215 freeway leading to Lake Las Vegas and looked for a likely place to stage an accident.

"You train the executive protection teams to avoid ambushes," Drake said. "Where would you stage an accident?"

Norris moved the cursor on the screen of Drake's laptop along I-215 to the exit for East Lake Mead Parkway and on through the town of Henderson, Nevada, then stopped. He enlarged the satellite image and said, "There, that open stretch before you reach Lake Las Vegas Parkway. It's open, there are no houses around, and no one to come running to see if anyone's hurt. By the time an ambulance or the police could get there, they would have time to plant drugs in our car."

"Is it realistic to think they'll try something like this?" Drake asked. "Everything would have to go perfectly for them to get away with it."

"What else can they do? Trying to get Chris in bed with the escort didn't work. Hacking his online poker account didn't work. If you're right about the drugs Shelton brought here being the confirmation of something else, then a car accident makes sense. If we're wrong, we'll have a nice drive to the lake and wait for them to try something else."

"It's your field of expertise. Let's try it."

"While we're giving them time to get organized, do you mind if I shower?" Norris asked. "I didn't have time in Seattle before we flew here."

"Sure, go ahead. I'll call Liz and see how she's doing."

It was late Friday morning, and he'd been gone for only two and a half days, but it seemed longer. Maybe it was because he didn't sleep alone as well as he did when he was home. Whatever it was, he was ready to get home.

"Morning, Liz."

"Why didn't you call me last night? I told you I didn't care how late it was."

"Oh, Liz, I'm sorry. Last night was crazy. I just forgot."

"What was crazy about it?"

Drake took a second too long to answer, and she asked, "What aren't you telling me?"

"The dirty tricks got a little dirtier last night," he said. "I had Mike fly in a protection team for Chris Patterson and his family this morning. We stayed with them at Patterson's condo last night. When the team flew in this morning, I had them take the Pattersons to their home in Summerlin."

"Are they in danger? Are you in danger?"

"No, they're not in danger, and neither am I."

"What's going on, Adam?"

"The opposition, whoever they are, and I have a pretty good idea who they are, hacked into Chris's online poker account and made it look like he was losing badly and in debt. Kevin caught it, and we changed the numbers. I'm looking for the man responsible to let him know we're onto him, that his dirty tricks aren't going to work."

"When you find him, will that end this?"

"That's the plan."

"I don't like what I'm hearing, Adam. I don't like any of this."

"I know, and I'm sorry you're worrying about me, but I'm fine."

"Will you be home sometime Saturday or Sunday?" she asked.

"Just as soon as I can get out of here."

"All right, call me tonight, like you didn't last night."

"I promise."

Norris returned and asked, "Was that Liz?"

"Yes."

"How's she doing?"

"She's fine."

"Then I take it she doesn't know about you being in the ER the other night."

"No, she doesn't, and I don't want anyone telling her. I'll handle it when I get home."

"Be careful. Keeping secrets from my wife was one of the reasons we divorced. She knew I couldn't tell her everything I was doing with HRT, but it didn't make a difference. She didn't trust me because of it."

"Got it," Drake said. "We've given them enough time. Did you bring a Glock for me?"

"I'll get it," Norris said and went to his duffel bag he left in the bedroom where he showered.

When he returned with a Glock 19 Gen5 MOS with a red dot sight in a leather and Kydex IWB hybrid holster, he asked, "I thought you liked your Stacatto CS?"

"I do, but I left it at home. I didn't want Mike picking it up and Liz asking why I needed it."

Norris shook his head and said, "Man, I don't envy…"

"It's time to go," Drake said, cutting him off. "Wear the clothes Chris was wearing and bring the Byrne gun. It might come in handy. I'll call the parking valet for the Dark Horse. You'll drive."

"Yes, sir."

"I'm sorry, Dan. I didn't mean to sound like that. I don't envy me either when I get home."

Chapter Twenty-Seven

THEY LEFT Veer Towers at noon and joined slow-moving traffic fleeing the city. People were leaving work early to avoid the congestion when the race fans flooded in to watch the race that night.

Drake adjusted his passenger-side rearview mirror to watch for Braxton's men.

"They'll use two vehicles," Norris said. "Something big enough to ensure they walk away, and we won't. They'll want this car disabled so it can't leave the accident scene. Watch for SUVs moving in tandem or big sedans."

"When they followed us in Red Rock Canyon, two of them were in a big pickup," Drake said.

"Right, pickups, too."

"Have you heard from the protection team?"

"Reynolds reported in when I stepped out of the shower," Norris said. "No suspicious activity to report, and Mrs. Patterson is baking cookies for them."

Drake watched an Alaska Airlines flight with Chester the Eskimo's smiling face on its tail take off from Harry

Reid International Airport as they drove by on I-15. "With any luck, the Pattersons will be able to return to a normal life after today."

"Principals never enjoy being protected," Norris said. "They find a way to deal with it like Mrs. Patterson does with her cooking."

Drake's phone vibrated, and he saw that it was Kevin from PSS.

"I have more information about Marcus Braxton and his company. Is this a good time?" Kevin asked.

"Fire away, Kevin. Dan Norris and I are sightseeing, and you're on speaker."

"Great. Well, the Braxton Group does work for Franklin Analytics, as you suspected. It also does work for the CIA."

"What kind of work?" Drake asked.

"Surveillance, Mr. Drake," Kevin said. "Surveillance of individuals on watchlists identified by Franklin Analytics and suspected of providing material support for terrorists or terrorist organizations."

"What kind of material support?"

"I looked it up, and the material support statute, 18 U.S.C. Sec. 2339B, includes any support that may encompass humanitarian aid, medical training, expert advice, and other services such as political advocacy."

"So, the Braxton Group gets a list of people Franklin Analytics has identified and the CIA sends him out to spy on those people."

"That's what it looks like."

"Is there anything else?"

"Mr. Braxton is leaving Las Vegas tonight with four other men. He sent an email to his personal assistant's computer telling her to contact the catering service at the airport. He wants dinner for five delivered and on his plane by seven o'clock tonight."

"He must think his work will be finished by then," Drake said. "Thanks, Kevin. You are the best."

"That's what you pay me for, Mr. Drake."

Norris checked his rearview mirror to see if he could spot Braxton's men before saying, "The timing's good. An accident this afternoon will give Braxton's men plenty of time to make it to the airport and leave town with him."

"Unless we mess things up for them," Norris said. "Two sedans just moved in tandem and pulled in behind us three cars back. This could be them."

Drake reached over and changed the Mustang's GPS display to pull back and show more of East Lake Mead Parkway up ahead. They were passing through Henderson, Nevada, and getting closer to the stretch of the road where they expected trouble.

"We're maybe five minutes from where you thought they'd hit us," Drake said.

Norris recognized the first car as a white Dodge Charger by its hood scoop and headlights. The second car looked like a Chevrolet Tahoe or GMC Yukon when it followed the Charger and cut in front of a sixteen-wheeler that flashed its lights and blasted its air horn.

"They're using two cars, one that's fast and the other with a larger mass," Norris said. "They'll try to sandwich us and make it look like it's our fault when we didn't see a car ahead stopping. I think we can make that work for us. They won't know we're expecting this."

"You're the driver. What do you want me to do?"

"Get out of the cars as quickly as possible. Make sure they don't get close enough to plant something in this car."

"Copy," Drake said.

Three minutes later, Norris watched the white Charger pull into the passing lane and accelerate past them. The GMC Yukon followed but stayed in the passing lane fifty yards behind it.

"The Charger is their lead car," Norris said. "The white Yukon is hanging back in the passing lane."

When the white Yukon accelerated and pulled behind them two hundred yards before the exit ramp onto the Lake Las Vegas Parkway, Drake said, "Here they come."

The Charger turned off the Lake Mead Parkway and slowed down, closing the gap between them to thirty yards. Then, it slammed on the brakes and slid sideways, blocking their path.

Norris braked as well, slowing down as if he was going to stop. When he saw the Yukon accelerate and speed toward them, he waited until the last second before he pushed the gas pedal to the floor. The Mustang shot forward and slammed into the right rear of the Charger, spinning it around and sliding past it on the left.

The Yukon's speed was too great to stop the bigger SUV in time, and it crashed into the passenger side of the Charger, pushing it down the exit ramp.

Drake turned to see what was happening and said, "Keep going, Dan. They're not going anywhere. We'll let them tell the police why they ran into each other."

Chapter Twenty-Eight

NORRIS STAYED on the Lake Las Vegas Parkway and turned off at the first exit to examine the damage to the Mustang. The right front fender was smashed in but not pushed back far enough to rub on the front tire. It was drivable.

"We can't keep driving it," Drake said when he joined him. "We'll get pulled over with no headlight and this much damage. I'll call Chandler and ask him what he wants us to do with it."

"We could leave it somewhere and get a cab back to Las Vegas," Norris suggested.

Drake shook his head no and called Chandler Patterson. "We have a problem. Your Mustang was in an accident. We can't keep driving it."

"Are you okay? What happened?"

Drake explained and asked him what he wanted them to do with his car.

"Take it to my dealership in Henderson," Patterson

said. "Ask for my manager, Ron Elwood. I'll text the address to you. He'll take care of it and get you something to drive."

"Thanks, Chandler. Sorry about your car."

"It can be repaired. Where are you going from there?"

"Back to your condo," Drake said. "Braxton and his men are flying out tonight. I think this was their last shot at Chris. Before they leave, I want to deliver a message to them to leave your son alone."

"Let me know if I can help with that."

"I will."

Norris leaned against the passenger side door and asked, "What did he say?"

"He wants us to take it to his dealership in Henderson. He'll send the address."

"What kind of message are we sending Braxton?"

"One he won't forget," Drake said. "Not sure what that will be, but we'll think of something."

An hour later, they drove a two-year-old Ford Taurus loaner from Patterson's dealership back to Las Vegas. The new Mustang Dark Horse was being repaired in the dealership's auto body shop, and its damaged front fender was thrown in the shop's parts recycle bin where it wouldn't be seen.

On the way, they tossed ideas back and forth about the best way to send Braxton a message.

Norris wanted to confront him face-to-face.

Drake wanted him arrested and jailed but didn't have the evidence to get him charged with a crime.

Before they got back to Patterson's condo, they agreed to compromise and do what they both wanted: find Braxton, tell him to leave Chris Patterson alone, and provide the evidence that would get him arrested before he left Las Vegas.

"I think Braxton's staying at the Paris Las Vegas Hotel and Casino," Drake said. "If he's leaving tonight, we might get lucky and be there when he checks out. There's a lobby bar with a view of the front desk.

"But before then, there's something I want to do. Braxton sent Shelton to plant drugs in Patterson's condo. Why don't we return the favor and plant the drugs on his Bombardier before he leaves Las Vegas? At a minimum, his plane will be searched. He'll have to explain why there are oxycontin pills and cocaine on his plane."

"How do we get the drugs on his plane?" Norris asked.

"Kevin said in the email to his assistant that he told her to have the airport caterer deliver dinner for five at seven tonight. We'll have the caterers deliver the drugs along with their dinner."

"How do we get them to do that?"

"Steve Carson is staying at the Santa Fe Station Hotel and Casino out by the airport playing blackjack," Drake said. "He could take something to the caterers and say it belongs to Braxton, and please return it to him."

"Like what?"

"Work with me, Dan. The drugs are at the condo. We need to go there before we drive to Steve's hotel. We'll come up with something, take the stuff to Steve, and find Braxton. Then we'll have an expensive dinner and go home."

"All in a day's work," Norris said. "Sure, why not."

Drake suggested they change out of their road-trip attire before they went to the Paris Las Vegas Hotel and Casino lobby and saw Braxton. Norris's duffel bag was in the bedroom Chandler Patterson and his wife stayed in the night before, and while he was changing his clothes there, he found what they were looking for lying on the bed.

"Drake, what about this? It was in Chandler's

bedroom," he said as he walked down the hallway to the other bedroom where Drake was changing clothes. Norris was holding a new Red Bull Racing F1 Team rain jacket on a hanger inside a clear plastic cover.

"This is something Braxton might have left behind. Steve can say they gave it to him in the terminal and asked him to return it to Braxton's Bombardier when he goes out to the G-280."

"Perfect," Drake said. "I'll ask Chandler if he'd like to donate it to a good cause."

Drake finished dressing and went to the kitchen area to get a bottle of Pellegrino and call Chandler Patterson. "We made it to your condo. Thanks for taking care of the Mustang and finding us a ride."

"The Mustang's in the paint booth. I gave it to my manager to drive for a while."

"I have a favor to ask," Drake said. "You left a Red Bull Racing Team jacket in the condo. I want to give it to our nemesis with the drugs he tried to plant in the condo in one of its pockets. He's leaving Las Vegas tonight on his plane. It's parked next to ours at the airport."

"Why let him leave with evidence you could use against him?"

"He won't leave with it, but it will be evidence used against him. As soon as it's on his plane, the police will get a tip that he's using his plane to traffic drugs."

Chapter Twenty-Nine

STEVE CARSON, the pilot who flew the PSS G280 to Las Vegas, was waiting in his room at the Santa Fe Station Hotel and Casino for Drake and Norris.

"Are you winning?" Drake asked when Carson opened the door.

"Breaking even," Carson said. "I'll do better tonight with a little luck."

"That will have to wait until another time, Steve," Drake said. "We need to fly home tonight, but I need you to do something first."

"Okay, what?"

Drake took the Red Bull Racing F1 jacket Norris was holding and handed it to Carson. "Get this onboard the Bombardier parked next to us before we leave tonight."

"How am I supposed to do that?" Carson asked.

"The Bombardier belongs to Marcus Braxton. He ordered catering to bring dinner for five to the plane by seven o'clock tonight. We order dinner from catering and have it delivered at the same time. When the caterers get there, tell them the jacket isn't yours. Someone in the terminal made a mistake, and it was delivered to the wrong plane. Ask them to take it to the Bombardier."

"Why this jacket?"

Norris took the jacket from Carson, sat on the end of the bed, and laid the jacket beside him.

"One of Braxton's men tried to plant drugs in the condo where Drake was staying. We caught the guy in the act, kept the drugs, and wanted to return them to him. Those drugs are here," Norris said, patting the jacket's left pocket.

"Braxton will know I gave the caterers the jacket," Carson said.

"It won't matter, Steve," Drake said. "He can't try to blame it on us. He doesn't want us to tell the police what he's been doing in Las Vegas. He knows we will if we're forced to. We'll leave after the jacket is on board and the police arrive."

"All right, I'll call in the catering order and file a flight plan. Is the protection team coming with us? Should I order dinner for seven?"

"What do you think, Dan?" Drake asked. "Should they stay with Chris a little longer?"

Norris leaned forward with his hands on the bed and put his head down before answering. "We don't know how crazy Braxton is or if he will back off on this. I recommend keeping the team with Chris until we get him back to D.C."

"I agree," Drake said. "Just dinner for the three of us, Steve. Departure at seven-thirty. We'll be there by seven fifteen."

"I'll be ready and waiting," Carson said. "Anything special you want me to order for dinner?"

"We haven't eaten anything since this morning, and I'm

hungry. Order the best steaks they have and a good bottle of red wine, Steve."

"You got it. See you in three hours."

When they left, the sky was clear, and the temperature was warmer than in Seattle. The weather had originally been a concern for the race when it was scheduled, but the forecast was much the same as it had been all week: dry and clear skies at night.

Drake drove Chandler Patterson's Ford Taurus loaner back to Veer Towers to leave their guns there before walking to the Paris Las Vegas Hotel and Casino. Casinos didn't allow guns on the premises, even with concealed carry permits. They didn't think they would need them anyway. After all, they only wanted to talk to Braxton.

"If Braxton is checking out and going directly to the airport from the hotel, he'll do that at the last minute," Norris said. "We have an hour or so to kill. Time for a drink before we leave?"

"Patterson said to drink whatever I wanted, go ahead," Drake said. "I'm going to call Liz."

He walked one last time to the floor-to-ceiling window spanning the length of the room to look across the Las Vegas Strip to the Paris Las Vegas Hotel and Casino and its half-scale replica of the Eiffel Tower in Paris, France. The hotel's recurring light show started at sunset and was mesmerizing, as the Eiffel Tower towered forty-six stories above the other dazzling lights along the famous street. Las Vegas was gaudy and beautiful at the same time, in a way that only Las Vegas could manage.

Drake turned his eyes away from the sight and called his wife. "Good evening, beautiful."

"I knew you would call because you promised you'd call

last night and didn't," she said. "But the sun's not set yet. Is something wrong?"

He had to laugh. "Liz, nothing is wrong, and you don't need to worry just because I called earlier than you thought I would. I wanted to tell you that I'm coming home tonight. It might be late, but it will be tonight."

He heard her gasp in surprise and sob softly. "Thank you," she finally said.

"Liz, are you okay?"

"I am now, but why aren't you staying for the race?"

"I will have finished what I came here for tonight," Drake said. "I can record the race and not have to stay up until midnight to watch it."

Liz laughed and said, "What happened to that young man I married?"

"Nothing, he just wants to get home to be with his wife."

"And she couldn't want anything more. Be safe and hurry home."

"See you tonight."

Chapter Thirty

DRAKE AND NORRIS left the Veer Tower condo at quarter to six o'clock that evening and walked to the Paris Las Vegas Hotel and Casino on the other side of Las Vegas Boulevard. They agreed the best place to see Braxton at the hotel when he checked out, if he hadn't already, would be the lobby or a nearby bar with a view of the main entrance. Taxi service and valet parking were just outside the hotel's doors.

When they entered the ornate white lobby with its hand-laid mosaic tiles and crystal chandeliers, Drake looked across it and nodded toward the *Le Central Lobby Lounge*. "There," he said.

When they were seated at a small table and had scanned the cocktail menus, Drake asked for a Modelo Negra, and Norris opted for a Sam Adams Boston lager when they saw that both beers were on tap at the lobby bar.

"Are you a gambler?" Norris asked when their waiter left.

"Not really. I played poker in Afghanistan. That's about it. You?"

"I played street craps with the guys I grew up with. Never played craps in a casino."

Service in the lobby bar was speedy, and soon, they were sipping beer and looking for Braxton in the stream of people walking in and out of the hotel lobby. Quite a few of them were wearing Formula One team gear to support their favorite team or driver when they attended Free Practice 3 later that night.

"Why do you think Braxton chose to lure Chris here this week?" Norris asked.

"Chris used to race. With the Grand Prix racing in his hometown, it would be hard for him to say no to," Drake said. "His routine in D.C. wouldn't give them the opportunities they needed to set him up. Here, they could control the activities they planned for him to attend. Las Vegas was perfect for what they tried to do."

"Do you think Braxton planned all of this?"

"He might have, but my money's on Daniel Franklin."

"Why Franklin?"

"The report Chris put together could hurt data brokers like Franklin Analytics," Drake said. "It wouldn't stop him from gathering and analyzing personal data, but he wouldn't have his biggest customer any longer if Congress closed the loophole he's exploiting."

"Who else does he sell to?"

"Corporations, other governments and criminal organizations buy it on the dark web. With a digital economy, personal data is the new gold."

"And does Franklin sell to criminal organizations?" Norris asked.

"I don't know, but I intend to find out," Drake said. "How about ordering some bar food to snack on while we wait for Braxton?"

"Sounds good."

Drake turned to wave over their waiter, and when he turned back, three angry-looking men were walking toward them. Arnold Shelton, the man they found planting drugs in the condo, was the man in the middle. The men on either side of him had bruising on their faces.

Shelton stopped in front of Drake and crossed his arms across his chest. "Mr. Braxton sent us over to tell you this isn't over. You were lucky once. You won't be lucky again."

Drake smiled and said, "You're right, Arnold. This isn't over. Why don't you join us? Your friends look like they could use a drink."

"Screw you," the man on Shelton's left said and sent Drake's glass flying off the table with a swipe of his hand.

Drake and Norris stood up, and Norris said, "You guys are slow learners. You picked a fight with the wrong guys. Leave before you regret it."

"Or what," the man said.

Drake saw two burly security guards running their way and said, "You'll be tossed out of here."

The guards moved in and grabbed the man's arms. "Okay, let's go."

"It's okay, we're leaving," Shelton said.

Marcus Braxton was on the other side of the lobby, and Drake waved to him. "You should hurry, or you'll miss your ride with Marcus," he told the men.

Braxton was hurrying toward the hotel's doors, pulling his rolling luggage.

Drake said, "Let's give them a few minutes and head back to the condo to get our things. I want to be at the airport when the caterers arrive to make sure the jacket gets on his plane."

"Who gets to let the police know Braxton has drugs on his Bombardier?"

"I do," Drake said. "Kevin installed an anonymous calling app on my phone a while ago in case I ever needed it. You might want to have him install one on your phone."

When Norris finished his beer, Drake called for the waiter to bring their check to sign out so they could leave the lobby bar. The tab for two beers surprised him. It would have been more expensive in a hotel lobby bar in Paris, France, but not by much.

When they left the hotel, there was no sign of Braxton or his men when they were outside. The temperature was still in the high fifties Fahrenheit, making the walk to Veer Towers comfortable and pleasant in the bright lights along the Las Vegas strip.

Chapter Thirty-One

DRAKE PARKED the Ford Taurus borrowed from Chandler Patterson's dealership in the North Las Vegas Airport parking lot and walked to the terminal building. Someone from the dealership would come and pick it up the next morning.

Steve Carson had finished his pre-flight inspection of the PSS Gulfstream G280 and was on the flight deck waiting for them when he called. "The caterers called five minutes ago to say they were on their way," he told Drake. "Braxton and his men are already onboard."

"We're going to the Sunshine and Tailwinds Café. There's something I have to do," Drake said. "I'll call you from the viewing deck when I see the caterers arriving."

"Copy that," Carson replied. "I'll be waiting to give them the jacket."

The café remained open for another hour, but there were no customers. Drake stopped at the counter to order two coffees and followed Norris to the windows.

They had a clear view from there of Braxton's

Bombardier tied down next to their G280, but not of the path the caterers would take to reach the planes.

Drake laid a ten-dollar bill on a table by the windows to pay for their coffees and walked outside to the viewing deck. The Bombardier's interior lights were on, and he could see movement inside.

Norris pointed and said, "The caterers are here."

Two white vans with matching logos on their sides were driving across the tarmac toward the planes.

"The caterers are arriving," he called to alert Carson. "You're on."

The G280's door opened a moment later, and the airstairs came out and extended down. As soon as they touched the tarmac, Carson came down holding the navy-blue Red Bull Racing Team jacket and walked around the tail of the Bombardier to meet Braxton's caterers.

When the jacket was handed off to one of the caterers and Carson was back in the G280, Drake took out his phone and called the North Las Vegas Police Department.

"Narcotics Division, please," he said.

"May I ask what this is about?"

"There's a Bombardier jet on tie-down at North Las Vegas Airport that's trafficking drugs."

"How do you know the jet is trafficking drugs?"

"I saw them being loaded on the plane from a caterer's van just now. Find out for yourself. But hurry and get here before they take off."

"May I have your name, sir?"

Drake ended the call.

"Let's get aboard before the police get here," he told Norris.

They used the gate cards Steve Norris gave them to access the tie-down area and walked nonchalantly across the tarmac with their luggage. A caterer was talking with the pilot when they passed behind the catering company's van delivering dinner to the Bombardier. When the pilot walked away, he held the Red Bull Racing Team jacket on a hanger inside a clear plastic garment bag.

The caterer's van started backing away, and Drake and Norris boarded the G280.

"Be ready to leave when the police arrive," Drake called out to Steve Carson on the flight deck. "I don't want Braxton to have the opportunity to get us involved in this."

"I'm not sure he knows this is our plane," Norris said. "If he does, he's smart enough not to say anything."

Drake looked out the window, waiting for the police to arrive.

When the caterer's vans were out of sight, he walked through the galley and asked Carson if the Bombardier was ready for takeoff. He was worried that Braxton's plane would leave before the police arrived.

"The pilot is warming up the engines," Carson said. "He'll need five minutes minimum before he's ready for takeoff."

Drake returned and said to Norris sitting in his club seat, "It'll be a shame if this doesn't work, and he skips out of here before the police arrive."

"That's if they get here at all," Norris said. "They might not respond to a call from someone who didn't give them his name."

"Having the police show up was frosting on the cake. Returning the drugs he tried to plant on Chris shows him we know what he was doing. Waving goodbye while he's being questioned by the police is just having a little fun."

Norris leaned closer to his window and pointed. "Looks

like you'll get to see if Braxton thinks it's funny. Flashing lights are headed this way."

"Steve, wind them up," Drake called out. "We'll leave in five."

Four white SUVs with their light bars flashing sped into the tie-down area and stopped, two in front of Braxton's Bombardier and two behind it. One officer jumped out of his vehicle in front of the plane and signaled with a slashing movement across his neck for the pilot to shut the plane's engines down.

The G280 was the last plane on the tie-down row, twenty yards between its wingtip and the Bombardier's wingtip. There was nothing to keep it from taxiing to its assigned runway for takeoff.

Drake told Carson to take off and watched the NLVPD officers take positions around Braxton's plane. They were waiting for its passengers to come out to search the aircraft and answer questions about an anonymous tip that they were trafficking drugs.

Chapter Thirty-Two

AFTER ENJOYING a steak dinner and glass of the Stag's Leap Cabernet Sauvignon, Drake, and Norris sat in two chairs behind the forward galley to talk about Las Vegas and Marcus Braxton before landing in Seattle in an hour.

"When President Ballard asked you to see if Chandler Patterson's concerns about his son were valid, is that all he asked you to do?" Norris asked.

"Explicitly, yes," Drake said. "I'm sure he knew if Chris was in danger, I'd do something about it. Why?"

"Braxton didn't get the results he wanted, but he didn't suffer any consequences for trying. That doesn't sit well with me. Neither does his goons putting you in the ER. It's unfinished business, as far as I'm concerned."

"What would finish this?"

"I don't know, but something should," Norris said and reached for the bottle of wine. "More?"

"Sure," Drake said.

He watched Norris fill his glass and knew he thought the same thing. Going after Chris Patterson the way Braxton did wasn't new. Cancel culture and gotcha politics were the new normal. Braxton's firm was highly paid for its opposition research that was used to destroy reputations, livelihoods, or a candidate's hope of being elected.

Learning that the Braxton Group also spied on individuals for Franklin Analytics based on personal data acquired from social media tech platforms and corporations was unsettling. Especially if the CIA and the intelligence community paid them to do it.

Norris was right. This was something they couldn't walk away from.

But where to begin? The U.S. intelligence community included seventeen different agencies, from the CIA, FBI, DIA, State Department, Treasury, DHS, and DEA to the National Geospatial-Intelligence Agency that found the compound in Pakistan where Osama bin Laden was hiding.

"Dan, this is bigger than the Braxton Group and Franklin Analytics," Drake said. "What they tried to do to Chris was for the benefit of the entire U.S. intelligence community. The IC will always find a private contractor to do what it isn't allowed. Going after Braxton or Franklin won't stop what the IC is doing.

"The incestuous relationship between our government, the media, and big tech violating our right to privacy is what has to end."

"That's something Congress will have to do," Norris said.

"Congress can, if it knows what's really going on. The president wants to know who's involved in this conspiracy to circumvent our laws. Who else could he trust to find out?"

"If you volunteer to do it for him, you'll have to beef up the company."

"What else do we need?" Drake asked. "How different

would this be from what we did last year sorting out what China was doing slipping commandos across the border?"

"Mike might not want us to tackle this," Norris said. The pushback from the power elite in and out of government would be enormous."

"I know," Drake said. "I'll talk with Mike before I call the president."

"When you mentioned powerful people, who are you thinking about?"

"The agencies in the intelligence community because they're using the data now. I'm also curious about people like the ones Franklin takes on a cruise every year from San Francisco to Cabo San Lucas and back. Elite billionaires from Silicon Valley, media moguls, politicians. The people who think they're smarter than the rest of us and need to be the ones running the country."

Drake looked out his window and saw pinpoints of light on the ground from cars traveling on I-5 seconds before Steve Carson announced they were descending on approach to Boeing Field in Seattle. He knew what he was suggesting and what it could mean for the company, but would they be able to say no to the president if he wanted answers?

"Fifteen minutes from touchdown, gentlemen."

Chapter Thirty-Three

BY THE TIME the Gulfstream G280 was parked in the company's hangar at the north end of the runway at Boeing Field, it was half past ten on Friday night. Drake and Norris each drove away from the airport in the vehicles they left parked in the hanger: Drake's Porsche Cayman GTS and Norris's Dodge Charger SRT.

The lights in the condo were on, and Liz had the garage door open when he got home to let him park beside her company car, a Cadillac XT6 SUV.

Drake laughed as she rushed to him and wrapped her arms around his neck. "I've only been gone three days," he said before kissing her.

"Seems longer," she said and hugged him tighter.

Lancer, Drake's German Shepherd, was standing beside her right leg with his tail wagging.

"Did you miss me too?" he asked Lancer, reaching down to pat his head.

"Why didn't you stay for the race?"

"Let's get you inside, and I'll tell you," Drake said. He

reached in to unlatch the front trunk lid, grab his luggage, and follow Liz into the lower level of their three-floor condo.

"How are you feeling?" he asked on the stairs to the main living area and kitchen.

"I'm fine. Would you like something to eat or drink?" Liz asked.

"No, I had a nice steak on the flight back, thanks."

"Well, I'm going to have something. You can tell me about Las Vegas while I eat." She opened the refrigerator and got a cup of mixed berries and a small dark chocolate bar.

Drake set his luggage and joined her at the breakfast table.

"Okay, tell me everything," she said, unwrapping the chocolate bar.

By the time he finished telling her about Las Vegas and convincing her it was time to go to bed, it was midnight.

At five thirty on Saturday morning, Drake slipped out of bed to go running without waking Liz. He put on his gear in his walk-in closet, including a belly belt with his holstered Stacatto CS pistol inside under his black Nike jacket, and motioned for Lancer to join him.

Thin white Cirrostratus clouds high overhead predicted it would rain the next day, but the temperature was in the upper forties and pleasant enough for a nice run. Lancer knew the route to the Cross-Kirkland Corridor path that ran the length of Kirkland, from the south to the north, and stayed half a body length ahead of Drake.

Lancer turned his head back every ten yards to see if his master was ready to run faster. Drake knew better than to accept the challenge, at least this early in their five-mile morning run. If he did, he would have nothing left for the last hundred-yard sprint Lancer enjoyed winning to claim his trophy, the treat Drake always had in his pocket.

The fresh air and the rhythm of the run cleared Drake's mind to think about what he would tell Liz when she noticed the bandage covering the stitches on the back of his head she missed seeing the night before.

Liz wanted him to stop putting himself in harm's way because she didn't want to raise a child as a single parent. He understood that. Before joining the Department of Homeland Security, she was an FBI agent. She'd been at his side the year before when a Chinese triad attacked their home with grenade launchers. She knew the danger his adventures, as she called them, exposed him to. And she wanted it to end now.

But he couldn't see himself sitting behind a desk and letting others do what he knew he was good at doing. There had to be a compromise Liz could be happy with, and he had to think of what it was going to be soon.

Lancer stopped ahead with his tail wagging at the halfway point of their run on the Corridor path, looking back at him, asking if they were turning back or going farther.

Drake answered Lancer's question by turning on the path and returning home. "That's enough today, Lancer. Let's get back in time to fix Liz breakfast in bed. Lead on."

As Dan Norris mentioned, the answer might be to expand the capabilities of the PSS intelligence contractor division.

His responsibilities didn't need to change much. His role could still require hands-on involvement when his men were on assignment in the field. Like a general near the frontline who needed to see what the enemy was doing to develop a battle plan, he'd still have an active role in what they were doing.

A new role with new responsibilities might let Liz stop worrying about him. But in the end, it would be what he did, not what he promised he wouldn't do, that would matter.

Chapter Thirty-Four

WHEN DRAKE and Lancer returned to the condo, Liz was in the shower humming a tune he didn't recognize when he checked to see if she was awake and out of bed.

"Let's go," he told Lancer and left to feed him and fix her breakfast. When he looked back to see if Lancer was following him, he saw he wasn't.

Lancer was sitting on his haunches at the ensuite door, watching Liz to make sure she was okay, as he'd done since the beginning of her pregnancy.

Good boy, Lancer, he thought, *I know you love her too.*

Drake started the grind-n-brew coffeemaker, took eggs and spinach out of the refrigerator to make the omelet Liz liked, and put a whole-grain English muffin in the toaster. On the refrigerator door was a list of the foods she allowed herself to eat, and his eggs and spinach omelet had four stars next to it.

The weekends for the last two months had been devoted to preparing the nursery and stocking up on what a newborn needed. Liz had a list and, one by one, checked each item off when it was purchased and stored away at home.

The weekend before he left to fly to Las Vegas was the last time they'd gone shopping together. When she checked the last item off her list when they got home, she declared she was as ready as she could be to bring a baby home from the hospital.

Drake, on the other hand, wasn't sure that he was. Liz was organized and prepared. She and her doctor had a plan, but he didn't have a coach to tell him what was expected of him. Hearing Mike assuring him that he would be a good father and not to worry about it wasn't enough.

His Green Beret father had been deployed overseas for most of his childhood, and he didn't remember much about his father's day-to-day role when he was home, especially in his early years. His father had taken him fishing and hunting, and he'd been there to watch his football games. Maybe that's all that being a father amounted to, but he wanted to be the best father he could be and wished he knew more about what that required.

Drake got a skillet, a cutting board from under the kitchen island, and a medium onion from the refrigerator. After chopping a couple of tablespoons of the onion, he added a little canola oil to the skillet and placed it on a burner set on medium-high heat. He added the chopped onion and some Italian seasoning to the skillet when he heard Liz come down the stairs from their bedroom on the floor above.

She was wearing her two-piece lounging sweatsuit and carrying her hospital go-bag. "Would you like to drive me to the hospital?" she said with a grin. "It's time."

Drake spun around and asked, "Are you sure? I thought your due date wasn't until two weeks from now."

"I'm sure, Adam. My water broke while I was in the shower."

"Right, okay," Drake said. "Do you have everything you need?"

Liz held up her hospital go-bag and said, "Turn off the burner."

"Yes, okay. I'll get your car started. Stay right there. I'll be right back."

"Adam, I can walk down the stairs to the garage by myself. You need to relax and drive me to the hospital. I called the Maternity Center and let them know I'm coming. Everything is under control."

And it was. Drake drove Liz to the Evergreen Health Family Maternity Center without getting a ticket and led his wife to a birthing suite where Doctor Susan Morgan was waiting for them.

Drake waited out in the hall while Dr. Morgan performed a preliminary examination of her patient, and a nurse prepared her for having her baby. When he was invited back into Liz's birthing suite, it was nine thirty Sunday morning.

He stood beside her bed or wandered around for the first six hours as Liz's contractions became stronger, more predictable, and closer together. When she began feeling pain and wanted to push the baby out of her body, he held her hand and kept her focused on controlling her breathing when she was told to wait a little longer.

And when it was time to push the baby through the birth canal, he was sweating with her. With Dr. Morgan's coaching, Liz began breathing in quick, shallow breaths to help her relax and ensure the baby had plenty of oxygen. He knew it was painful for her because her fingernails were digging into the back of the hand she was holding onto.

Drake was vaguely aware that twenty minutes had passed when Liz groaned through clinched teeth one last time to help Dr. Morgan pull the head and shoulders of their baby out of her body.

When baby boy Drake was held up for his mother and father to see, they were both crying when Drake leaned down and kissed her forehead. It was a moment he knew he would never forget.

Then, when their baby was handed to the nurse and cried out for the first time, they were both laughing and crying together.

Drake stayed at Liz's side until their baby was laid on her bare chest, and mother and baby were covered with a warm blanket before he excused himself and left the birthing suite.

He wasn't expecting the wave of emotion he was feeling and walked without caring where he was going or if anyone noticed his tears. His son's head had been turned toward him when he was lying on Liz's chest, and his eyes were open wide, staring at him.

He was a father now and never felt more humbled than he was by the inexplicable magnificence of God's creation and the birth of his son.

Chapter Thirty-Five

DRAKE WAS HOLDING SEVEN-POUND, ten-ounce Alex Thomas Drake in his arms and talking to him softly when Mike and Megan Casey came into hospital.

"Congratulations, you two," Casey said, walking over to look at a young Drake. Megan went to Liz's bed and squeezed her hand.

"You look wonderful," she said. "How are you feeling?"

"I'm tired but otherwise fine," Liz said. "My labor was half as long as my mother's."

"How did Adam do?"

"He stayed right with me, didn't pass out or anything."

When Megan laughed at hearing that, Drake sighed and shook his head. "Mike, I think the conversation in this room is venturing into a territory where we don't belong. Let's take a walk before it gets any worse."

"Bring that baby over here before you do," Megan said. "I want to hold him."

Drake handed her his son gently and told Liz he'd be right back.

Outside in the hall, Casey asked how Liz was feeling.

"Exhausted. I don't know how they do it."

"Tell me about it. Megan was in labor with our first for twenty-six hours."

Drake pointed to a sign on the wall with directions to the hospital cafeteria. "I need something to eat. You hungry?"

"For the first time I can remember, I have to say no. We had a big breakfast with the girls before we came here. How was Las Vegas? Carson told me about the prank you pulled at the airport."

"The president did the right thing by sending me there," Drake said as they entered the cafeteria. "I'll tell you about Las Vegas when I get back."

Drake left and walked through the service line, picking out a deli ham and cheese sandwich, a small fruit bowl, and a cup of coffee. When he paid for his order, Casey sat at a table looking at his cell phone.

When Drake sat down, Casey held up his cell phone with a frown and said, "Kevin's text says someone's trying to infiltrate our IT system. He's never seen an attack like this."

"Have they done any damage?"

"No, they didn't get in. Kevin's trained everyone well enough to keep us from making the usual mistakes cyber gangs try to exploit."

"I might be responsible for this, Mike," Drake said. "I poked a hornet's nest in Las Vegas. This might be how they're reacting."

"Who?"

"Franklin Analytics, the Braxton Group, and maybe our intelligence community."

For the next half an hour, Drake recounted the events in

Las Vegas and told Casey what he learned from the attempt to discredit Chris Patterson and his PIAB report.

"Daniel Franklin is a data broker, and Marcus Braxton does contract surveillance work for the CIA. But coming after us doesn't make any sense. They know they'd be the first ones I'd think of."

"I can't believe our intelligence community would risk being involved. If they are half as good as they think they are, they must know the president is your friend."

"The president and the IC aren't exactly friends, Mike. They may think their surveillance programs using personal data from brokers like Franklin Analytics are too important to risk losing."

"Have you talked with the president about Las Vegas?"

"Not yet," Drake said. "I was going to call him today."

Casey looked past Drake and raised his hand when he saw his wife enter the cafeteria, looking around for him. "Looks like Liz sent Megan out looking for you."

Drake looked at his watch, picked up his half-eaten sandwich, and carried the fruit bowl to the self-bussing station.

"Is she okay?" he asked Megan.

"She's fine," Megan said and patted his arm. "Her nurse gently reminded me when she finished feeding Alex that she needed to rest and asked me to leave."

"Thank you for staying with her, Megan. I lost track of time."

"You should rest too, Adam," Casey said. "You won't get as much sleep as you're used to when you get Alex home. And don't plan on coming to the office tomorrow, or next week for that matter. Stay home and take care of Liz and Alex."

"What about Kevin's text? We need to…"

"Kevin's working on identifying who's behind it," Casey said. "When we know that, we'll talk about what we'll do about it. It might take him some time, so stay home. I'll let you know when he finds something."

"All right," Drake said, man-hugging Casey and kissing Megan goodbye.

When he got back to Liz's room, her eyes were closed, and a nurse was standing next to her bed checking her vital signs. His son was asleep in a bassinet next to her bed, covered with a baby blanket, and had a small blue knit cap on his head.

The nurse whispered, "You might want to rest yourself, Mr. Drake. Your son will probably sleep for a while. I'm keeping an eye on them. Don't you worry."

He nodded and silently mouthed thank you as he walked over to the beige recliner chair on the other side of the bassinet.

What a day, he thought. Liz was resting peacefully with a little smile on her face, and his son was the best-looking baby he'd ever seen. And he was his father.

Chapter Thirty-Six

A CRYING baby woke Drake up from his nap, and when he opened his eyes, he saw that it was his baby in the bassinet next to him.

"Welcome back," Liz said.

"How long was I asleep?"

"Only an hour or so. You were jerking around like you were fighting with someone."

Drake ran a hand through his hair and sat up in the recliner chair. "Did I look like I was winning?" he asked with a smile.

"Did you?"

"Did I what?"

"Win the fight in Las Vegas you forgot to tell me about. When you rolled over on your side, I saw the bandage on the back of your head."

"Minor skirmish, nothing more. How are you feeling?" he asked.

"I'm fine. Dr. Morgan says I can go home the day after tomorrow. I'll feel better when you tell me about Las

Vegas."

"I will, I promise, but now I think he needs your attention," Drake said when the nurse came into the room and lifted Alex out of the bassinet to be fed.

"While I feed him, why don't you phone your in-laws and tell them they have a grandson."

"Good idea," Drake said and got up to leave.

"When you return, I want to see what's under that bandage."

He patted her toes as he walked by the end of her bed and headed to the visitors' waiting room to get a cup of coffee. Senator Hazelton and his mother-in-law, Meredith Hazelton, were in Georgetown, Washington, D.C., and would be home from church by now to hear the news.

In the short amount of time that he was married to their daughter, Kay, before she died from an aggressive form of breast cancer, Senator Hazelton and his wife had become "Mom and Dad" to him. His parents died before he graduated college and now the Hazeltons were the only family he had, besides Liz and Alex.

"Hello, Adam," Meredith Hazelton said brightly when she answered. "Are you here in D.C.?"

"No, Mom, I'm in Seattle," Drake said. "In a hospital."

"What are you doing in the hospital? Are you all right?"

"Better than all right. You have a grandson!"

"Robert," she yelled, "We have a grandson!"

"Tell me everything," she gushed. "What is his name? How much does he weigh? Is Liz okay?"

Drake recited Alex's vital statistics and told her Liz was fine when Senator Hazelton took the phone from his wife.

"Congratulations, son. We're very proud of you and Liz. When do we get to see some pictures?"

"I'll send them today."

"Excellent. Excellent," Senator Hazelton said. "We're flying to Portland to host a Thanksgiving dinner for my office staff. Would it be okay with you and Liz if we stop in Seattle on the way home to see our grandson?"

"We would love it."

"Send us those pictures. We can't wait to see them."

"Right away, sir. You'll have them within the hour."

Drake checked his watch and saw that he'd only been gone for ten minutes. He was alone in the visitors' waiting room and had the time and privacy to call the president and tell him about Las Vegas. And buy a little time before he returned and had to tell Liz how he got the stitches hidden under his bandage.

He gathered his thoughts and called the number for a private and secure conversation with the president.

"Adam, I was expecting your call," President Ballard said. "Congressman Patterson told me how you kept his son out of trouble in Las Vegas."

"Then you know most of the story," Drake said.

"What's the part of the story I don't know?"

"Daniel Franklin is using personal data he collects as a data broker to identify Americans that require surveillance by the CIA. The CIA then pays the Braxton Group to provide that surveillance. The CIA is spying on American citizens without warrants, sir."

"Can you prove this?" President Ballard asked.

"Some of it."

"Then I want your company to investigate Franklin, Braxton, and everyone else involved. Give me a full report that I can use when I call on Congress to end this."

"You will have a lot of it when you receive Chris Patterson's report from the President's Intelligence Advisory Board," Drake said.

"I want all of it, Adam. I know you will dig deeper than Chris could do. Be thorough and take as much time as you need, but get it to me before the next Congress is sworn in."

"Yes, sir," Drake said. "I will be out of the office next week, but I'll get it started tomorrow."

"Vacation?"

"No, sir. I'm taking some time to be home with Liz and our new baby."

"Well, congratulations. Boy or girl?"

"Boy, sir."

"Send me the announcement. I'll see if I can find something to send that he might enjoy having someday."

"Thank you, sir."

Drake knew what the president was asking and knew Dan Norris was right. If they were going to investigate Franklin, Braxton, and the CIA's domestic surveillance programs, the company would have to grow and expand its capabilities, manpower, and facilities.

It would be an understatement to say it would be David versus Goliath to do what the president asked. But it was what the president wanted. Sound Security and Information Services, the smallest private intelligence company in the U.S., would have to find ways to get the job done.

Chapter Thirty-Seven

DRAKE STAYED at the hospital Sunday night until Liz made him go home to sleep and come back in the morning. Rushing to get Liz to the hospital, he'd forgotten to bring the car seat and the diaper bag with Alex's coming home clothes.

When he walked into Liz's room, Dr. Morgan reviewed her post-partum instructions and complimented her on how well she was feeling and what a healthy baby she had.

"That does not mean I want her to do anything but rest and take care of herself when she gets home, Mr. Drake," she said when she saw him.

"I'll make sure she does, Doctor."

"Did you bring the car seat I approved for Alex?"

"It's in the car," Drake said.

"All right, then. Liz is ready to leave as soon as she dresses Alex with the clothes you brought," she said. "Why don't you go get your car? We'll have Liz and Alex out front in fifteen minutes."

Drake went to Dr. Morgan and shook her hand. "Thank you for taking such good care of Liz, Doctor."

"You're welcome," she said. "You have a beautiful wife and baby, Mr. Drake."

"I know," Drake said, looking at Liz, who was holding Alex in her arms. "And please call me Adam."

Drake left, took the elevator down to the first floor, and walked to the parking lot to bring Liz's car around. Her Cadillac XT6 SUV wasn't exactly a family car, but it did have a back seat big enough for a baby's car seat.

Liz's car would be okay for a while, he thought. Then they'd talk about trading it in for something more family-oriented and accommodating for their needs, like a minivan. The thought of them buying a minivan made him smile.

While he waited at the front entrance for Liz and Alex to come out, he saw it was the top of the hour and turned on the radio to 570 AM KVI to hear the news.

"The U.S. House and Senate Select Committees on Intelligence announced today joint hearings would be held next year. The committees will investigate the need to reform section 702 of the Foreign Intelligence Surveillance Act, or FISA, to prevent warrantless searches of U.S. citizens. Personal data obtained from data brokers is being used to spy on Americans, it's being reported. U.S. intelligence agencies are currently prohibited from collecting personal data, but under the current law, they can obtain personal data from data brokers. The Chairman of the U.S. House Permanent Select Committee on Intelligence, Congressman Matthew Bridge, and the Chairman of the U.S. Senate Select Committee on Intelligence, Senator Robert Hazelton, say it is time to end this abuse to protect the American citizens' right to privacy.

Wow, Drake thought, *that didn't take the president long.*

The CIA and the intelligence community weren't going to like being called before Congress. It might also explain why Puget Sound Security was hit with a massive penetration attack on its IT system.

Someone had learned about his conversation with the president or realized his interference in Las Vegas meant someone anticipated the attempt to discredit the PIAB report to the president.

Whichever it was, someone was a couple of steps ahead of him. The next year promised to be an interesting one.

The hospital's front doors slid open, and Liz was wheeled out in a wheelchair with Alex in her arms. He jumped out of her car, thinking next year couldn't hold a candle to how interesting the next several weeks would be.

Drake took Alex from her arms and waited for her to thank the nurse before walking with him to her car idling at the curb. "How are you feeling?" he asked as he opened the rear door to put Alex, who was asleep, in his rear-facing car seat.

"A little sore and a little teary, but most of all, ready to be home," Liz said, moving in behind him to make sure Alex was secure in the car seat.

"Make sure the chest strap isn't too tight," she said.

"Got it," he said, slipping one finger under the strap to check.

He opened the door for Liz before walking around the back of her car to put her go-bag and the diaper bag in the back seat across from Alex.

When he slipped into his seat as quietly as he could, Liz's eyes were closed and her head was back against the headrest.

"Don't worry, I'm just resting," she said.

"Keep resting. We'll be home before you know it."

Drake looked back to see if Alex was okay and pulled away from the curb.

"He'll let you know if he needs something," she said with her eyes still closed.

Drake grinned and wondered how she could be so comfortable with a baby to care for in the back seat.

He was still gripping the steering wheel too tightly when he turned off their street and punched the overhead control to open the garage door of their townhouse condo.

Liz opened her eyes as they drove into the garage and sat up straight. "You forgot to tell me why there's a bandage on the back of your head," she said.

"It's complicated," he said.

"Take all the time you need to uncomplicate it," Liz said, opening her door. "I'm not going anywhere for a while, and neither are you until you tell me."

Chapter Thirty-Eight

THE FOLLOWING two days were busy for Drake, ensuring Liz could rest while he cooked, cleaned, and washed dirty diapers.

On the third day, when he said he was going to his office to retrieve his laptop, she smiled and told him to take a seat and tell her about Las Vegas.

"Okay," he said, sitting in the rocker beside their bed. "What do you want to know?"

"How did you get the stitches?"

"It turned out Chandler Patterson was right to worry about his son," Drake said.

"How did you get the stitches?"

"It was nothing serious."

"Adam…"

"Some guys tried to take me for a ride. I resisted and got whacked on the head."

"A one-way trip to the desert?"

"That's probably what they wanted it to be."

Liz got up and sat on the edge of the bed facing him. "Why didn't you tell me?"

Drake sighed and said, "Because I didn't want you to worry. Chris Patterson was the one in danger."

"So were you, it seems."

"Not from then on. That surprised me. I had Mike send a close protection team to Las Vegas."

"What about the next time and the time after that? You made me a promise. What's going to change?"

Drake spent the next hour explaining the changes they needed to make at PSS and his role at the company when they did. "Trust me, Liz. I want to be around to see Alex grow up and be grandparents someday."

He knew she wasn't convinced and wanted to hear specifically how things would change when they heard someone ringing the doorbell chimes downstairs.

Drake went downstairs, grateful that he'd literally been saved by the bell, and was surprised to see Senator Hazelton and his wife when he opened the door.

Robert Hazelton was a handsome and distinguished-looking elder statesman with more gray hair than the last time Drake had seen him.

His beautiful wife, however, hadn't changed a bit.

Merideth Hazelton hugged him and said, "I made him fly here instead of home to Portland. I couldn't wait any longer to see my grandson."

"Come in." Drake smiled and shook hands with Senator Hazelton. "I'll let Liz know you're here."

"I'll get Alex," Liz said loudly over the intercom. "I'll meet you in the living room."

Drake hung their coats in the closet and ushered them upstairs to the main living area of the condo.

"How are you doing?" Senator Hazelton asked, walking behind his wife on the stairs.

"I love being a father," Drake said, "But I'm still adjusting to a new sleeping routine."

"I remember," Senator Hazelton said. "Kay didn't sleep through the night for weeks."

"Oh, he's beautiful," Meredith said when she saw Liz holding Alex in the living room.

"Say hello to your grandmother, Alex," Liz said, holding him out to Meredith.

Senator Hazelton moved closer to see his grandson and put his arm around his wife. "I get to hold a lot of cute babies, but Alex is the best-looking one of them all."

"Have a seat," Drake said, motioning to the white leather sofa and champagne-yellow chairs near the window. "Can I get you anything, coffee or tea?"

"Nothing for me," Senator Hazelton said. "I had my coffee quota for the day on the plane."

"Mom?" Drake asked his mother-in-law, who was whispering to the baby in her arms.

"We're fine, Adam, thanks," Senator Hazelton said. "This is the first time I've been here. Very nice."

'Come with me. I'll show you around."

Drake led Senator Hazelton up the stairs to the third floor and showed him the master bedroom, the second bedroom, now Alex's nursery, and the study.

"There's a rooftop deck with a great view of the Seattle skyline across the lake," Drake said.

"Do you have time to tell me about Las Vegas?" Senator Hazelton asked.

"Sure," Drake said, motioning toward the study.

The senator sat in one of the leather armchairs and asked, "Did you see the news that we're holding hearings next year on the use of personal data and domestic surveillance of Americans without a warrant?"

"I did."

"The president said you learned some things about the problem while you were in Las Vegas," Senator Hazelton said. "Care to share?"

"The president asked me to investigate two parties involved, Daniel Franklin and Franklin Analytics, and Marcus Braxton and the Braxton Group. Franklin is a data broker who supplies personal data to the CIA and identifies Americans he thinks may be a security risk. The CIA then asks the Braxton Group to conduct surveillance of those individuals."

"Can we prove this?"

"Yes, but not with what we have at the moment."

"How does Franklin identify these security risks?"

"I don't know. I assume he analyzes the personal data he collects."

"How are you going to get the evidence you need?"

Drake smiled but didn't answer.

"Right," Senator Hazelton said. "Is there anything I can do to help?"

"Let's keep in touch. Maybe we can help each other."

"I'm sure we can, Adam," the senator said, looking at his watch. "We'd better get back downstairs. I haven't held my grandson yet, and we need to get back to Portland tonight."

"You're welcome to stay. There's a guest bedroom on the first floor."

"I'd like to, but we can't tonight. Maybe after Thanksgiving on our way back to the capital, if the inn's still open."

"We'll make sure that it is."

Senator Hazelton took his turn holding baby Alex and

told Liz how happy they would be to babysit whenever she and Adam needed a vacation.

When they left, Liz nodded upstairs and said, "Let's continue our conversation about the changes you're making when you return to work."

Chapter Thirty-Nine

MARCUS BRAXTON SAT at the gated entrance of his home in Langley Forest, Virginia, at eight o'clock Wednesday night, waiting for the black iron security gate to slide back. The long hours he worked to keep his company at the head of the pack of private intelligence contractors the intelligence community used made it possible for him to live in the exclusive neighborhood and drive a dark Champagne-colored Range Rover.

He smiled at the sight of his Tudor home, with its stacked stone walls, six bedrooms, and a four-car garage where he kept a restored black Jaguar XK120, black Jaguar E-type, and black BMW K 1600 GT motorbike.

He hadn't always lived this well, but as a CIA para-military operations officer, he recognized the opportunity to become wealthy when the intelligence community began outsourcing work to private contractors. Six years after leaving the CIA and starting the Braxton Group, he was living large.

Of course, he owed part of his success to Daniel

Franklin and his work for Franklin Analytics. Franklin was a member of the elite ruling class in Washington, and the people Franklin knew in the intelligence community opened doors for him that would have been slammed in his face without Franklin's backing.

That's why the debacle in Las Vegas worried him. Franklin hadn't spoken to him since he returned home. Franklin knew everything and would certainly know that the police had detained him after they searched his plane at the airport for narcotics. But the bigger problem was that he'd screwed up their plan to discredit the PIAB report to the president. Franklin had warned him there would be consequences for failure, and he feared Franklin's silence was an ominous sign.

He parked the Range Rover next to his motorbike in the garage and entered the house, dropping his coat on the kitchen island and walking to the den to end the day with three fingers of Woodford Reserve Bourbon in a glass over a single ice cube.

With his drink in his hand, he settled into the black leather armchair next to the wet bar and raised the remote from the side table to listen to "Hotel California" by the Eagles on his favorite rock album.

His phone's ringtone interrupted the song's opening guitar riff, and he ignored it until he saw who the caller was.

"Put a team on Drake," Daniel Franklin said.

"Why?" Braxton asked.

"It wasn't a coincidence he was in Las Vegas. The president sent him. Adam Drake isn't just someone you knew in the army. He's a friend of President Ballard, and I want to know everything there is to know about him."

"Don't you have a file on him?"

"There's not much in it," Franklin said. "He doesn't use

social media or have an online presence. He wasn't on our opposition list. I'll send you what we have in his file. It's enough to get you started."

"I'll assemble a team tomorrow."

"Do it tonight, Braxton."

"What's the rush?"

"The Congressional Intelligence Committees are starting their investigations. Our friends think the committees know more than they should. They think it's because you screwed up in Las Vegas."

"It was your plan, remember? I wanted the kid to have an accident."

"The plan was solid. You let Drake interfere. It's your mess to clean up," Franklin said, ending the call.

Braxton finished his drink and poured another.

If Adam Drake was a friend of the president, he should have been on the enemy list, or opposition list, as Franklin called it. Franklin's dream was to have a file on every person who might stand in his way someday, as J. Edgar Hoover did when he was the director of the FBI.

Franklin's opposition list included the president's friends and family members, as well as his political allies and world leaders. Franklin said that with the internet and the ability to purchase personal data from social media companies and corporations, secrets are easy to find if you know how to look for them—and Franklin knew where to look.

Braxton finished his glass of bourbon and called the surveillance team night manager at Braxton Group operational headquarters in Maryland.

"Leo, I need a surveillance team assembled for tomorrow," Braxton said. "Wheels up at 0700 hours, target lives in Seattle. I'll have more information for you before the team leaves."

Leo Watson was a former FBI Surveillance Specialist who worked there for twenty years and retired early to find a better-paying position in the public sector.

"Anything special about this assignment?" Watson asked.

"Read the Las Vegas report. He's a former Tier One operator with Delta Force. Do not engage. Watch and report."

"Roger that. 0700 hundred hours. Team for Seattle."

Braxton selected a Fuente Fuente OPusX cigar from the humidor and went outside to smoke it under the covered patio beside his swimming pool. He cut the cigar cap with a stainless-steel double Guillotine cutter and drew on the cold cigar several times before lighting it. Holding the flame under and close to the cigar, he savored the first puff.

Light rain made a dimpled pattern on the surface of the pool's water, mesmerizing Braxton as he smoked his cigar. If the president had assigned Adam Drake to protect the PIAB's report, Drake would have been working as a civilian unless there was something about the arrangement they didn't know about.

Braxton was right; they needed a lot more information about Adam Drake to prevent him from interfering in their plans again.

Chapter Forty

THURSDAY MORNING, Drake left home in his gray Cayman GTS 4.0 to drive to PSS headquarters to return to work for the first time since becoming a father. He'd promised Liz he would limit the times he exposed himself to danger by reassigning some of his duties at the company.

The problem was he wasn't sure how he could do that. Agreeing to help the president when he called wasn't something in his job description.

The reality was, his Special Activities Division wasn't needed after the company created its intelligence contractor division. Mark Holland, the former head of the NYPD Counterterrorism Bureau, was the right person to lead the division and assign work to the people he was hiring.

As the company's special counsel, the new division allowed him to spend more time on legal work, which was mainly boring compared to what he wanted to do.

Except for his current project, developing a new training facility for the company's intelligence contractor division at the old Hood River ranch. He had a long list of requirements for the facility that Director Holland had left on his desk, and it was time to find a person to see to it that those requirements were met.

When he drove through the security gate at PSS headquarters, he knew the name of the person he wanted to manage the development at the Hood River ranch, but he had no idea how to make the changes he promised Liz he would. At his core, he was a soldier and always would be.

All the employees he met on his way to his office greeted him with a smile and congratulations, and when he opened the door, he saw why. A box of Pampers diapers with a red ribbon and bow on top was sitting on his desk, next to a blue and purple box of ZzzQuil nighttime sleep aids and a bottle of Pendelton Midnight Whisky.

When he stepped back into the hallway, Mike Casey and the executive floor staff stood outside the breakroom clapping.

"Thank you, thank you," Drake said and smiled. He didn't want to tell them he'd been washing cloth diapers for four days.

Mike Casey walked toward him and said, "I didn't expect you back so soon."

"Liz was tired of being asked if she needed anything and said it was time for me to get back to work."

"How's Alex?"

"He's good," Drake said, waving Casey into his office. "He hasn't smiled at me yet. My repertoire of funny sounds sucks."

Casey laughed. "My Donald Duck did too."

"Mike, what do you think about asking Paul Benning to manage the development of the Hood River facility?"

"We need someone on site. Would Paul be able to stay

there until it's completed? If he is, ask him. I can't think of anyone I trust more than Paul to keep an eye on things."

"I feel the same," Drake said. "I'll call him."

"Have we closed the deal on the ranch?"

"Yes, the ranch belongs to PSS. No more papers for you to sign."

"Let me know when you head down that way," Casey said. "I'd like to go with you."

"Roger that."

Drake moved his baby shower gifts off his desk and called Paul Benning in Portland.

"Paul Benning Investigations," Margo Benning said.

'Hi, Margo. It's Adam. Is Paul around?"

"Why don't I have new pictures of Alex?"

"I sent a bunch of them to you from the hospital."

"That was four days ago."

"Sorry, I'll send more when I get off the phone. Is Paul around?"

"When do I get an invitation to come see Alex?"

"Margo, you don't need an invitation. Come whenever you want, okay?"

"Thank you. Here's Paul."

Margo Benning was Drake's first and only secretary when he was in the Multnomah District Attorney's office in Portland, Oregon. When he left to open his law office, Margo left with him to become his office manager and legal assistant. She looked after him as if he was her son and frequently corrected him like he was.

"Good morning, Adam."

"Hi, Paul. Margo wanted to know when she could come and see baby Alex. Why don't you drive up and make her happy? I want to talk to you about something. You can make it a business trip."

"If I mention this to Margo, we'll be headed your way today," Benning said. "Is there anything I need to be prepared to talk about?"

"No, just come," Drake said. "Plan on spending the night if you can."

"You'll probably see us later this afternoon if I tell her. Is today okay?"

"Today is fine. I'll let Liz know. She'll be delighted to see you both. Go to the condo when you get here. I'll meet you there."

"All right," Benning said. "I'll let you know when we leave."

"Great."

Paul Benning would be the perfect person to oversee the development of the training facility. If he could persuade Margo to move there, he would also be the perfect person to stay on as the facility manager.

Benning was a retired senior detective with the Multnomah County Sheriff's Department and a former officer in the Military Intelligence Corps. When he retired from the Sheriff's Department, Drake convinced him to work on a retainer for PSS while he developed his private detective practice in Portland.

He was street-smart and experienced, and he managed the detective division of the Sheriff's Department for the last ten years before he retired. Paul Benning was also a friend. It would be a pleasure to create a position for him at PSS.

Working with Paul Benning to get the training facility up and running would keep him busy for a while, but sooner or later, he would have to decide how to redefine his new role at PSS to keep his promise to Liz.

Chapter Forty-One

DRAKE LEFT his office early after Liz called. Paul and Margo Benning had arrived, and she said he needed to stop at the wine shop and bring home a bottle of unoaked Chardonnay. Margo forgot to bring a bottle and needed it for the paella she was making for dinner.

When he walked upstairs from the garage to the second floor of their condo, Liz was sitting on a stool, drinking a glass of white wine, watching Margo Benning cook.

Drake kissed Liz on the cheek and said, "Hello, Margo."

"Did you bring the wine?" she asked without turning around.

He walked around the white waterfall island and set a bottle of the Chardonnay she ordered on the counter beside her.

"Nice to see you too, Margo," Drake said, peeking over her shoulder at a lobster cooking in a pot of boiling water.

Margo bumped her head against his and said, "I don't want to overcook the lobster. You'll have to wait for a hug."

Drake laughed, squeezing her shoulder. "Right, we don't want overcooked lobster."

"Where's Paul?" he asked.

"He's up on the deck, enjoying the view," Liz said.

"How's Alex?"

"I just fed him. He's sleeping."

"I'll say hello to Paul," Drake said.

When Drake left, Margo took the lobster out of the pot and put it on a chopping block on the island. "How's he doing?" she asked.

"He's wonderful. If I let him, he'd have Alex in his arms every moment he's awake."

Paul Benning was standing at the rooftop deck railing, looking at the Seattle skyline.

"Hi, Paul," Drake said, crossing the deck to stand beside him.

"A black Mercedes sedan followed you home," Benning said. "There's a white Honda Civic parked at the curb down the street with two men inside, and a gray Toyota Tacoma parked at the intersection. You're under surveillance."

Drake could see the white Honda without turning his head and leaned against the railing to see the truck. "How long have the Honda and the Toyota been there?"

"They were parked there when I came up here fifteen minutes ago. Do you know who they are?"

"I have no idea," Drake said.

"Let's see if we can find out," Benning said, slipping his phone out of his pocket and turning it on camera mode. He stepped back and took a picture of the Honda Civic. When he turned toward the intersection, the Toyota Tacoma pulled away from the curb, allowing him to get a shot of the rear of the truck and its license plate. The Honda pulled away from the curb and left as well.

Drake took his phone out and called Kevin McRoberts at PSS. "Kevin, find out who these two vehicles are registered to." He held out his phone and had Benning recite the license plates from the pictures on his phone.

When Benning finished, Drake said, "Someone has staked out my home. I need to know who they are."

"I'm on it, Boss," McRoberts said.

"Paul, while we're here, let me run something by you," Drake said. "We bought the old ranch at Hood River to develop it as a training facility. We want you to be our project manager. The county walked away from it two years ago, and it's a mess. The only problem I see is the manager needs to be onsite 24/7. There's a great ranch house you could live in."

"You mean stop working as a private investigator and become a project manager? What would I do with my office and our apartment?"

"You would still be on retainer as our investigator," Drake said. "The manager position would be an addition to that, as an employee of PSS, with all the benefits and perks that come with it."

"How long would the position last? Until the project is finished? I can't make that kind of a change for the short term."

"When the facility is operational, we'll still need a manager to coordinate activities, develop training exercises, and manage the staff there. The position will be permanent for as long as you want. You and Margo are family, Paul. We're growing the company, and we need you."

"I appreciate that. You know I do. But Margo is a city

girl. She's always lived in Portland. Moving her to a ranch outside a small city, like Hood River, will be a tough sell."

"Is it something you're willing to consider?" Drake asked. "If it is, we'll find a way to make it attractive to Margo."

"It would have to give her something meaningful to do," Benning said. "She's bored running my office. There isn't enough work to keep her busy. You remember what she was like as your legal assistant in the DA's office. The more cases she had to work on, the happier she was."

"Then we'll create a position for her at the ranch. We have twelve hundred employees, adding another five hundred in the intelligence division. People will be coming and going all the time at the ranch, so there will be plenty for her to do."

"What do you have in mind for the salary?"

"What will it take?"

"Seriously?"

"Talk it over with Margo and let me know. I'll see if we can make it happen," Drake said.

Benning turned and looked across the lake at the skyline in the distance. "I wasn't expecting this, Adam. When I left the Sheriff's Department, I thought I'd find a hobby and settle into retirement. Then you asked me to investigate some things for you, and now I'm a private investigator with my own office. Then, you ask me to run a training facility for bodyguards and spies. Will I ever get to retire?"

"You know the saying, 'When you retire, you expire.' Margo wants you to stay around as long as possible. I'm just trying to help make sure you do."

Chapter Forty-Two

THE NEXT MORNING, after feasting on Margo's paella and an evening listening to her stories about all the years she shepherded Drake through his legal career, Benning drove Drake to PSS headquarters in his red Ford F150 truck.

When they passed a blue Toyota Camry that was parked in the same place as the white Honda Civic the night before, Drake recognized the man behind the wheel,

"I know that guy," he said. "He was at the Paris Las Vegas Hotel and Casino, one of Marcus Braxton's guys. These are Braxton's watchers."

"Who is Marcus Braxton?" Benning asked.

"He's a private intelligence contractor."

"Why does he have a surveillance team watching you?"

Drake turned around and saw the Camry wasn't following them. "I played a dirty trick on Braxton in Las Vegas, planted drugs on his plane, and called the police. I'm sure he'd like to get back at me, but he could find out where I live and work without sending a surveillance team to Seattle."

"What else happened in Las Vegas?"

"That's a story for another time, Paul," Drake said. "I'll have a protection team sent here when I get to the office. Turn around and take me back to the condo. Stay there until they arrive. I'll get the plans for the training facility in my office and bring them back. You don't need to come to headquarters to see them."

"All right," Benning said, pulling into a driveway to turn around and return to the condo.

"Did you tell Margo about managing the training facility?"

"No, not yet. I thought I'd tell her on the drive back to Portland."

"Let me know as soon as possible, Paul."

The Camry was still there, and Benning slowed so Drake could get a better look at the driver.

Drake waved to him as they drove past and said, "Yeah, the same guy."

Benning pulled behind the duplex condo and waited while Drake called his wife on his phone.

After explaining to Liz why the protection team was coming and that Paul Benning would remain there until he returned, Drake backed his Porsche Cayman out of the garage and left.

Two blocks away, the gray Toyota Tacoma truck turned off a side street, slotted in behind the Cayman two cars back, and followed him to PSS headquarters.

Drake wondered what Braxton was up to. The stunt at the airport in Las Vegas was retaliation for what he and his men tried to do to Chris Patterson. There was no need for Braxton to respond to it unless there was more in play than he realized.

He parked his car in his assigned space in underground

parking at PSS headquarters and took the stairs two at a time to his office on the third floor. Once there, he pushed the button on his desk console for the protection division, arranged for a detail to be dispatched to his home, and walked down the hall to Mike Casey's office.

Casey's door was closed, but his assistant's next door wasn't.

Captain Peter Marshall was a helicopter pilot who lost both of his legs when his AH-640 Apache helicopter crashed in Afghanistan. He was the first employee Casey hired at Puget Sound Security when he took over the company from its owner when he retired.

"Pete, when he's finished with what he's doing, will you tell him to come see me?" Drake asked.

"Sure thing," Marshall said. "It shouldn't be long."

Drake returned to his office and called Kevin McRoberts, the head of the IT division on the floor below.

"Kevin, do you still have access to the Braxton Group's IT system?" Drake asked.

"If I don't, I can get back in. Why?"

"He has a surveillance team watching me. I want to know why."

"How deep do you want me to go?"

"I want it all," Drake said. "Who he's working for, who's paying him, who his employees are, where he lives, where his offices are, everything."

"How soon do you need this?"

"I need it now."

"I'm on it," Kevin said.

Mike Casey rapped twice on the open door and asked, "You wanted to see me?"

Drake waved him in and told him to shut the door. "Marcus Braxton has a surveillance team watching me."

"Why, because of Las Vegas? I'm sure he was embarrassed by what you did at the airport, but why go to the expense of surveilling you?"

"I know, it doesn't make sense," Drake agreed. "I'm pretty sure he was behind the cyber attack the other day. He knew we couldn't prove he was responsible. Why send a team that isn't hiding the surveillance. They're parked down my street, where I'll see them."

"What are you doing about it?"

"I sent a protection team to the condo. Kevin is visiting Braxton's IT system. He'll get me everything he can find."

"Do you think the guy he was working for in Las Vegas, the personal data guy, is involved in this?"

"To what end? He doesn't have a bone to pick with me like Braxton does."

"Braxton's a loose cannon," Casey said. "Be careful. Why don't you drive one of our armored SUVs for a while, just in case."

"Good idea. I'll stop and see if one's available. I'm going home. Paul's staying around until the protection team arrives."

"Did you talk with him about managing the training facility?"

"Yes, last night. I think he's interested. I don't know about Margo yet."

"Let me know," Casey said. "If we want it ready by next summer, we need to get moving on the project," Casey said.

Drake put the plans for the training facility in the leather messenger bag hanging on the back of the door and went downstairs to see the fleet manager on the first floor.

Chapter Forty-Three

DANIEL FRANKLIN WALKED to the net to shake hands with his friend, Ruben Marek, a Harvard philosophy professor, after their weekly Friday afternoon tennis match at Boston's Tennis and Racquet Club.

"Drinks are on me next week," Franklin said

"You say that whenever you win," Professor Marek said. "I just wish it wasn't every week."

"It lets you indulge your taste for the club's selection of Polish vodka more often if I win."

"Which selection you helped expand, I've learned. Your generosity is appreciated."

"My pleasure, friend. Enjoy your weekend," Franklin said, walking to his bench to get his tennis bag and shower.

Ruben Marek was more than Franklin's friend. He was a classmate, fellow campus radical at U.C. Berkeley, and the political commissar of a cell of American Marxists who wanted a second revolution. America wasn't a functioning democracy, and the sooner the country's low-information citizens realized it, the better off they all would be.

Franklin and the others were working to shape public opinion to achieve that goal. His contribution was collecting and analyzing Americans' personal data to create content for social media influencers on TikTok and other social media platforms to use and influence public opinion.

The data he analyzed was also used to create their list, separate from the list he created for the CIA, of citizens who opposed their goal and needed to be monitored. By labeling those individuals and adding them to the list he provided to the CIA as "potential security threats" for the agency to use in its domestic surveillance programs, the government was their unsuspecting silent partner.

Project Consensus, as they called it, had unlimited resources, thanks to the wealth its members had at their disposal. With their resources, they generated trends and topics that went viral, shaping the stories traditional media networks picked up and influencing public opinion in the way they wanted.

Today, Franklin skipped a round of drinks with his friend after showering to rush home and change for dinner with Senator Wayland Morris, California's junior first-term senator. He'd promised to take the senator to dinner at the Contessa in exchange for information.

Contessa was the reigning queen of restaurants in Boston's Back Bay, sitting atop the glamorous Newbury Boston hotel, and it cost him a small fortune to change his monthly reservation on short notice to accommodate the senator.

Senator Morris was a retired army general who wanted to be president. He was a member of the Senate's Committee on Armed Services, and the best chance Franklin had to get his hands on the classified military records of Major Adam Drake, former Delta Force Tier

One operator, a friend of the president, and an enemy he needed to know more about.

Whatever the reason for his being in Las Vegas, Drake discovered what Braxton's men were doing in a single day and prevented them from accomplishing what he had sent them to accomplish. He'd even turned the tables on Braxton by anticipating an ambush and planting drugs on Braxton's jet.

If Drake's charge from the president was broader than just protecting the PIAB staffer in Las Vegas and included investigating Braxton or himself, he would have to determine what could be done with Mr. Drake. For that, he needed to understand who Drake was.

When he arrived, Senator Morris sat at a small table near Contessa's bar with a Glencairn Whiskey glass held to his nose, inhaling the aroma of a dark amber liquid.

Senator Morris raised his glass and asked, "Do you drink Scotch?"

"I prefer vodka."

"A glass of this 29-year-old Glenfiddich Grand Yozakura will change that," Morris said, holding his glass up. "Thanks for the room. This is a nice hotel."

"I thought you might like it," Franklin said, nodding to the bartender before sitting down. "How's your campaign doing in California?"

"The Republican who will probably be my opponent is wealthy, he's good-looking, and that's about it. He's getting some attention, but it's because he's a new face, and no one knows anything about him."

"Can I help with that?"

"How?"

'I could send you his file and tell you what skeletons are in his closet."

Senator Morris cocked his head to one side and waited until the bartender set a Grey Goose vodka martini with a lemon twist down and left before asking, "You already know what they are? He only announced that he was running two weeks ago."

Franklin winked and smiled. "You would be surprised to find out who I have files on."

"Including me, I suppose?"

Franklin tasted his martini and nodded. "Even you."

"Is that why you invited me here?" Morris asked. "To tell me you have a file on me and get something you want? It won't work, Franklin."

"Relax, Senator. I want you to be president someday. I'm not telling anyone what I know about you, but there is something I want."

"You don't know anything about me, and I don't care what you want."

Franklin shook his head and said, "It doesn't have to be this way, Senator. I'm not threatening you, but you should understand that I find out things that no one else knows. It's what I do."

"Things like what?" Senator Morris said sarcastically. "There are no skeletons in my closet."

"What about the money in your Cayman account? I know where it came from."

Morris choked and spilled his glass of Scotch. "There's no way you could know that."

"I know about the Afghan growers you protected in Afghanistan when the Taliban declared war on the opium trade," Franklin suggested.

Senator Morris raised his glass to get the bartender's attention and asked softly, "What do you want?"

"You're the chairman of the Senate's Committee on

Armed Services. I want you to get the military records of a former Delta Force operator, Major Adam Drake."

"Those records are classified. Why do you want them?"

"Drake's a problem," Franklin said. "He's poking his nose where it doesn't belong. I need to find a way to get him to back off."

"What in his army records would make him do that?"

"Someone I know said he was being investigated for something before he left the army. I want to know what it was."

"You'll have to find another way to get them," Senator Morris said. "Records of Tier One Special Forces operators are classified at the highest level for national security purposes. I'd go to jail if they ever found out I gave them to you."

"Find a way, Senator, unless you want to spend the rest of your days in Leavenworth after the army court martials you for what you did in Afghanistan."

"You...!"

"Be a gentleman, Senator, and quiet down. The grilled Mediterranean Branzino is excellent. You should try it," Franklin said and left.

Chapter Forty-Four

DRAKE WAS BACK at PSS headquarters Saturday morning to meet with Kevin McRoberts and hear what he discovered when he accessed the Braxton Group's IT system.

He was surprised to find a cup of coffee and a bagel on Kevin's desk instead of empty energy drink cans.

Kevin smiled at the look on Drake's face and said, "My girlfriend is trying to get me to eat better. The coffee's her idea."

"I didn't know you had a girlfriend?"

"She's a member of my cycling club. She's helping me train for the Seattle to Portland ride next summer."

"I didn't know you were a cyclist," Drake admitted.

Kevin grinned. "I was spending too much time gaming. I still love it but needed to get out more to improve my social life."

"It looks like you succeeded. Congratulations," Drake said and sat in the chair beside Kevin's desk so he could see around the two massive monitors on it.

"I didn't find much we didn't already know about Braxton, Boss. The surveillance team was sent to Seattle from Braxton Group's Maryland headquarters: three men and one woman. Nothing about why they're here."

"Is there any mention of Las Vegas or emails from Braxton while he was there?"

"No, sir."

"Okay," Drake said. "It's a long shot, but see if you can find anything at Franklin Analytics. I saw Braxton with Franklin in Las Vegas."

"Do you want me to see if there's anything on Braxton's or Franklin's personal computers? They're probably connected to their company's IT systems."

"Anything you can find, Kevin. I don't like having a surveillance team staked out around my house. I want to know why."

Drake walked through the IT division with the weekend staff busy at their stations, pleased that his genius hacker and IT division director had a social life and angry that someone was messing with him and his family. Braxton should know that involving a man's family crossed the line. If he didn't, he was going to find out.

He found Wayne Beardon's cell phone number in his contacts list and called him back in his office.

"Hi, Wayne. Are you home?"

"Yeah, watching my alma mater losing. We're two touchdowns behind," Beardon said. "Do you need me to come in?"

"No, you can work on it from home," Drake said. "I want you to organize surveillance of an individual and his company. The man lives in McLean, Virginia, and his company headquarters is in Maryland. I'll send you the details. He has a surveillance team following me and watching my home."

"Why?"

"I have a good idea. He's the CEO of a private intelligence contractor that does surveillance work for the CIA. Be prepared; his men don't always play nice."

"Understood. When do you want us to leave for the East Coast?"

"Monday's fine. Meet me in my office before you leave. I may have more information for you by then."

"See you Monday," Beardon replied.

Drake sat back and crossed his arms over his chest. Marcus Braxton knew who he was and where he lived. What else did he think he would learn by sending a surveillance team to keep an eye on him? If he wanted revenge for keeping Matthew Patterson safe in Las Vegas or embarrassing him at the airport, he didn't need a team of watchers to help him do it.

Braxton was more of an in-your-face, smash-mouth kind of guy. He wasn't subtle or patient by nature. That's what got him in trouble in Afghanistan when he tortured the Taliban fighter instead of taking time to break him and get information that was reliable and actionable.

If Braxton wasn't going to learn anything by having him watched, then who would? Daniel Franklin? Keeping Chris Patterson's PIAB report from being discredited wasn't the only reason House and Senate Intelligence Committees were investigating government agencies for domestic spying. Two U.S. Senators had been doing the same thing for months.

There was another reason, something more sinister than data brokers losing money.

Social media platforms use personal data to decipher an individual's preferences and opinions. When they knew what music you liked, what news you watched, and whether your politics leaned left or right, they knew how to influence your choices and profit from that knowledge by selling you what they knew you wanted to buy, hear, or watch.

Were Braxton and Franklin working to preserve the government's means of influencing or controlling public opinion? Or did they have another agenda?

Chapter Forty-Five

SENATOR WAYLAND MORRIS put the Sunday edition of the *Washington Post* newspaper down next to the half-eaten chocolate croissant on the round window table in his bedroom at the Pendry Washington Hotel at the Wharf and went to the door.

A young man wearing a long black wool overcoat, gray crew neck sweater, and black pants took a thick file from a carrier bag hanging from his shoulder and handed it to him without saying a word, and left. Judging by the cut of his hair, Senator Morris knew the man was delivering the file from the Pentagon he wasn't supposed to have.

Before he opened the file, he stopped, looked out the large picture window at the boats moored at the Wharf Marina, and congratulated himself again for choosing to live in the best hotel in the hottest new neighborhood on the Potomac when he was in D.C. It was expensive, but he deserved it after all his years in the army serving the country.

Senator Morris poured another cup of coffee from the

stainless-steel coffee pot provided by room service and carried it with the file to the seating area adjacent to his bedroom. With his coffee cup in his left hand and the file in his right, Morris sat in the white reading chair to discover why Daniel Franklin was so interested in Adam Drake's military records.

He remembered Drake and his partner, Mike Casey, because he was their commanding officer when they killed a village chieftain in Afghanistan. Men from the village claimed their leader had been captured, tortured, and beheaded by the two soldiers. Drake's and Casey's after-action reports said the chief was on the kill list and died from a single sniper round Casey fired from a ridgeline thirty-five hundred meters away that exploded the man's head in a burst of pink blood.

To keep the peace with the local Afghans who provided intelligence about the location of Taliban fighters and the movements of Taliban leaders, he appointed a command investigator to investigate the allegations. After the investigator's report was submitted with a he-said, she-said conclusion, he'd considered what was at stake and signed an order to convene a military court.

Before he filed a formal preferral of charges with the court, he was informed their defense counsel had filed discovery motions to obtain the records of all his visits to villages suspected of being involved in the country's opium trade and a list of all the village chieftains he met with.

To protect his career, he let it be known that if Drake and Casey resigned their commissions, he would let them leave the army with their rank and benefits intact and return home as soon as the paperwork was completed.

Franklin knew why he allowed Drake and Casey to leave the army without being tried in a military court for killing the local Afghan chieftain. So, what did he hope to find in Drake's classified records?

Senator Morris went through the file page by page, impressed with the number of high-value targets the two men sanctioned as a hunter-killer team. Halfway through the thick file, he refilled his coffee cup, finished the croissant, and returned to the task at hand, finding what Franklin was looking for in Drake's file.

An hour later, he was still baffled when he picked up a hand-written note from the trial counsel prosecuting Drake's court martial and stared at it.

Defense counsel says he has evidence the reason the commanding officer is preferring charges has nothing to do with the tribal chieftain who was killed. He wouldn't say what it was.

Senator Morris stopped breathing, took a deep breath to calm himself and read the note again. Franklin knew what he'd done in Afghanistan and used it as leverage to get what he wanted. But no one would know the truth if he did what Franklin wanted.

But if Franklin used something he found in Drake's file against Drake and Drake found out how Franklin got his hands on his classified records, his political career would be over. He'd spend the rest of his years in a federal prison in Leavenworth.

He got up and walked to the door and back to the suite's picture window, with his eyes fixed in a thousand-yard stare as he looked across the Potomac.

Franklin wouldn't believe him if he said he couldn't get Drake's classified records. Franklin said he knew everything about him, and he believed him. Afghanistan wasn't the only skeleton in his closet. He made deals in California when he entered politics that were almost as bad.

Nothing he could think of would prevent Franklin from

using the information in Drake's classified records if it helped him deal with the problem he had with the man.

There had to be a way to quiet Drake and his sniper partner, Mike Casey, and prevent the news of his misdeeds in Afghanistan from interfering with his dream of becoming the president.

A dream, he thought, Daniel Franklin might share as well. If he did, and he was president, the secrets Franklin claimed to have would give him control of the government and the power to make the changes Franklin liked to talk about on his yacht each spring, sailing to Cabo San Lucas with their friends.

Senator Morris walked to the other room and picked up his phone on the nightstand. If Franklin was willing to cooperate and help him deal with Drake and Casey, getting Drake's classified records might be the key to making his dream come true and a way to get rid of the biggest obstacle there was that could keep him out of the White House.

"Daniel, we need to talk," Senator Morris said. "Would you come to Washington tomorrow?"

Chapter Forty-Six

SENATOR MORRIS GLANCED at the simple Panerai Luminor watch with its plain brown strap on his wrist and saw that it was eight o'clock. The Moonraker restaurant on the fourteenth floor of his hotel closed at nine o'clock on Sunday nights, and Daniel Franklin's flight from Boston landed at Reagan National at a quarter past seven o'clock.

He hoped it wasn't delayed. He was counting on Franklin's love of Japanese cuisine and Moonraker's menu to help persuade Franklin to agree with him in the time they had before the restaurant closed.

Adam Drake and his partner had to be dealt with. He'd learned from a friend at the Pentagon that Drake had worked closely with the FBI and President Ballard the year before to defeat China's false flag operation to frame a secret militia group for an attack on America's power grid. Drake's name was also mentioned in a Defense Intelligence Agency file about a Chinese industrial spy operation targeting the development of satellite surveillance using artificial intelligence for military operations.

Drake's relationship with the president and his history of working independently on national security threats made him someone they couldn't trust to keep his nose out of their business. Analyzing and using personal data in domestic surveillance programs run by the intelligence community and the military was necessary to protect the country. If Drake was working for the president in Las Vegas to keep the PIAB report and its writer from scrutiny, as Franklin believed, then Franklin had a reason to want Drake off the playing field.

He had his reason for wanting Drake taken care of, and Franklin knew what it was, but he suspected Franklin had more at stake than he was letting on. The big hitters he invited to sail with him to Cabo each year hinted at it when they'd had too much to drink, but he knew what they wanted. They wanted to run the country, and if he wanted to ride along with them and be their president, that was okay with him. For that to happen, though, Franklin had to help protect his reputation.

Daniel Franklin followed the maître de to Senator Morris's table and pulled his chair back to sit without making eye contact.

"Thank you for coming," Senator Morris said.

"I have a meeting tomorrow," Franklin said. "What do you want to talk about?"

Senator Morris nodded at the waiter approaching their table and asked, "Would you like something to drink?"

Franklin waited for the waiter and said, "Haku vodka, neat."

"The yellowtail sashimi is excellent. You should try it."

Franklin stared at Morris and then grinned. "Touché. Now, why am I here?"

"We have a problem I thought we should discuss."

"You mean your Afghanistan problem? I will help you deal with that."

"That's part of it," Senator Morris said. "Drake may have found out what I was doing and has evidence to prove it. If you try to use something from his classified records, he isn't going to back off."

"Let me be the judge of that."

"You don't understand. When a Chinese triad tried to take him out, its Dragon Master winds up rotting away in a maximum-security prison. When the head of a Chinese drug cartel in Mexico goes after him, he hightails it back to China to escape."

"How do you know this?"

"The Defense Intelligence Agency has a file on him," Senator Morris said. "The CIA has one, too, I'm told."

"Why will any of that make a difference to me?"

"Because if you try to make him go away by using something from his classified records, he will find out about it and come after me. And then he will come after you when he finds out I gave you his classified records."

Franklin's vodka arrived, and he took a sip. "There has to be a way to discourage Drake from getting any closer than he was in Las Vegas."

"From what I can find about the man, the only way you're going to do that is by taking him off the playing field," Senator Morris said quietly.

Franklin shook his head no. "That's not something in my wheelhouse, even if I agreed with you."

"It is in the wheelhouse of people you know," Senator Morris reminded him.

"Maybe in some other country, but not here."

"You're not that naïve, Daniel. They've done it before."

"Why would they want to? Drake's my problem, not theirs."

"Because Drake's doing the president's bidding. President Ballard doesn't trust the intelligence community. If he sent Drake to Las Vegas, as you believe, the president won't tell him to stop now. Drake will keep digging until he finds out what you and the intelligence community are doing. And he'll help the president put an end to it."

Franklin signaled for another round of vodka and laughed. "I get it. You want me to get their okay to have someone eliminate your problem. What do they get out of it? What do I get out of it? What's the quid pro quo, Senator?"

"I will organize and lead the opposition in the Senate to block any legislation that will make it illegal for a government agency to purchase personal data from third-party data brokers like Franklin Analytics."

"No, if Drake is 'taken off the field,' as you call it, the president will know who's behind it. Our friends will never go for it."

"I think they will if they make it look like someone else had a score to settle, someone like a Chinese triad or the CCP; he's embarrassed both of them recently."

"And create an international crisis? They won't risk that."

"Daniel, you're good at what you do but you're not a politician. My constituency is the military. It exists because the country wants to be protected from its enemies. It needs an enemy, and an international crisis puts a face on one."

Franklin sat back in his seat and shook his head. "I had my doubts about you, Senator. You might make a good president after all."

"Do we agree on what needs to be done?" Senator Morris asked.

"Yes," Franklin said.

"Excellent. A courier will deliver his records to your office. You shouldn't travel with them in your possession."

Chapter Forty-Seven

WAYNE BEARDON, the head of the surveillance team, was in the breakroom down the hall from Drake's office when Drake walked by.

"How do you take your coffee?" Beardon called out.

"Black," Drake said and turned back to join him. "You're here early."

"I had things to do before I meet the team at eight."

Drake took the coffee mug Beardon handed him and said, "I see Mike's here. Bring a pastry if you want."

"Thanks," Beardon said, following Drake to his corner office with a maple bar in his hand.

Drake hung his coat on the back of the door and opened the laptop on his desk before he settled in his chair.

"Steve's at Boeing Field getting the G280 ready. Call him when you're ready to drive the team there. How many are you taking?"

"Eleven, including myself."

Drake opened the file on his laptop and scanned it.

"Braxton lives in McLean, Virginia. His company, the Braxton Group, has its headquarters in Bethesda, Maryland.

"Kevin also found a Braxton Group facility located west of Seneca, Maryland. The note says it's a rural location near a wildlife management area, but it doesn't say what the facility is used for."

"What do you want us to focus on, Braxton or his company?"

"Braxton *and* his company. I want to know who Braxton meets, where he goes, and what he's doing. I also want to know who his watchers are and where they're based. Braxton's doing surveillance on Americans for the CIA. I want to learn as much as possible about that before I report to the president."

"How long do you want us back there?"

"As long as it takes to understand what Braxton and his men are doing. Be prepared for anything. They attacked me in Las Vegas. Assume they will come after you if they're told to."

"Is there anything else I need to know?" Beardon asked.

"That's all I have. I'll send you the addresses for his residence and company locations. If we learn anything else, I'll send it to you. Be careful, be safe, and tell me when you're finished and heading home."

Beardon got up and shook Drake's hand. "On my way, then."

Drake picked up the coffee mug on his desk, thinking about Marcus Braxton and the surveillance team he was flying across the country, and was reminded that Braxton's men were still here in Seattle watching him.

Why? he thought. They weren't hiding their presence, and they weren't learning anything new about him since they arrived. They knew where he lived and worked. Why were they still here?

He decided to find out and called Pat Reynolds, the head of the company's Executive Protection Unit.

"Pat, come see me when you have a moment," Drake said. "I have something I'd like you to do."

"Give me five, and I'm on my way."

"Thanks."

Reynolds was a former Marine Corps Force Recon officer, one of the world's deadliest and elite military units. Force Recon's mission was to gather intelligence deep behind enemy lines for the corps command element. Its motto was "Swift, Silent, Deadly," and only a few hundred men were qualified and selected to serve in the unit.

Reynolds knocked on Drake's doorframe and stepped into the office.

"Thanks for organizing a team so quickly to protect Liz and my son," Drake said. "I appreciate it, especially when I'm sure everyone had plans for the weekend."

"It wasn't hard. Everyone in the unit volunteered."

"Has anything changed?"

"No, two cars are still watching your home, with one car following you wherever you go. They're not hiding; they want us to know they're out there."

"I want to find out why," Drake said. "Use our DJI Phantom drones with the audio feature and listen to their conversations. We might hear something that will tell us why they're here."

"Do you want pictures to go with the audio?"

"Sure, let's identify them and run background checks. Let's also find out where they're staying. Coordinate with the surveillance unit. We'll find out who's paying for their lodging."

"We can handle that."

"Okay."

"Is there anything else?"

"Not right now," Drake said. "I'm sending Wayne and a team to watch the man who sent these guys. I'll let you know if anything changes."

Drake leaned back in his tall leather office chair and stared at the vivid colors of the abstract print of the Seattle skyline on the wall Liz bought to bring some color into his office.

He liked it better when he was the hunter and not the hunted. When he and Mike were sent out as an Omega hunter/killer team in Afghanistan, they knew their target. They didn't know his exact location. Completing the mission required time and patience, but they knew who they were looking for.

He wasn't sure who he should be looking for now. Marcus Braxton was too obvious, as was the man he saw Braxton talking to in Las Vegas, Daniel Franklin. Braxton had worked with Franklin before, Kevin had said, doing surveillance for the CIA on Americans on Franklin's list of security risks. But he was sure they were acting on behalf of someone else.

The CIA didn't need Franklin or Braxton to go after Chris Patterson and his report. The PIAB report might have been an annoyance it didn't want to deal with. Still, the CIA and the Intelligence Community had plenty of skilled professionals they could have used who would have done a better job than Braxton and Franklin did in Las Vegas.

Squaring off against Congress over domestic surveillance programs happened every time Congress considered a bill restricting the sweeping powers the Act gave to the government. The Intelligence Community had prevailed every time.

Something more significant was in play, and he was determined to find out what it was. Franklin, Braxton, and the IC were involved, but he was beginning to believe they weren't the only ones.

Chapter Forty-Eight

DRAKE WORKED all morning approving plans and orders for the new training facility until noon when Kevin McRoberts called on the company's secure VoIP system and asked if he could come to his office.

"I'm going home for lunch, Kevin," Drake said. "Can it wait until I get back?"

"I won't take long. I found some things you'll want to hear about."

"Does it involve Franklin?"

"Yes," Kevin said, "and Braxon too."

"All right, come up."

Two minutes later, Kevin was sitting in a chair in front of Drake's desk with his laptop resting on his knees.

"Three things, Mr. Drake. First, Daniel Frankin has hundreds of encrypted files in a 'People' folder. I can get you a list of names from the index, but I haven't tried to get into those files. Do you want me to try?"

"Any idea what's in these files?"

"No, but because they're encrypted, it's something he

doesn't want anyone to see. They're important people in the U.S., and some names I recognize in Europe."

"Let's leave them alone for now."

"Second, what's more interesting is an annual report Franklin Analytics sends to the CIA identifying Americans for consideration as security risks. There are attachments to the report that map the connections these people have with each other. He's using Artificial Intelligence to determine who they meet, where they go, what churches they attend, what clubs and groups they belong to, and even where they go for dinner. It's all on a map with colored connecting lines."

"Is the map used to monitor these people?" Drake asked.

"It probably is, but using AI expands the number of people considered security risks to everyone they're connected to. His next report to the CIA will likely include those people as well."

"And the list of security risks keeps growing until it includes everyone. Just like it was in the U.S.S.R. with Stalin," Drake said. "You said you found something about Braxton?"

"It has nothing to do with this report about security risks," Kevin said. "When I went back to see if there was anything new in the Braxton Group's system, I found an email asking for a quote from a company that's a little weird. This company manufactures and sells Lethal Miniature Aerial Missile Systems, the little killer drones. Why would the Braxton Group want something like that?"

"And why would they think they can buy them?" Drake asked. "The LMAMS were developed for the military. They're not available to non-governmental buyers like the Braxton Group."

He was familiar with loitering munition systems, also known as kamikaze drones. One of their clients was a defense contractor that bid on the Defense Department contract to manufacture the revolutionary class of weaponry that was changing modern warfare and battlefield operations.

Loitering munitions were unmanned aerial vehicles (UAVs) designed to loiter over battlefields, scanning for targets until a suitable one was detected. First developed by an Israeli firm, its Hero-30 was a tiny drone launched from a man-portable pneumatic carrying tube that flew up to 115 miles per hour. It had a stabilized camera and thermal imager in its nose to beam back video to an operator. Capable of loitering overhead for thirty minutes, it could locate and track an enemy target as far away as five kilometers and deliver a one-pound warhead with deadly precision that limited collateral damage.

"Find out what you can about the company they asked for the quote from and what the response was," Drake said. "Braxton worked for the CIA's Special Activities Center, the company's tactical paramilitary unit. These are the weapons covert operators love. I want to know why Braxton wants one."

"Okay," Kevin said and got up to leave. "Before I forget it, Daniel Franklin emails some influential people around the country. Would you like to know who they are?"

"Sure, I want to know as much as possible about the man. Thanks, Kevin."

Before he followed Kevin, Drake jotted down some things on the legal pad on his desk that he wanted to do when he returned.

There was only so much Kevin could learn about Daniel Franklin and Marcus Braxton using his skills as a hacker who was unsuccessful only once when he was caught hacking into Microsoft's IT system.

He needed the kind of inside information he could only get from a person who had been in Washington long enough to hear the rumors and had the resources to find out what people like Franklin, Baxter, and the Intelligence Community might be doing.

Someone with friends in and out of government, his father-in-law, Senator Hazelton.

The cobalt-blue armored GMC Yukon was idling in its assigned parking space, thanks to the remote start key fob he was carrying. He drove up the ramp from underground parking to the headquarters compound's security gate and looked for the watcher's car. It was parked halfway down the street where it had been Saturday.

He was tempted to drive down the street and say hello but turned to the right instead and followed his regular route home. They knew his routine. He'd thought about running a surveillance detection route, but they already knew where he lived. Until he had a better understanding of what Braxton was doing, he'd keep to his routine.

They might know where he lived and worked, but he knew they were out there. When Reynolds hovered a drone over their car and recorded their conversation, he would also know something about them. When he did, he'd decide what to do with them.

Until then, he would ignore their presence, wait for his surveillance team to report back, and learn what he could about Daniel Franklin and Franklin Analytics.

Chapter Forty-Nine

DRAKE WAS BACK in his office by two o'clock, after enjoying the chicken Cobb salad Liz had prepared for their lunch and checking on his son, who was asleep in his crib. He'd seen Braxton's two cars parked in their usual spots and Reynold's black Yukon parked around the corner half a block away.

Senator Hazelton had a delegation from Oregon cities and counties in his office concerned about the lack of federal funding to help law enforcement deal with street gang violence when he called. Thirty minutes later, the senator returned his call using the Signal encryption app they used to keep their conversations private.

"Hello, Adam. How's our grandson doing?" Senator Hazelton asked.

"He's fine, sir. Eating, sleeping, and needing his diapers changed more often than I thought was possible."

"How are you and Liz doing?"

"We're fine, learning how to be parents."

"I remember. Merideth read all the books, and we still didn't have the answers we were looking for. We never did find them, come to think of it."

"Senator, your Intelligence Committee hearings are about government agencies buying personal data from data brokers. Can you tell me what the committee's investigators know about one of the data brokers?"

"You mean Franklin Analytics? The president told me you helped him with something in Las Vegas."

"Yes, Franklin Analytics and a private intelligence contractor he works with, the Braxton Group," Drake said.

"I know about Franklin Analytics but not much about the Braxton Group."

"Marcus Braxton is the CEO and founder of the Braxton Group. He was with Franklin in Las Vegas. His men tried to lure a Congressman's son, Chris Patterson, into a honey trap with an escort from Paris, France. They also tried to take me on a one-way trip to who knows where."

"I didn't hear about that."

"I should have expected they would try something. I interfered with their plan, and I know Braxton. The CIA uses the Braxton Group in its domestic surveillance program."

"Do you have evidence of that?"

"I do, but it's nothing you can use."

"I see," Senator Hazelton said. "What do you want to know about Franklin and his company?"

"My home is under surveillance, and I'm followed wherever I go. I recognize one of Braxton's men from Las Vegas in one of the cars. I think Franklin's behind it, but I don't know why."

"Franklin attended some of the Intelligence Committee's hearings, and I was surprised to learn that he has friends on both sides of the aisle. I didn't expect it with his background. So, I had one of my investigators check him out. It's public knowledge that he was a campus radical at U.C. Berkeley and became a billionaire when he sold the Silicon Valley software company he started.

"For two years after he sold his company, he sailed around the Pacific Rim and the Atlantic in a yacht he bought. At various times, the guests on his yacht included some of the day's leading Marxist philosophers and writers. Most were university professors or campus activists but not outright revolutionaries.

"The brand of Marxism they're known for is 'Cultural Marxism,' the values and goals the New Left are espousing. The enemy is no longer the bourgeoisie and capitalism, but it's white males and white supremacy or white privilege and racism. All success is unearned in our racist society, and wealth needs to be redistributed to the oppressed, those who are not white and privileged."

Senator Hazelton stopped and apologized. "Sorry, I didn't mean to lecture you on Marxist wokism and progressive mantras. Franklin is one of this city's most popular philanthropists, and the recipients of his generosity are mostly the usual Far Left causes and activist groups. And he contributes to several nonprofit organizations that funnel dark money to their favorite candidates."

"You said he gives money to Far Left causes and activist groups 'for the most part,'" Drake said. "Who else does he give money to?"

"A nonprofit in San Franciso called the 'Collective,'" Senator Hazelton said. "According to the nonprofit's mission statement, the goal is to preserve the poster art of the 1970s Free Speech Movement at Berkeley."

"He's a supporter of the arts. Isn't that what billionaires do?"

"If that's the real goal. The board of directors is a Who's Who list of tech billionaires. They sail each year to Cabo San Lucas on Franklin's yacht. Franklin and one Harvard professor are the only board members who attended the University of California at Berkeley."

"Why do you think preserving poster art isn't the real goal?" Drake asked.

"You can get prints of that poster art online. They're not preserving anything. I don't know their goal, but it's not preserving art."

"What about Franklin and the Intelligence Community? He's doing more for them than selling personal data. He provides the CIA with a list of Americans he says are security risks, and the CIA includes them as targets for domestic surveillance."

"And you have evidence of that as well?"

"Yes, but again, it's nothing you can use."

"How far are you going with this?" Senator Hazelton asked.

"The president asked me to investigate Franklin and the Braxton Group," Drake said. "What they tried to pull in Las Vegas would have benefitted the Intelligence Community as much as it would have Franklin if he pulled it off. President Ballard wants to know if Las Vegas was something the IC farmed out to Franklin or if he acted alone."

"What can I do to help with that?"

"If your committee's investigators come across anything else about Daniel Franklin or his involvement in the IC's domestic surveillance programs than what you've told me, I would appreciate hearing about it."

"Likewise, I would appreciate hearing about anything

you learn that will help my investigators," Senator Hazelton said.

"Of course."

"Say hello to Liz and Alex."

"I will," Drake said.

Chapter Fifty

AN HOUR after talking with his father-in-law, Pat Reynolds called him.

"They left," Reynolds reported. "I thought the SUV parked down the street from headquarters pulled back because they knew where you were, but the cars watching your home are also gone."

"Have they regrouped somewhere?"

"They left before we could follow them to wherever they were staying. They might still be in Seattle, but I don't know where to look for them. We ran the Washington plates on the four cars they were driving. They were never issued here in the state. They were all fakes."

"It was worth a try," Drake said. "Keep a team with Liz and Alex until we know they're not in danger."

"Copy that."

What game was Braxton playing, he wondered. Showing his hand by sending a surveillance team just confirmed that Braxton knew he was responsible for the drugs on his jet and calling the police. It was a warning, but why? If Braxton wanted to get back at him, why telegraph it by parking a surveillance team at his doorstep? To show him he had the resources to do it?"

Two could play that game. Braxton would know that soon enough.

Drake opened his contact list on his phone and called Wayne Beardon.

"How's the weather on the East Coast?" he asked.

"Cold and gloomy. They're predicting snow later this week."

"Before Christmas?"

"It's global warming."

"Of course," Drake said. "Are your teams in place?"

"I have one team at Braxton's home in McLean to follow him, one team watching his office in Bethesda, and one team at the Braxton Group facility in rural Maryland."

"Where's Braxton?"

"If he's driving his Range Rover, he's at the facility in Maryland."

"What's that like?"

"Two large buildings located in the northeast corner of forty acres surrounded by forested land on three sides west of Bethesda," Beardon said. "A parking lot with fifty to sixty cars and a black Bell 525 Relentless helicopter on a pad next to the main building. Two colossal satellite dishes next to that building with antennas on its roof. There's a manned guard shack and a security fence with concertina wire around the place. It looks like his operations center."

"Let me know what Braxton's doing," Drake said. "Get pictures of the employees and send them to Kevin. We'll see how many of them he can identify."

"Roger that."

"Wayne, if you need anything, let me know."

"I didn't expect this facility to be isolated and this well protected. I could use a Black Hornet nano drone if you want more information about this location."

"On its way," Drake said. "Anything else?"

"Not that I can think of."

"All right, keep me informed."

"Will do."

It was four o'clock, and Mike Casey would want to know that Braxton had pulled his surveillance team.

Drake walked down the hall to Casey's office and found him reading a file he held in his hands.

Casey looked up when Drake knocked and opened the door. "Have you seen this?"

The front of the blue file Casey held was embossed with a gold seal Drake didn't recognize. "No, I haven't. What is it?"

"A potential client wants to know if one of their employees is spying for the Chinese."

"Who's the client?"

"The university?"

"Which one?"

"Washington."

"Why us?" Drake asked and sat down. "Why don't they ask the FBI to investigate it?"

"They did. They want us to take another look," Casey said. "Take the file and tell me what you think."

"Okay," Drake said and reached across to take the file. "Braxton pulled his surveillance team."

"When?"

"Just now. I asked Reynolds to take one of our quad-copters and listen to what they were saying. When he got there, they were gone."

"I don't understand why they were there in the first

place."

"I think Braxton wanted to send a message," Drake said. "I know you put the drugs on my jet, and there will be retribution."

"Like what?"

"I don't know. He tried to take me out in Las Vegas. He might try again. I'm going to keep driving the armored Yukon. I think you should drive one until I know more. Wayne and his team might learn something."

"Why me? I wasn't in Las Vegas."

"No, but he knows where I work. He knows we were a team in Afghanistan."

"How does that figure into any of this?"

"I don't know," Drake admitted. "But I don't think we should let our guard down until we do."

"Okay, if you think that's what I should do. You know the guy better than I do."

Drake returned to his office, thinking it wasn't true. He didn't know much about Marcus Braxton. He knew why he was booted out of the army and what he tried to do in Las Vegas. But that didn't give him the measure of the man.

Braxton worked as a paramilitary officer for the CIA, but he knew other good men who did. As a private intelligence contractor, the CIA would have vetted him carefully before giving him any work—at least, he hoped they had.

He also worked for Daniel Franklin, a high-profile player in Washington who was involved in Braxton's misadventure in Las Vegas. Franklin had a reputation in Washington to protect. He wouldn't risk tarnishing it by sending Braxton's surveillance team to Seattle. There was nothing he would gain by it.

Then what was Braxton doing? Was he off the reservation with a personal agenda Franklin didn't know about?

Chapter Fifty-One

MARCUS BRAXTON INITIALED the last field surveillance report and slipped it in the out tray for the weekly report to the CIA. He didn't agree with some of the names Franklin had on his list, but as long as the CIA kept paying for the surveillance teams he had in the field, who was he to disagree?

A yawn prompted him to check the time on his Suunto Core Stealth watch. He wore it to remind employees he was the company's alpha male. He wasn't a desk jockey CEO. He was a former Special Forces operator, a better man than anyone he recruited and hired to do the government's dirty work.

That's why he wasn't concerned that Daniel Franklin was worried about Adam Drake after what happened in Las Vegas. Franklin's plan failed because Franklin was afraid to do what needed to be done. Accidents happen. If he had been allowed to take care of the president's staffer the way he wanted, the matter would have been over and done with before Drake had a chance to interfere. And make him look like a fool by planting drugs on his jet.

Braxton turned the light off in his office, locked the door, and walked past his Surveillance Division's room on the third floor of the BG Operation Base's main building. Men on the night shift were watching video feeds on split-screen monitors from surveillance cameras trained on two hundred Americans the CIA was paying him to spy on.

He took the stairs down to the second floor, where the Intelligence Division was located, and continued to the first floor to talk with his man in Field Operations.

The briefing room was dark, and he checked to see that no one was in the equipment locker room and that the armory door was locked.

The staging area was at the end of a long hall, a vast open space with four roll-up service doors that spanned the width of the room's eastern exterior wall. When he opened the door, he heard country western music coming from the machinist's room to his right. Johnny Cash and Willie Nelson were singing "Highwayman."

The loud music covered the sound of his footsteps across the cement floor. When he reached the door to the machinist's room, he knocked to announce his presence.

Carl Marston was a jack-of-all-trades and a CIA assassin. There wasn't a way to kill someone Marston didn't know, but he'd never operated a loitering munitions drone before. Braxton asked for him because he trusted him to do the honorable thing if he was arrested or captured.

Marston was also a man you didn't sneak up on.

"Evening, Carl," Braxton said. "Have you figured out how to use that thing?"

Marston looked up and smiled. "Piece of cake. When your man shows up in his SUV, he's toast. All I do is get this hovering over his headquarters building, and it does the rest."

"How close do you have to be when you launch?"

"It has a range of nine miles, but I'll get within a couple hundred yards."

"When can you leave?"

"Right now, if you want."

"Great," Braxton said. "The Bell 525 is out on the pad. It will take you to our hangar at Reagan National. The Bombardier will take you to Denver. Then you're on to Seattle in a Kodiak Air Claw we use for aerial surveillance. When you complete the mission, the Air Claw will fly you back to Denver."

"What do you want me to do if this drone doesn't perform as advertised?"

"We'll think of something else."

"I can improvise."

"Just get back to Denver."

"Roger that," Marston said. "I'll call you from there."

"Make sure you do," Braxton said, then returned to his office to confirm the mission to his client.

"He'll leave tomorrow morning."

"There can't be any repercussions from this?"

"For you or me?"

"For either of us."

"There won't be. We routed the package from Israel to Mexico. A friend brought it across the border. The only trail that can be traced ends in Mexico."

"What about your man?"

"He doesn't exist. They erased any evidence he ever lived. Nothing links him to me. They route his pay through an account in Belize."

"What about a backup plan?"

"The same one we talked about," Braxton said. "We'll use one of my clients on the Dark Web. He's made enemies. Getting one of them to help us won't be hard."

"Call me when it's done. We can't let him get any closer."

Braxton started to say something and realized Franklin hung up on him. The man was a genius in many ways but an idiot regarding tactical planning. His plan for Las Vegas was too complicated. When there's an obstacle in your way, you remove it. The way he was going to with Adam Drake.

You didn't finesse the play to defeat an enemy. You used overwhelming force and annihilated him. Drop a one-pound warhead on his head that he couldn't see coming and forget about picking up the pieces. There wouldn't be any.

That was the lesson America forgot in Iraq and Afghanistan. You don't defeat a death-cult enemy by sending the ones you capture to a Caribbean resort. You give them what they want and send them on to enjoy their virgins in paradise.

If Franklin didn't want Drake getting too close, don't send the man a message and hope he'll back off. You take a man like Drake out so he can't interfere again.

Chapter Fifty-Two

DRAKE LEFT for work late Tuesday morning after driving to the pharmacy and back home with a cool-mist humidifier for baby Alex's first cough and cold. He had turned the sound down on the baby monitor next to his bed so Liz could sleep, but every time Alex had a coughing spell, he woke up to check the video screen or get up and check on him.

He'd shortened his run with Lancer and skipped breakfast that morning, but when he drove through the security gate at PSS headquarters, he was still thirty minutes later than usual when he parked the armored SUV he was driving.

Mike Casey was passing out a report when he entered the conference room and apologized for being late to the staff meeting.

"We skipped your item on the agenda," Mike Casey said. "Get some coffee. You look like you could use it. We just got started."

"Thanks, Mike."

Drake jogged down the hall to get his initial report about the University of Washinton's espionage concerns and returned with a mug of coffee from the break room to sit beside Casey.

Mark Holland, the head of the company's Sound Security and Information Systems intelligence contractor division, was reporting on the division's new hires. When he finished, he asked if anyone had any questions. Before anyone responded, an explosion rattled the windows in the room.

Drake ran to the conference room door with Casey behind him and sprinted down the hall to the stairs.

"That was outside," he shouted over his shoulder.

"See if anyone was hurt," Casey replied. "I'll call 911."

Drake hurried down the stairs to the underground car park and ran up the ramp to look outside. Dust was settling over a car-sized crater in the center of the headquarters' overflow parking area. Glass from shattered car windows and debris littered the asphalt around the cars.

Drake walked toward the crater and saw white fragments scattered around it. The crater caused by the explosion was two feet deep and four feet wide. At the bottom was what was left of the bomb: tiny pieces of metal, copper wiring, and what appeared to be a small piece of a printed circuit board.

Mike Casey walked beside him and squatted at the crater's edge. "Drone with an IED?"

"Possible," Drake said. "The cartels are using C4 with their drones. They'll use a mortar shell if they can get their hands on one. We'll know when we have these fragments tested."

"Who do you want to use?"

"The university is working on a new counter-drone technology for the Air Force. They might do it if we agree to find out if their employee's a Chinese spy."

"We have other clients who could do it."

"The university will be faster."

"Any idea who did this?" Casey asked.

Drake walked over and picked up a fragment that was white on one side and black on the other. "Entry-level drones have plastic frames. Commercial drones or drones made for the military use carbon fiber or aluminum. This looks like carbon fiber. With companies worldwide developing drones for the military, it will be hard to determine who made this."

"And all of them are for sale on the black market," Casey added. "So, who did this?"

Drake tossed the white fragment in the air and caught it in his hand. "My money's on Marcus Braxton."

Casey took his arm and led him away from the crowd of employees gathering around the crater. "Why Braxton? He sent a surveillance team to let you know he blamed you for the drugs planted on his jet. That doesn't mean he'd go this far."

"It's Braxton."

"Why?"

"Kevin found a request on Braxton's IT system for a quote from the Israeli company that sells the Hero 30 loitering munitions drone," Drake said. "I couldn't think of why he wanted one. I do now."

"He can't think he could get away with using a loitering munitions drone. Why would he try?"

"I don't know, Mike. A drone like that can be launched a mile away or up close by an operator with a remote control. If it was up close, we can find out where and maybe who did it."

"How?"

"By using a dog to search the scent of the explosive in this crater for a location near here," Drake said.

"A dog like Lancer?" Casey asked.

"Yes."

"And then what?"

"We'll know that when we know who did this."

The sound of sirens approaching prompted Casey to order everyone back inside.

"You don't need me here," Drake said and picked up a larger bomb fragment from the ground. "I'm going home to get Lancer. I'll be back in twenty."

"Tell Liz not to call Megan," Casey said. "I want to be the one to tell her that I'm okay. You know how she worries."

Drake did. After Mike was poisoned by mistake in San Francisco by a female assassin sent to kill him, it took months of psychotherapy for her to get over seeing him paralyzed in the hospital. Since then, she told Liz she worried every time he left home to drive to work. The compromise they worked out resulted in Mike stepping away from being involved in anything that promised to be dangerous.

Mike hadn't always been able to keep himself out of harm's way. Learning that a bomb exploded outside her husband's office building wasn't going to ease her fears for his safety.

Liz handled it better than Megan, with her experience and training as an FBI special agent. But hearing about a bomb exploding at headquarters would only reinforce her argument that he had to do the same thing Mike had promised to do for the sake of their family.

He'd promised he would, but if he learned the bomb was meant for him, he would have to make Liz understand. The way to keep their family safe was to eliminate the threat so they wouldn't become collateral damage if someone tried again.

Chapter Fifty-Three

CARL MARSTON WALKED to the terminal building at Paine Field north of Seattle after returning his Toyota Rav 4 rental to Avis Rent a Car. He had time to have lunch and a Bloody Mary before contacting his handler to see if he was returning to Denver.

The drone had failed to perform as advertised, and the only explanation was that a counter-drone system had been installed at PSS headquarters or in the SUV Drake drove to work. The drone was hovering over the compound before Drake arrived and programmed to target his black GMC Yukon. When it disappeared down the ramp, the drone had failed to respond to its remote control commands and remained hovering overhead for another five minutes before it crashed and exploded on impact.

When he entered the bar near the departure area, he smiled at the cute bartender and ordered a Bloody Mary before looking for an empty table. There wasn't one, but a last call for a departing Alaskan Airline flight emptied half the room, leaving plenty of places to sit.

"Would you like to see a menu?" the waitress said without making eye contact when she brought his Bloody Mary.

"Sure," Marston said. "What's good?"

"It's all good for an airport bar," she said and went to get him a menu.

He knew what that meant. The hamburger wouldn't kill you, and the fries would be limp and greasy.

The Bloody Mary wasn't bad when he tried it, and he decided to take a chance and ordered a hamburger.

Marston watched people come and go in the departure area while he waited for his hamburger and considered what he would say if they wanted him to stay in Seattle and finish the job. Using the drone had been a risk he'd been willing to take when they suggested it, but it wouldn't have been his first choice.

Learning that the target's SUV was drone-protected means it was likely armored as well. A kill would require getting close to a target like Drake unless they provided him with a sniper rifle. If they did, it would be ironic that a sniper's bullet took out a former member of an Omega hunter/killer sniper team in Afghanistan. Getting close would be difficult unless Drake was lured out of his protected cocoon.

Marston was wrong about the hamburger; it was as greasy as the French fries and cold. He finished his Bloody Mary, put two twenty-dollar bills on top of the thirty-nine-dollar bill, and left the bar.

The departure lounge wasn't crowded across the way, and he stopped there to contact his handler. From the far end of a row of empty chairs, he sent him a cryptic message on his iPhone and waited for a reply.

No joy.

Mission compromised?

No.

B will want u to try again.

Target will be wary.

Can it be done?

Possible but a long shot.

Meaning?

Meaning it would be a long shot with the right gear.

Find a place to stay. Pilots on standby until I hear back.

Roger that.

Marston smiled and slipped his phone in the pocket of his jacket. Contingency planning means having a backup plan. He had a reservation for a room with a view at the Silver Cloud Hotel on Puget Sound that he made before he left Maryland. And the number of an escort service he'd saved on his phone.

If Braxton had listened to him, he wouldn't have wasted his money using a drone. A round from his favorite 6.5 Creedmoor Tikka T3x TACT A1 rifle would have done the job. But Braxton wanted to make it look like one of Drake's enemies used a narco drone to do the job. It wouldn't take Drake long to discover the drone was a Hero 30 loitering munitions weapon system made in Israel.

Marston left the departure area and walked toward the baggage claim area to look for a cab waiting outside. Whatever Braxton wanted him to do, it wouldn't interfere with his night. He would enjoy a few tequilas, have a good steak, and invite a beautiful young lady to spend the night in his room.

Something had changed, and he needed to know what it was. Braxton wanted him to return to Denver, but his CIA handler wanted him to stay in the area. Who was calling the shots?

Braxton was a contractor the Pentagon used for domestic surveillance, but he'd never been given a kill order for a U.S. citizen living in the country. The military's secret undercover army, the sixty-thousand people in the program they called its signature reduction force Braxton Group was a part of, only carried out domestic assignments. He'd never heard of a kill order given in one of its domestic assignments.

As a freelance operator, he was careful which clients he worked for. When he was contacted, he was told Marcus Braxton was the client. His agent, the man he called his handler, had never lied to him, but he'd been around long enough to know there was a first time for everything. Was this it?

If Braxton wasn't calling the shots, then who was? Someone Braxton worked for? Someone Braxton worked for who worked for someone else?

Until he knew the answer, he was satisfied to walk away with the money already deposited in his account and live to work another day. Life was short enough in his business, and he didn't need the money.

But he knew he wouldn't walk away. The challenge of killing a man like Drake would look so good on his resume.

Chapter Fifty-Four

WHEN DRAKE RETURNED HOME, he parked the armored Yukon in front of the condo's garage door and called Liz before he opened the door so she wouldn't be alarmed.

"Liz, it's me."

"Did you forget something?"

"No, I'll explain in a minute," he said, opening the garage door.

A minute later, he was standing in the kitchen on the second floor where she was feeding his son.

Drake leaned down and kissed her on the cheek. "I need to take Lancer with me to do some tracking. There was an incident at work. A drone crashed in the parking area, and I want to see if I can find out where it came from."

Liz looked up and said, "What? When?"

"Just after I got there. Nothing for you to worry about. No one was hurt."

Liz gave Alex another spoonful of sweet potato baby food and stood up to face him. "What exactly happened?"

"The drone left a small crater when it crashed," Drake said. "It was carrying an explosive of some kind."

She crossed her arms over her chest and asked, "Is this about Las Vegas?"

"Liz, I don't know."

"But it's possible?"

"It's possible."

"What are you going to do?"

"Right now, I'm taking Lancer with me to see if we can find where the drone was launched and if there's anything left there to tell us who launched it," Drake said. "We'll send a fragment from the drone to the university to see if they can identify its manufacturer."

"Was this a narco drone from one of the cartels?"

Drake stepped forward and rested his hands on her shoulders. "Liz, I don't know."

"Are we safe here?"

"If this was about Las Vegas, I was the target. We'll keep the protection unit here until we know more."

"They can't protect us from a bomb."

"If you want to move somewhere, I'll talk with Pat and see what he recommends."

"I don't want to live like this, Adam."

"I know," Drake said. "Mike would like to tell Megan about this before she hears it from someone else."

"Of course. Take Lancer and call me if you find anything."

Drake pulled Liz close and hugged her. "I'm sorry."

"I know."

Drake signaled for Lancer to follow and walked down the stairs and through the garage to the armored SUV.

When Lancer was sitting in the passenger seat, he

stroked his head and said, "She's worried, Lancer. I'm counting on you to make her feel safe, okay?"

Drake returned to PSS headquarters and parked inside the compound by the security gate. "Time to go to work, boy," he said when he opened the SUV's passenger side door. After picking up his running shoes from the floor and putting them on, he walked over to the bomb crater with Lancer at his side.

"Take a good smell," he said, holding the drone fragment down for Lancer before giving him the command in German to track the scent. "Zook."

Lancer ran past the security gate and turned east, with Drake following him on the sidewalk. Two blocks later, they reached the Cross Kirkland Corridor. Lancer veered onto the familiar trail and continued running south for ten minutes.

When Lancer reached the trail that led to NE 53rd Street and the entrance to Carillon Woods, a neighborhood park, he sat on his haunches and waited for Drake.

"Is this it?" Drake asked when he arrived. "Good boy. Zook."

Lancer took off down the trail a short way and turned into the entrance to Carillon Woods.

Drake followed and saw Lancer fifty yards ahead of him on the paved trail through the park. When he reached a small playground with a green slide and climbing structure covered in leaves, Lancer had stopped ahead in front of a bench at the side of the trail, with a large fir tree behind it.

"What did you find?" Drake asked when he got there.

Lancer moved around the bench and sniffed at something on the ground next to the tree covered with leaves.

Drake joined him and brushed off the leaves covering

the launch tube of a manpack Hero 30 loitering munitions drone.

"Good boy, Lancer," he said, petting his dog. "Steak for you tonight."

He stepped back and searched the area for anything the drone operator had left behind. He only saw footprints in the soft earth leading from the trail to the launch tube. When he placed his running shoe beside the footprint, he judged the operator's shoe size to be a size nine and a half or ten.

Drake took his phone out and called Mike Casey.

"Mike, is the fire department there?"

"And Kirkland's finest," Casey said. "Did Lancer find where they launched the drone?"

"Yeah, not far from headquarters. We're at Carillon Woods, a hundred yards down the trail east of the park entrance. Who's investigating this, the fire department or the police?"

"The police for now, but they called your friends, the FBI."

"Terrific! Send someone from the fire department over here to take custody of this thing," Drake said. "When the FBI get there, tell them I'll stop by and tell them what I know later."

"Where will you be?"

"I'm going to take Lancer home and stop by the university. Do we know anyone there who would run tests on my fragment from the drone?"

"They might be doing research for the DOD on counter-drone technology somewhere, but I don't know in which department. You might try the Department of Aeronautics and Astronautics. They might should know something about UAVs."

"Do you know anyone in the department?"

"I don't, I'm sorry. I do know someone at Boeing who might be able to run a test. Ken Burch. I'll get his number for you."

"Thanks," Drake said. "I told Liz what happened. Have you told Megan?"

"I did. She wasn't pleased to hear what about it."

"Liz wasn't either. Happy times at home tonight."

"Right," Casey said. "Here's Ken's number. I'll let him know you're coming."

"I'll be back before you head home tonight. Maybe we'll know more by then."

"I hope we do. The sooner we know who did this, the sooner we'll know how to respond."

"I already know, Mike. We'll talk about it when I get there."

Chapter Fifty-Five

DRAKE LEFT the Carillon Woods Park with Lancer and returned to PSS headquarters when the Kirkland Fire Department bomb squad arrived to take custody of the drone's launch tube. He referred them to Mike Casey and ignored their questions. Anything he said would be included in their report and passed on to the Seattle FBI office, meaning he'd spend time sitting for a lengthy interview by FBI agents he'd crossed swords with in the past.

He parked his SUV on the street and walked with Lancer past the guard station, nodding to the guard on duty. Using the public entrance to PSS headquarters, he avoided the fire, police, and FBI personnel standing around and inspecting the crater in the employee parking area.

Mike Casey was standing at his assistant's desk when Drake found him.

"Where's Lancer?"

"In my office."

"The *Seattle Times* wants a statement," Casey said. "What do I tell them?"

"Just say it's under investigation," Drake replied. "You don't know what exploded or why it landed here."

"What did you tell them at the park?"

"Nothing." Drake smiled. "I referred them to you."

"Thanks," Casey said and hooked a thumb over his shoulder toward his office.

Drake followed him and closed the door. "I don't need to talk to your friend at Boeing. The drone was a Hero 30, like the one Braxton wanted to buy."

"That doesn't mean it was Braxton."

"Not Braxton, he's not that stupid. Someone he sent."

"Did you find anything in the park?"

Drake shook his head and sat down across the desk from Casey. "A footprint. I don't think they'll find anything on the launch tube. It wouldn't have been left in the park if there was."

"What do you want to do?"

"Find Braxton and put an end to this."

"We can't prove it was Braxton."

"I don't need proof, Mike. He sent a team of watchers to follow me, and now this."

"You don't need proof, but the FBI will."

"I can't wait for them to build a case," Drake said. "He might try again when I'm with Liz and Alex. I have to find him before then."

"What about Liz? She won't want you to go after him."

"I know. I don't have a choice. She'll have to understand."

"Did you promise her you'd do what I did and let someone else do the heavy lifting?" Casey asked.

"Yeah, I did."

"Then let them. Put a team together to go with you to find Braxton."

"I already have a team watching him."

"Wayne's men are surveillance specialists. Take men from your Special Projects unit or Mark Holland's intel division."

"We already have ten men there from Wayne Beardon's unit."

"Take as many more as you need," Casey said. "It's not good for business when a security firm can't keep people from dropping bombs on them."

Drake stopped at the break room for a soup bowl and filled it with water for Lancer before walking down the hall to his office.

"I have a few calls to make before I take you home, Lancer," he said when he set the bowl down. "I won't be long."

He opened the Thinkpad X1 laptop on his desk and scrolled down the list of operators in his Special Projects file. He selected four of them to go with him to Maryland.

Dan Norris, a former FBI HRT commander, was Drake's Special Projects team leader. The FBI Hostage Rescue Team is the elite hostage rescue team in the world and trains to the same standards as the military's top special operations units. HRT is also the only full-time counter-terrorism force in the federal law enforcement system.

Marco Morales was a former U.S. Army long-range reconnaissance patrol soldier. As a LRRP, he was a member of a small, well-armed recon team trained to patrol deep behind enemy lines. When the army decided to replace dismounted reconnaissance with other technologies, like unmanned aerial vehicles (UAVs) and satellites, Morales left the army and looked for another way to use his training and skills. Drake hired him and Marco had been with him on all of Drake's Special Activities missions at PSS.

Carol Sanchez was a former undercover cop with the Denver Police Department. She was thirty-one years old, stood five feet five inches tall, and weighed one hundred and twenty pounds. She punched well above her weight class and was a Krav Maga black belt. Sanchez could get into places the other men he was taking couldn't.

Drake closed the file on his laptop and sat back in his chair to think. Braxton had muscle with him in Las Vegas and demonstrated that he would use violence and didn't play by the rules. That was fine. He knew how to deal with men like Braxton, and so did the people he was taking with him.

The goal was to prove that the drone was Braxton's and discover why he escalated their disagreement. Braxton was in a hurry for some reason. He needed to know why.

He wouldn't find that out by using force and storming Braxton's castle, although he wouldn't rule that out. He would have to find a way to sneak in and find the answer.

Kevin McRoberts would have to go with him. Kevin had gained access to the Braxton Group's IT system. They would have to find a way to dig deeper and gain access to Braxton's PC or laptop. Maybe his smartphone. Kevin could do some of that at a distance, but some of it would have to be closer to the target in Maryland.

Kevin McRoberts, the head of the PSS IT division and their young genius hacker, would be the fourth member of his team.

Chapter Fifty-Six

DRAKE FINALIZED the arrangements for the team's equipment and flight plans and left PSS headquarters by noon to return home and tell Liz what he was planning to do.

Lancer was in the passenger seat of the armored SUV with his eyes fixed on the traffic ahead when Drake gave him his assignment. "It's your job to keep Liz from worrying about me when I leave tomorrow, Lancer. I don't care how you do it. You keep me from worrying about her. Now, do the same thing for her. Okay?"

He shook his head and realized he was telling his dog to do something he knew he wouldn't be able to do himself. Liz would worry when he told her what he was doing, and there was nothing he could do to change that.

Drake let Lancer go ahead, walking up the stairs from the garage. When he reached the second floor, Liz was sitting in the breakfast nook on her phone. He knew she was talking with Megan Casey when she turned to face him.

"Adam's here," she said. "I'll call you back."

"Megan?"

Liz nodded. "What did you find?"

"Lancer found a drone launch tube in the park at Carillon Woods."

"Then it wasn't a kid with a fireworks rocket strapped to the bottom of his drone."

"No."

"Could you tell what kind of drone it was?"

"The launch tube looks like one for a Hero 30 loitering munitions drone," Drake said. "Kevin found a picture when he saw that Marcus Braxton was trying to buy one."

Liz looked at him emotionlessly for a long minute. "Why?"

Drake sat across from her and reached for her hands. "I don't know."

"Will he try again?"

"He's shown his hand. I think he has to."

"Can you stop him?"

Drake nodded. "I have to."

"How?"

"Wayne Beardon has a team watching Braxton and Franklin," he said. "I'm taking a team with me tomorrow to find him. We'll make sure he doesn't try again."

Liz dropped her head and stared at their hands. "Will you keep your promise?"

"I'll try, Liz. That's the best I can do."

———

CARL MARSTON OPENED the door and stepped onto the small balcony of his king bedroom at the Silver Cloud Hotel

– Mukilteo Waterfront to watch a ferry pass by on Possession Sound. He was still waiting for his handler to call.

He wasn't worried. With his plans to pass the time until he called, he didn't care how long it took them to make up their minds. As long they did it within twenty-four hours. When an assignment went off the rails, people got nervous and start thinking about ways to minimize blowback. He knew from experience that often meant eliminating anything that could be traced back to them. Or anyone.

No one knew where he was, but they could quickly find him with their resources.

Relax, he told himself, stepping back into the room and refilling his glass with Jack Daniels and more ice. There was no one better than he was, and anyone they sent after him knew it.

Marston turned on the television and looked for a news channel until he stopped on King 5 News. A young black reporter was standing on the street with her cameraman focusing over her shoulder at the scene beyond the security gate at Puget Sound Security headquarters.

"The Kirkland Fire Department's Hazardous Devices Unit is still here investigating a crater inside this compound caused by an explosion this morning," she reported. "The Fire Department won't say what caused the crater, but it's believed to be something that fell from the sky."

Marston threw back his head to laugh and swallowed the ice cube he was sucking on. "That's rich," he laughed. "Something that fell from the sky! If these clowns are the best they have out here, I don't have anything to worry about."

He continued watching to see if the reporter revealed anything else worthy of the 'Breaking News' headline that ran at the bottom of the screen when his phone beeped to signal that he'd received a text message.

Return home ASAP. Fly commercial

Why?

Something else planned.

For D?

Yes. See me before you see BG.

Tomorrow okay?

Be here by noon ET.

So much for the night he planned. Marston opened his laptop and searched for an American Airlines flight to get him to D.C. in time. There was only one, and it left at 12:35 A.M.

Whatever. He called the escort service and asked for an earlier visit, then called room service and ordered a steak with French fries and another bottle of Jack Daniels.

It wasn't the first time the target had changed on a mission. Braxton was adamant that Drake had to be stopped. Then why was he being recalled to Washington when Drake was in Seattle? He never knew the big picture for an assignment but always heard enough to figure it out.

On this one, his handler let Braxton give him the mission details and backed away, saying Braxton's the client and it's his show. That wasn't the way the CIA worked. It was always the CIA's show if they loaned him to someone for a mission.

Until now, he hadn't figured out why Drake was a target the CIA cared about. If they wanted him back in D.C., maybe they didn't care. Or if they did, maybe killing him wasn't the plan any longer.

He would be disappointed if that was true. Drake was a kill he wanted.

Chapter Fifty-Seven

STEVE CARSON HAD the Gulfstream G280 ready to take off from Boeing Field when Drake pulled into the PSS hangar with his team at 7:00 A.M. PT, Friday morning. Ten minutes later, with their gear loaded and seat belts fastened, they were in line to take off.

"Where is Braxton now?" Dan Norris asked from his seat across the aisle from Drake.

"Wayne said he stayed late last night at the Braxton Group facility and drove home to his residence in McLean at midnight," Drake said. "He's still at home."

"Does he usually work that late?"

"No, surveillance says he leaves his office in Bethesda by six every night like clockwork. Last night was an anomaly."

"Where do you want to take him?" Norris asked.

"I'd like to know more about this BG facility, if he goes there again," Drake said and shrugged. "But we'll follow him, see where he takes us, and then decide."

"But ultimately, the goal is a face-to-face meeting with Braxton."

"That is the goal," Drake affirmed.

When Carson announced they had reached cruising altitude, Drake got up and walked to the galley for coffee. Carol Sanchez followed him.

"Thanks for inviting me," she said.

He raised a cup and asked, "Coffee?"

"Yes, please."

She watched him fill her cup and waited until he handed it to her before asking, "Why did you?"

"Why did I what?" Drake asked.

"Bring me?"

Drake smiled and leaned against the galley counter. "Carol, you're as capable as any of the guys in the Special Projects unit, and you have undercover experience. I thought we might need you to get close to Marcus Braxton."

"Where?"

"He has an office in Bethesda, near the Intelligence Community Campus. There are people there who will know me, and Dan was at Quantico when he was HRT. They probably won't recognize you, but even if they do, they won't know why you're there. You might have to find Braxton for us."

"What will I do if I find him?"

"Tell him I want to meet him. That's all."

"Couldn't you tell him you wanted a meeting without going to Washington?"

"Braxton was the one who dropped the bomb on us at headquarters, Carol. He might think we want to do more than talk with him."

"Do we?"

"I guess that depends on what he says," Drake said.

Sanchez nodded and said, "Roger that, boss."

He watched her return to her seat across from Marco Morales and rested her hand on his shoulder before she sat down. The two had worked together when she was new to PSS and she'd embarrassed Morales on the mat before she told him she had a black belt in Krav Maga. Since then, they'd become good friends.

Sanchez leaned across the aisle and said something to Morales that made him look at Drake and walk down the aisle to the galley.

"Hey, jefe, Carol says all you want to do is talk with Braxton."

"That's right," Drake said. "Don't worry, it doesn't mean I'm raising a white flag. He needs to hear this is a battle he's not winning."

"If he doesn't listen?"

"Then we make him."

"Amen to that, Boss," Morales said and left.

Drake saw Kevin McRoberts get up with his laptop and head his way.

"Braxton sent twenty thousand dollars to an account in Belize two days ago," Kevin said. "Do you want me to find out who owns that account?"

"Can you?"

"I can try. Braxton's office account says the 20k is for services rendered by CM. If I keep looking, I might find out who CM is."

"Keep looking," Drake said. "Is there anything new from Wayne?"

"Not since we took off."

"Let me know when there is."

Drake knocked on the door of the flight deck and stuck his head in. "You guys need anything?"

Steve Carson said no, but his new co-pilot, Joe Ryan,

said a cup of coffee with cream would be nice. Ryan was a former A-10 Thunderbolt II "Warthog" pilot Mike Casey met in Afghanistan and hired him when he left the Air Force.

Drake stepped back into the galley, filled a cup, and returned with it for Ryan.

"Flying us around is safer than flying rescue missions in the Warthog but not as exciting," Drake said. "How are you adjusting to civilian life?"

"Life is good, Major," Ryan said. "I'll take safer any day, and so will my wife."

"Glad to have you with us, Joe."

"Thanks, glad to be here."

Drake returned to his seat and looked out at the endless gray carpet cloud cover below the plane. He had a team of professionals on board with a combined skill set capable of accomplishing anything he asked them to do. They were asking, each in their own way, what that would be when they landed. *What's the plan?*

He didn't have one except to find Braxton. Ask him why he had people following him. Why target him with a loitering drone that had an explosive warhead? Why try to kill him for a third time?

That wasn't the real reason, he admitted, shaking his head. He wanted to smash his teeth in, bloody his lip, and leave him moaning on the ground. He wanted revenge. But that wasn't a plan. That was the way people got killed, following a leader without a plan.

Why was he flying across the country then? Just to find Braxton?

He stared out the plane's window and answered the question. To uncover the reason Braxton was in Las Vegas in the first place and who the people were who wanted him

244

dead. Any report he gave the president wouldn't be complete if it didn't answer that question.

So, what was his plan? It was simple, really: find Braxton and get him to talk, discover who's behind the curtain pulling strings, and then expose whatever it is they're doing,

Who needed a more detailed plan when it was that simple?

Chapter Fifty-Eight

THEY LEFT the Signature FBO at Reagan National Airport at four o'clock that afternoon in two silver Ford Explorers and a black Badlands Ford Bronco.

Drake drove the Bronco with Dan Norris riding shotgun across the Potomac River on the Arland D. Williams Memorial Bridge. Then northwest up the Potomac River Freeway to the Embassy Suites by Hilton Hotel in Bethesda, Maryland.

Wayne Beardon and the surveillance team had rooms at the Bethesda Marriott not far away.

"Tell the others to meet in the bar when everyone gets checked in," Drake told Norris when he stopped to unload their luggage in front of the Embassy Suites. "I'll call Wayne and see if he's available to brief us."

The two Ford Explorers pulled up behind the Bronco, and Norris walked back to greet them.

Drake got out and leaned against the driver's side door. "We're at the Embassy Suites. Can you come to brief us?"

"I'll be there in ten."

Drake used the Bronco's key fob to open the tailgate, pulled out his slate gray REI Centurion duffel bag, and set it on the ground. Norris had a matching duffel bag, and so did Morales, Sanchez, and McRoberts, who were unloading theirs from the two Ford Explorers.

Each bag, except Kevin McRoberts', who didn't have a security personnel license to carry, contained a SIG P320 M18x pistol, a Benchmade Claymore tactical knife, a Motorola APX Next two-radio, and tactical clothing.

Drake handled registration and check-in for the team, found his room, tossed his bag on the bed, and was the first one down in the empty bar ten minutes later when Wayne Beardon arrived.

"Everyone here?" Beardon asked.

"Our pilots will join us later," Drake said. "The others will be here soon. What have you learned since your last call?"

The bartender looked annoyed when Drake waved to get his attention.

"Get you guys anything?" he said when he approached their table.

"Beam on the rocks," Drake said. "Wayne?"

"Are we finished for the night?"

"Yes, unless you have something that needs attention."

"Vodka with a lemon twist," Beardon ordered.

When the bartender left, Beardon said, "Braxton's still at his office. Nothing's happening at the Braxton Group facility. Braxton's routine hasn't changed, so I can't think of anything that needs to be done tonight."

"Does Braxton travel alone?"

"He has so far. Drives his Range Rover to his office. Last night, he went to his facility west of here with someone before driving to his home in McLean, but that's the only thing he's done after leaving his office."

"What about his office?"

"He has the nineteenth floor of the Avocet Tower in Bethesda," Beardon said.

"Security?"

"I found a business news article that reported Braxton was installing Google's new face recognition system. I don't know what else his office has."

"What about his facility west of Seneca?"

"Forty acres with a ten-foot-tall security fence with concertina all around, CCTV cameras, a manned guard booth at the gate and floodlights. Why?"

"Kevin found that he was trying to buy a Hero 30 loitering munitions drone, the same kind that cratered the parking area at headquarters yesterday," Drake said. "If I want to prove it was Braxton's drone, we might have to get in there."

"That won't be easy."

"Did you bring a few of the Hyperfire IR cameras you use for fixed surveillance?"

"Yes."

"Set them up around his facility. Take Morales with you. Maybe we'll find a way to exploit in his security system."

Norris and the rest of the team entered the hotel bar together and stood around the table.

"Are we going out tonight?" Morales asked.

"Why, do you have plans?" Drake asked.

Morales smiled. "Only if you plan on us eating here tonight. Have you seen the menu?"

"No."

"Dan says there's a great seafood restaurant not far from here if you're open to suggestions."

"Anyone not like seafood?" Drake asked.

They all shook their heads no.

"Have a drink if you want, then we'll let Dan take us to dinner."

"You mean to drive you there?" Norris asked.

"Dinner was your idea," Drake grinned.

Chapter Fifty-Nine

IT WAS RAINING Saturday morning when Drake took the elevator to the first floor to have a made-to-order breakfast at Embassy Suites.

Drake was the last in line behind Norris and followed him to a table with a plate containing an omelet, bacon, fresh fruit, and coffee. Norris was already pouring syrup over an egg on top of his waffle.

"What are we doing today?" Norris asked with a fork halfway to his mouth.

"Wayne called and said Braxton changed his routine and drove to his office this morning. I'm sending Sanchez to ask him to meet with me?"

"Do you think he will?"

"It will save us time if he agrees, but I doubt he will," Drake said. "I want him to know I'm here."

"What about the rest of us?"

"Kevin's staying here. He has access to Franklin's PC. He's trying to find out who his friends are. Wayne is taking

Morales out to Braxton's facility to recon the place and set up his surveillance IR cameras."

"How did Kevin get access to his PC?"

"Franklin sent Braxton texts from his PC," Drake said. "Kevin got into Braxton's IT system."

"What do you want me to do today?"

"I called Kate Perkins this morning," Drake said. "I'm meeting her at ten for coffee. Would you like to join us?"

Kate Perkins was the Assistant Director of the FBI and the woman Norris left behind when he gave up his FBI HRT command and moved away. Drake knew Norris regretted his mistake and kept in touch with Perkins.

"Sure, if you have nothing else for me to do."

Drake finished eating and went to Carol Sanchez's table, where she sat with Marco Morales.

"Carol, Wayne Beardon will call you if they see Braxton leave his office," Drake said. "If he does, stay here until I get back."

"If he leaves his office, is it all right if she goes with me to Braxton's facility?" Morales asked.

Drake nodded and tried not to look surprised as he left to check on Kevin McRoberts.

Kevin's door was open, and he knocked to get his attention. "Kevin, did you have breakfast?"

Without turning around, Kevin said, "Yes, I wanted to get started early."

"How are you doing?"

"Franklin knows a lot of people, Mr. Drake. I think he's blackmailing some of them."

Drake looked over Kevin's shoulder to see what he was looking at. "Based on that email? It looks innocent."

"None of them are explicit. The attachment that

accompanied an earlier one was just a copy of a hotel receipt."

"Who did he send that one to?"

"A U.S. Court of Appeals judge for the District of Columbia."

"Did Franklin want something?"

"No, that's what is puzzling. It looks like he's just letting the judge know he knows something."

"Something that Franklin can use later?"

"That's what I think," Kevin said.

"Are there others?"

"I found two more, a Department of Justice prosecutor and a reporter for the *Washington Post*."

"I wonder what Franklin thinks he's doing?" Drake asked.

"I think he's copying what J. Edgar Hoover did, Mr. Drake, finding things he can use to influence people."

"Of course, by analyzing personal data he collects."

"That's what it looks like."

"Good work, Kevin. Get me a list of everyone you think he has something on when you finish going through his emails."

"Do you want me to find out where he's keeping this stuff?"

Drake put his hand on Kevin's shoulder. "Yes, if you can, but be careful. We don't know who Franklin's friends are."

Norris was waiting for him in the lobby. He was wearing a blue blazer, a blue chambray shirt, and khaki pants.

"Is there a new dress code at FBI headquarters?" Drake asked.

"No, I might meet someone I know from HRT," Norris said.

"And that's why you changed clothes?"

"I didn't think jeans and a sweater represent the new me."

Drake laughed and tossed the key fob for the Bronco to him. "You are so full of it, Dan."

"What?"

"Just drive us to the Hoover building. I'm sure Kate will appreciate the new you."

If Kate Perkins noticed anything new about Norris when they found her in the cafeteria, she didn't show it.

"Drake," she said, holding her hand out to him and nodding to Norris. "To what do I owe the pleasure of seeing you two again?"

"We're in Washington and thought we'd say hello," Drake said. "Can I buy you coffee?"

"Yes, Sumatra, no cream or sugar."

"Dan, would you get Kate's coffee?" Drake asked.

"Sure," Norris said.

Perkins walked to an empty table and sat down. Drake watched her eyes following Norris.

"How are you, Kate?"

When she pursed her lips and looked away, he had the answer.

"I heard you're a father. Congratulations."

"Thanks," Drake replied. "Liz said to say hello if I saw you."

Norris returned with Kate's coffee and sat across the table from her.

"Thank you," she told him and looked at Drake. "Why are you here, Adam?"

"What can you tell me about Daniel Franklin?"

Perkins raised the cup to her lips with both hands and turned her head slightly to see if anyone was close enough to hear their conversation. "Franklin is a personal data broker with friends in this city."

"Does the FBI check to see who the brokers sell personal data to?"

"We don't. Should we?"

"If they sell it on the Dark Web, you should."

"Does he?"

"Have you heard rumors that he analyzes personal data to find information, like Hoover did, to influence people in the city?"

"What kind of people?"

"Powerful people."

"Do you have evidence that he does?"

"Kate, I'm only asking if you've heard rumors because I have."

"If you find there's something to these rumors, would you tell me?"

"Would it be helpful if I did?"

"It might."

"Then I will," Drake said. "We'll be in town for a day or two. Would you like to join us for dinner before we leave?"

Her eyes flicked toward Norris and back before she said, "Maybe another time."

Chapter Sixty

NORRIS DROVE them back to the hotel without saying anything until Drake asked, "What's going on with Kate?"

"I wish I knew. Something's going on. She won't tell me what it is."

"Is it about her work?"

"I think it's personal. She's sad about something."

"If you need time to go see her, take it."

"Thanks," Norris said.

Drake left it alone and texted Carol Sanchez, asking if she'd seen Marcus Braxton.

He left his office.

Where is he now?

Driving to D.C., Wayne has a team on him.

Thanks.

Drake texted Wayne Beardon.

Where is Braxton?

He's headed south toward the Wharf District.

What's there?

Hotels, restaurants, shops, water taxi.

If he meets someone, can you record him?

The team has a shotgun microphone.

Do it. Let me know.

"Braxton's on the move," Drake said. "He's headed toward the Wharf District."

"It's a good place to meet someone. Want me to turn around?"

"Yes, I might get a chance to talk to him."

Norris took the next exit off I-395 and drove south toward the Wharf District, when Beardon texted again.

He turned into the Portal 2 Parking lot near the Wharf.

Follow on foot?

They're on it.

"Braxton pulled into a parking lot near the Wharf," Drake said.

"Which one?"

"Portal 2, Wayne says. His team is following him on foot."

"We'll be right behind them. We're five minutes away."

By the time they found a parking spot on the fifth level of the parking structure and walked down to the street, Braxton and the surveillance following him were fifteen minutes ahead when Drake stopped to read another text message from Beardon.

Braxton stopped at the Transit Pier. He's buying a ticket for the Potomac Water Taxi.

Where is he going?

Georgetown, the scenic tour.

"Braxton's taking a water taxi to Georgetown," Drake said.

"I've taken that tour. We can be at the Georgetown terminal when it docks." Drake texted Beardon:

Did your team make it onto the water taxi?

Yes.

Did he meet someone?

Yes, I'm sending you the video. The sound quality is poor, but they'll get closer with the shotgun mic.

"Let's go to Georgetown," Drake said, turning around. "Braxton met someone on the water taxi."

Norris dodged around people on the crowded sidewalk

to catch up with Drake. When he did, he asked, "Who's he meeting?"

"Wayne's sending me the video."

When they reached The Portals parking structure, Drake didn't wait for an elevator and took the stairs two at a time to the fifth floor.

While Norris was backing out of their parking slot, Beardon sent Drake the video of Braxton meeting an older man on the water taxi. Drake held his phone closer to watch the video.

The man sitting next to Braxton was wearing a Washington Commanders hat with a digital camo design, aviator-style sunglasses, and a black windbreaker with the collar turned up. Braxton was wearing a gray sports coat over a black turtleneck sweater and looked straight ahead while the man was talking.

Norris glanced over and asked, "Can you tell who that is?"

"Not from this."

"We'll get a better look at the Georgetown terminal."

Drake thought about that. "We will if they get off the water taxi. They could take it back to the Wharf terminal. Or one could stay on, and the other one get off."

"What's more important, learning who the other guy is or following Braxton to meet with him?" Norris asked.

Drake held the phone up again and studied the video. It was trained on the two men from the port side of the water taxi, fifteen or twenty feet away, at a 120-degree angle. The seats ahead of the two men were occupied, and the rows of seats extended to the port side. This was probably the closest shot they would get of the two men.

"Let's keep the surveillance team on Braxton," Drake

said. "When we get to Georgetown, we'll follow the other man. I want to know who he is."

When they got to Georgetown, Norris found a place to park the Bronco a block away from the Potomac Water Taxi terminal. There was plenty of time to buy two tickets for the return trip to the Wharf Terminal if their man stayed on for the return trip, and they were parked close enough to follow him if he took a taxi somewhere.

They watched the yellow water taxi come up the Potomac River from the upper deck of the terminal and reduce its speed to come alongside the dock.

Drake texted Wayne Beardon.

Wayne, did you record their conversation?

Yes, every word. Sound quality is good.

We're you able to identify the other man?

No, but we know he's a senator.

A current U.S. Senator?

Braxton asked him how he was able to get the classified military records he received. The man said, "Son, when you're on the Senate Armed Services Committee, you can get anything you want," close quote.

Drake was stunned that a sitting member of the U.S. Senate would say something like that, but he wasn't surprised. Leaking classified records was a crime that was prosecuted only when the leak became public, and someone's political interests took a hit.

Learning that Braxton was in possession of classified

military records was disturbing because he had a good idea whose records the senator was talking about. His records as a Tier One operator with Delta Force.

Drake sent Beardon another text.

Wayne, split the team. Keep one person on Braxton and have the other person follow the senator. I want to know who he is. Bring the audio recording to meet me at Embassy Suites.

Roger that.

Passengers were walking up the ramp from the water taxi, and Norris asked, "What do you want to do?"

"Return to the hotel," Drake said. "This just got a lot more interesting. The person Braxton met is a U.S. Senator. I think he gave Braxton my classified military records."

Chapter Sixty-One

DRAKE AND NORRIS waited for Wayne Beardon in the hotel lobby and rode the elevator with him to Drake's room on the fifth floor.

"Did you identify the senator?" Drake asked as soon as Norris closed the door.

Beardon gave Drake a mock salute and said, "Yes, sir, we did. You may recognize his voice. Listen to this."

He took an iPhone Pro Max out of his pocket and opened the camera function. "This was recorded using a Sennheiser MKE 400 shotgun microphone."

"Senator," a male voice said.

"Tell me what happened. I was told you could handle this," another male said.

"The device malfunctioned. It stopped responding to his commands."

"Can it be traced?"

"No, it was routed through Mexico."

"What about the man you used?"

"He's been recalled."

"How will you finish this?"

"They have a plan. He won't be a problem any longer."

"That's what Daniel told me if I agreed to get his records."

"Senator, how did you get his records?"

"Son, when you're on the Armed Services Committee, it isn't a problem."

"Is there anything else?"

"Tell him to keep his word. This man's a threat to both of us. Finish it."

"I'll tell him."

The video continued without any further conversation between the two because Braxton left and walked away.

"Braxton was the last person off the taxi at Georgetown," Beardon said. "The other man, the senator, stayed on the water taxi and returned to the Wharf. He has a suite at the Pendry Washington Hotel and the senator's name is…"

"Senator Wayland Morris," Drake said. "I recognize his voice."

"You know the senator?" Norris asked.

"He was my commanding officer in Afghanistan. He's the reason I left the army."

"Why is he involved with Braxton?" Beardon asked.

"Senator Morris and Franklin must know each other," Drake said. "Franklin is the 'Daniel' Morris referred to. Braxton does work for Franklin and Franklin Analytics."

"Then the man the senator asked about is the guy who operated the 'device' that malfunctioned," Beardon said. "Braxton sent the guy with the drone to take you out."

"I knew Braxton was responsible," Drake said. "That's why we're here."

"But why are you a threat to this senator?" Norris asked.

"Because he was dirty and took money from the

Taliban. If he's seen my classified records, he knows I have evidence to prove it. Proof that he collaborated with the enemy. It would end his political career if he was exposed."

"Evidence that he leaked classified military records would also end his career," Beardon pointed out.

"That's why I need to find out if Braxton has a copy of my records," Drake said. "Those records are classified for a reason. If Morris is willing to leak my records, he doesn't belong on the Armed Services Committee, let alone in the Senate."

"Assuming Braxton does, where would he keep them?" Norris asked.

"Wayne, of the three places you know about, which place is the most secure?"

"I would say his facility west of here. He has facial recognition security at his office, and his home will have some level of security, but the Braxton Group facility looks like a fortress."

Drake pointed to the two chairs near the window and sat on the end of the bed. "Have a seat. Let's talk this through. Wayne, did you get your surveillance cameras placed at that Braxton's facility?"

"We can see anything that moves outside the two buildings."

"Did Morales go out there?"

"Yes, while you were in D.C."

"Where is he now?" Drake asked.

"He may still be out there."

Drake took out his phone and scrolled through Contacts until he found Morales, Marco, and called him.

"Morales."

"Marco, are you at the Braxton Group facility?'

"I'm not far from there," Morales said. "I'm in the parking lot of a nature preserve across the road."

"Is Sanchez with you?"

Drake silently counted one one thousand, two one thousand, and waited for Morales to answer.

"Yes, she is," Morales finally said. "Do you want to talk with her?"

"No, I just wanted to know if she was there with you. Have you found a way for us to get into Braxton's facility without being invited?"

"Just through the fence or into the buildings?" Morales asked.

"Into his office, whichever building that's in."

"Boss, that won't be easy. We could get through the fence, but there are CCTV cameras everywhere. The employees use a palm recognition scanner to enter the buildings from the parking lot. The service doors are opened from the inside. There's a guard at the security gate checking ID. If there's a way in, I haven't found it yet."

"Keep looking," Drake said. "We're getting into Braxton's office tonight. He has something he shouldn't have."

"I'll keep looking."

"Take Carol with you. She can watch your six. Call me when you finish looking."

Drake heard Norris laughing and looked over. "What?"

"Watch his six?"

"Employee safety is a priority at PSS."

"Okay," Norris said. "Are we really going to break into Braxton's office?"

"No, I'm just trying to give Morales a little more time together with Sanchez," Drake joked. "Yes, Dan, we're going to break into Braxton's office if possible."

"Who's going with us tonight?" Norris asked.

"Let's wait to hear what Morales says. How long does it take to get out there, Wayne?"

"Half an hour."

"Do they work more than one shift?" Drake asked.

"Most of the employees work a day shift, 7:00 A.M. to 4:00 P.M. There's a smaller crew in the main building all night. From the dim lights on the second floor, they're probably monitoring computers."

"Is the main building where Braxton's office is located?" Norris asked.

"That's the building he enters when he goes there."

"All right, that's all until we hear from Morales," Drake said.

Chapter Sixty-Two

CARL MARSTON'S handler didn't look up when he slipped into the booth he was in at The Raven Grill, a dive bar in northern Washington, D.C.

"What's going on, Sam?" Marston asked.

"How was the trip back?"

"It was great. Love the place. Now, what's going on?"

"Do you enjoy your work, Carl?"

"What?"

"I ask you if you enjoy what you're doing?"

"Why would you ask me that? You know who I am and why I do what I'm doing. You recruited me?"

"You screwed up, that's why I'm asking. That's not like you. It can't happen again," Sam said.

"The equipment screwed up, not me."

"You didn't do your homework, Carl. You didn't consider they might have counter-drone protection at their headquarters. You had plenty of places you could have taken him out. Why there?"

"You said minimize collateral damage," Marston said. "The parking area at PSS headquarters was the best place."

"Get something to drink," Sam said when his phone buzzed in his coat pocket. "I'll be right back."

"What the hell," Marston said when his handler got up and walked outside to take the call. Sam didn't trust him enough to take a call in his presence? The drone wasn't his idea, but he was getting blamed for mission failure. Maybe it was time to find an employer who appreciated his talent and listened to him.

Marston slipped out of the booth and stepped to the bar five feet away to order a drink. "Jameson, neat."

Sam must live in the neighborhood. Why else would he tell him to meet him here? It was a Pabst Blue Ribbon beer kind of place, and Sam was a Scotch guy. Something was wrong.

Marston handed the bartender his American Express card and had it handed back to him. "Cash only," the bartender said, pointing to the sign behind him.

"My friend's paying," Marston said.

"When he comes back and pays, you get your drink," the black bartender said, setting his Jameson on the back counter.

Marston glared at the man and thought about grabbing him by the throat, when Sam returned.

"Pay the man," he said. "You picked a cash-only bar."

Sam grinned and said, "It's okay, Rollie. Put it on my tab."

Marston took his drink and waited for Sam to sit before he joined him in the booth.

"What's going on, Sam?"

"I'm giving you another chance, that's what's going on.

So, sit back and listen for a change. They don't want Drake killed. They want him arrested for killing Braxton."

"Is Drake going to kill Braxton?" Marston asked.

"No, you are," Sam said. "Drake has three surveillance teams watching Braxton. One team is camped out at his facility, where you picked up the drone. You're going to blow up his office when he's there. They'll make sure there's evidence that Drake and his men did it."

Marston shook his head and downed his drink. "That's crazier than trying to take him out with a drone. Let me have another chance."

"They wanted to use a drone to make it look like a cartel wanted him dead. There's a bigger picture now. Braxton met with someone he wasn't supposed to know about. They want Braxton out. This is your opportunity to make amends for Seattle."

Marston sighed and motioned to the bartender for another round of Jameson's. "How am I supposed to take out Braxton and make it look like Drake's responsible?"

Sam held up his phone. "That was the call I was waiting for. We just delivered enough C4 to Braxton's facility to take the place down. He'll meet you tonight to hear how you'll use it to kill Drake. Make something up. When you get the chance, use the tunnel I told you about to get out of there and detonate the C4 when you're on the other side of the security fence. His CTTV cameras are on a feed to an offsite location we know about. Video showing Drake's men at the facility will be discovered by law enforcement when they investigate the explosion, and he'll go down for it."

"What could go wrong with a plan like that?" Marston asked.

"Make sure nothing does, Carl. They're not going to give you another chance."

Marston grinned and looked away to keep from saying what he wanted to say every time a handler said something like that.

"If something goes wrong, Sam, what's the backup plan? Kill Braxton, and you'll find another way to deal with Drake? Walk away, and you'll figure out another way to kill Braxton and Drake? Who are we doing this for, Sam? This is a screwed-up way to solve a simple problem. Two bullets, and who cares who gets blamed? It doesn't have to be this complicated."

"Complicated is why they get paid more than we do," Sam said. "We'll never know why they do everything they ask us to do. No one's said anything about a backup plan, but I know Braxton is the one they're most worried about. If it goes bad, make sure you take him out. I'll worry about the rest later."

"All right. What time am I supposed to meet Braxton?"

"He's expecting you at 7:00 PM. It's Sunday night, so there's only a skeleton crew out there," Sam said. "Call me when you get back."

Marston nodded and got up to leave. "Same arrangement as before?"

"The money will be in your account tomorrow."

He walked outside and envied Sam. He was a loyal employee and lived in a neighborhood that wasn't like the rest of D.C.; it wasn't upscale and gentrified. The Raven Grill was the only bar, and it was straight out of the 1950s. It reminded him of the bar he frequented when he was fifteen and living in South Carolina. The bartender knew his ID wasn't real and let him buy beer anyway because his dad was a regular.

Someday, he would find a place like this when he stopped working. A place with real people who had real jobs and lived in a nice neighborhood. A place with a bar where you could drink cheap whiskey and have enough money in your pocket to leave with a woman for the night.

Maybe after tonight, he would look for a way out because this wasn't the work he signed on for.

Chapter Sixty-Three

WAYNE BEARDON DROVE Drake and Norris out to Braxton's facility and turned into the nature reserves' parking lot at half past nine Sunday night. Morales and Sanchez were waiting in the second Ford Explorer parked at the back of the lot.

Drake lowered his passenger side window when Beardon stopped beside the other Explorer and asked through Sanchez's open window, "Did you two find a way in?"

Morales opened his door and walked around to Drake's window.

"Not one that will go undetected," Morales said. "Sorry, Boss. We've been around the perimeter twice. We can cut through the fence, but crossing the open area means tripping the motion detectors and floodlights on the buildings."

"Are guards on duty?" Drake asked.

"We haven't seen any."

"Wayne said Braxton's here."

"His Range Rover is," Morales said. "We were on the

perimeter when he arrived a little before seven o'clock. He was alone, but another car followed him ten minutes later."

Drake opened his door and stepped out, wearing black tactical clothing that matched what Morales, Sanchez, and Norris had on. His SIG M18x pistol was strapped to his leg in a thigh holster, and he held a black balaclava in his left hand.

"Let's go take a look," he said. "Wayne, stay here and let us know if you see trouble headed our way. I'll call if we decide to cut through the fence."

Norris joined him and jogged across the parking lot, following Morales and Sanchez to the road.

"From here, it's a quarter of a mile through the forest on a deer trail we found," Morales said, pulling on his balaclava.

"Lead on," Drake said, and sprinted across the road behind Morales.

Morales found the trail ten yards north of the road and stopped to let the others form up. From there, it was an easy hike on a narrow path covered with wet leaves through a hardwood forest.

They stopped when Morales raised a clenched fist at the edge of a cleared strip of land that bordered the security fence. The two buildings were on the far side of the fenced area one hundred yards away.

"Braxton's office is in the big building," Morales said softly. "That's his Range Rover next to it."

Drake studied the area flooded with lights from the buildings' rooflines. At the southern end of the property, he could see the guard shack to his right and the parking lot with ten or fifteen cars at the northern end to his left. A dark strip of pavement ran along the property's eastern side from the guard shack to the parking area. Two large satellite dishes were in the open area south of the parking area, and a dozen antennas were on the roof of the larger building.

"Where did Wayne put the IR cameras?" Drake asked.

"There are two in the trees on each side of the fence, except along the road," Sanchez said.

Drake stared at the main building with his arms folded across his chest. "The only way in is from the air; we don't have time to set that up."

"If the senator gave Braxton a copy of your records, I'll bet he kept a copy for himself," Norris said. "Why not get them from the senator?"

"I'd like to prove Braxton has them," Drake said. "If we can't prove it was Braxton's drone, we could still get him for possession of classified material."

Carol took a pair of binoculars from the harness system she wore and raised them to her eyes. "Ten o'clock, man running from the main building."

Drake turned and watched a man wearing a tan jacket and dark pants running across the parking area toward the back security fence. When he stopped at the door of a small storage shed, he took something out of his pocket and pointed it at the main building.

A cloud of red fire engulfed the building, and a booming explosion rocked the night. Flames shot out of the windows on the top floor, and car alarms started blaring in the parking lot.

Drake looked away from the burning remains of the main building and looked for the man at the storage shed. He was gone, but the shed's door was open.

"Look," Morales said, pointing, "Someone else made it out of the building."

A second man was running toward the storage shed,

struggling to shrug off his coat with one hand and slapping at flames in his hair with his other hand.

"That's Braxton," Drake shouted, running along the fence line toward the storage shed where the two men disappeared.

He reached the end of the fence line ahead of the others and searched the area to see how the men escaped under the security fence.

"Spread out," he said when the others arrived. "Look for a tunnel they used to get under the fence."

Morales found it a hundred feet into the forest. A metal manhole cover with leaves kicked over it.

274

Chapter Sixty-Four

THEY HUDDLED AROUND DRAKE, watching the burning remains of the building on the other side of the security fence, while he called Wayne Beardon on his Motorola APX two-way radio.

"People will be here to investigate the explosion you heard. Retrieve your cameras before they arrive and meet us back at Embassy Suites."

"What happened?"

"An explosion in the main building," Drake said. "Braxton ran to a tunnel under the security fence and fled. We're going after him. Have a team see if he goes home or to his office."

"Roger that," Beardon said.

Norris, Morales, and Sanchez were huddled around him, watching the burning remains of the main building.

"It looks like Braxton and the other guy were the only ones who got out," Norris said.

"What'd they have in there?" Sanchez asked. "That was a massive explosion."

"But it wasn't an accident," Drake said. "Multiple explosions occurring simultaneously means someone wanted this to happen."

"Braxton?" Morales asked.

"We'll know the answer to that when we find him," Drake said. "You're our tracker, Marco. Let's see if we can catch up with him."

Morales used his SureFire G2X tactical flashlight to search the ground around the manhole cover and pointed to depressions in the wet earth. "They went this way."

"Both men?" Norris asked.

"Both men," Morales said and followed the trail leading into the forest.

They walked behind Morales for several yards down the trail until it widened onto a man-made dirt path a small tractor could drive on. Another hundred yards and the path ended at a gravel road that bordered a farm's plowed field.

Morales swept his flashlight to his right and left along the gravel road, saying, "One set of footprints ends here where a car was parked. The other set takes off in the other direction. They didn't leave together."

"They wanted Braxton to die in that explosion," Drake said. "He wasn't supposed to make it out of there."

"If he didn't leave in the car, where is he?" Sanchez asked.

"Running for his life," Norris said.

"Braxton worked for the CIA," Drake said. "He'd have planned for something like this to happen someday."

"Where to now?" Morales asked.

"I don't know, but we have to get out of here. Take the lead, Marco," Drake said.

Morales jogged to the dirt path, stayed on point through the forest, and led them back to the nature reserve parking lot with the sound of sirens in the distance approaching from the east.

When they drove past the Braxton Group facility, fire trucks, and EMT ambulances were streaming down the entrance road past the guardhouse to the burning building. Not far behind them on the highway, a line of patrol cars flashed by with lights flashing and sirens screaming in the night.

Drake watched them go by and called Kevin McRoberts. "Kevin, Braxton's on the run. See if Braxton owns properties around here. He won't be listed as the owner, but it might be something his company owns or leases."

"Are you looking for Braxton or where he might go?" Kevin asked.

"Where he might go."

"I can't tell you where he might go, but I can tell you where he is."

"How?"

"I have the billing statements from his cell phone service. I can ping his phone."

"How long will that take?"

"A minute."

"Kevin is pinging Braxton's phone," Drake told Norris. "He might be able to tell us where he is."

"If he's on the run, he won't use his phone. He'll use a burner," Norris said.

"If he panicked, he might have taken his phone with him when he ran out of the building. Kevin can still track it if he did."

Kevin called back and said, "He must have left his phone in his office. That's where it is now."

"Someone blew up his office building," Drake told

Kevin. "Braxton escaped. Keep looking for where he might be going."

"I'm on it," Kevin said.

A second string of patrol cars raced by on the highway toward Braxton's facility.

"Sooner or later, they'll get around to checking the CCTV surveillance videos," Norris said. "They might see us there when the building exploded."

"If we're lucky, the video recorder was destroyed," Drake said. "If it wasn't, Wayne's cameras will prove we didn't go near that building."

"I'm just saying, we'll need to explain why we were there."

"Understood."

Norris made sure he didn't exceed the speed limit on the way to the hotel and parked the Explorer in the Embassy Suites' back parking lot.

Kevin McRoberts was sitting in the lobby with his laptop to greet the team when they walked in.

Drake saw the hotel bar was still open and asked Kevin to go there to hear what he had to report.

The bartender was the only one there and ignored them when they came in, as Drake walked to the table at the back of the room anyway.

"I couldn't find properties around here he has, but I did find where he might go," Kevin said. "He owns a ski cabin in Killington, Vermont. It's an hour and a quarter by air or almost nine hours by car. You could be there in the G280 if he's driving there."

"Why do you think he'll go there?" Drake asked.

"My AI search engine found a Vermont probate proceeding that said Braxton inherited a cabin there from his uncle. According to court records in Rutland County, Vermont, the cabin is still in his uncle's name, Alfred Remington."

Chapter Sixty-Five

THE PSS GULFSTREAM G280's tires chirped softly when they hit the runway on touchdown at the Rutland-Southern Vermont Regional Airport at 7:20 AM Monday. As it taxied toward the small terminal building, Drake stood behind the pilots on the flight deck, looking to see if the two GMC Yukons he rented were waiting there, as promised.

The Enterprise Rental office was closed when he decided they'd chase after Marcus Braxton the night before. It opened just twenty minutes before they landed, and the hurried delivery of the second SUV to the airport had added an extra hundred dollars to the bill.

"They'll send another Yukon out for you guys later," Drake said when he saw the lone white SUV parked at the edge of the tie-down area. "If Braxton doesn't show up in a day or so, we'll fly back to D.C. Find someplace in Killington to stay and be ready to fly out of here on short notice."

"Where will you be?"

"Waiting in the woods for Braxton to arrive."

"Have fun," Carson said. "The new forecast says it will get down to 27 degrees tonight."

"Yeah, thanks for the update."

Braxton's mountain getaway was ten miles north of Killington, built in the middle of a three-acre lot at the end of a long driveway, the only entrance to the cabin. It was surrounded on three sides by dense woods, and the nearest neighbor was a mile away.

Morales studied a satellite map of the area and found a small opening in the canopy of red and sugar maples half a mile from the cabin where they could hide the Yukon. A short hike through the woods would take them to concealed positions around the cabin where they could wait for Braxton to arrive.

Drake returned from the flight deck and told the team about the weather forecast. "It's going to be chilly tonight and might even snow. Let's hope Braxton arrives before dark."

Morales raised his hand and said, "Braxton was Special Forces and might have booby traps in and around the cabin. I volunteer to clear the area and wait for him inside."

"I thought Texas boys were tough," Sanchez chided. "Afraid of the cold?"

"I am Texas tough, we're just not used to being cold," Morales said.

Norris leaned down, pulled a thermal blanket from his backpack on the floor, and tossed it to Morales. "Are you sure you were Recon?"

Drake got out of his seat when the plane rolled to a stop. "Let's go, boys and girls. Time to get to work."

He lowered the airstairs and led the team across the

tarmac to the white Yukon, where an Enterprise employee was holding a clipboard with a rental agreement for him to sign. Five minutes later, Drake was behind the wheel, driving them north on the airport road toward Braxton's cabin.

Morales pinned the cabin's location on his iPhone's Map and rode shotgun as Drake's navigator.

"Left at the intersection and right when we get to the highway," Morales called out.

"Copy," Drake said.

"If Braxton flew up here last night, he'll be ready for us," Norris said from the seat behind Drake.

"If he is here, he'll want to talk when he hears we saw what happened last night and who detonated the explosion."

"He might, but don't forget he's the one who tried to take you out with the drone," Norris said.

"Don't worry, I won't forget," Drake promised.

"One mile ahead, turn onto Coffeehouse Road," Morales said. "We're getting close."

After driving a quarter of a mile down the dirt road, Morales pointed ahead to an opening in the trees on the left side lining Coffeehouse Road. "The clearing is through there."

Drake slowed down to drive across a deep ditch and then on through trees brushing against the sides of the SUV. He stopped under the branches of a red maple and turned off the engine.

When they got out and quietly closed the doors of the Yukon, the only sound they heard was the distant sound of a dog barking.

White clouds of vapor rose in the air with their breath

as they listened for any sound of activity in the woods around them.

"There are two weeks left in deer season," Drake told them. "Watch for hunters. Marco, take point."

Morales checked the bearing locked on his Suunto Vertical GPS watch and started across the clearing. Drake followed him ahead of Sanchez and Norris.

Walking silently through the woods, Drake thought about the long marches over barren and rocky terrain in the dark of night he'd made in Afghanistan with Mike Casey. Sometimes, walking for a week or more to reach the location of a village where a high-value target was seen, only to find the HVT was no longer there.

He wouldn't be surprised if Braxton didn't show up; he would just be disappointed. A cabin hidden in the woods in Vermont that most people would never find out about was the logical place for him to go. But if he could find his mountain getaway, the man who blew up his office could find it as well.

Braxton might be anywhere, but it would end here with any luck. Braxton would show up, be smart, not try to fight his way out, and eventually tell him why he was doing what he'd been doing.

If it didn't work out that way, he'd have to find what he was searching for from Daniel Franklin or his old commander, Senator Wayland Morris. He didn't care who it was.

Today, he hoped it would be Marcus Braxton.

Morales raised his right fist and stopped next to the trunk of a large maple tree ten feet away from the end of the foliage. Beyond that was the brown grass of a winter lawn at the rear of Braxton's cabin that hadn't been mowed recently. A wooden deck five feet above the lawn on cement pillars spanned the width of the structure.

Dark burnt orange curtains were drawn across the windows on both sides of a sliding glass patio door, and the blinds on the patio door were closed.

Drake signaled for the team to stay under the trees while Morales moved in to clear the area around the cabin.

Chapter Sixty-Six

WHILE MORALES MOVED SLOWLY around the cabin, Drake took a pair of Steiner Commander Military binoculars from the case on his chest harness and searched the exterior of the cabin.

There was a dual-lens security camera above the glass sliding door with a panoramic 180-degree view of the rear yard and another camera on the wall to the left of the rear deck. Braxton had installed a satellite dish and ham radio antenna on the cabin's green metal roof and a weather station monitor on the deck railing.

When Morales appeared around the far corner of the rear deck, he radioed to the team that the grounds were clear. "Do you want me to try and get inside?" he asked.

"If he has security cameras inside, he'll know we're here," Drake said. "We'll surprise him when he gets here."

Morales moved to a concealed position on the other side of the cabin and radioed, "I have eyes on the road from here."

"Copy," Drake responded.

"I have the long driveway from here," Norris added.

"Carol?" Drake asked.

"I'm on the other side of the deck opposite you," she said.

"He might come through the woods like we did, so stay alert," Drake advised.

He flexed his fingers, shifted his weight from one foot to improve circulation in his extremities, and settled in to wait for Braxton to arrive. Driving from Maryland to Killington, Vermont, would take nine hours traveling at the posted legal speed limit, and it had been twelve hours since he used a tunnel to escape with his clothes on fire. Allowing enough time to get to a vehicle he had waiting somewhere or find one to steal, Braxton should be in Killington by now.

Drake pulled back the sleeve of his black tactical jacket and checked the time on his watch. If Braxton hadn't shown up by noon, he'd call Kevin McRoberts in Bethesda and ask if there was any new information about his location.

Finding Braxton quickly was imperative, but he couldn't keep chasing him much longer without more to go on.

Drake stretched his neck from side to side and twisted his body ninety degrees to each side to scan the woods behind him before turning back to look for Braxton to arrive.

At eleven o'clock, Drake broke the radio silence. "If he isn't here by noon, we're out of here."

"Roger that," Norris said.

"Boss, a car turned off the road," Morales said.

"Let us know if it's coming our way," Drake said.

Five seconds later, Morales said, "It is, lone driver."

An old Honda Civic drove down the long driveway slowly and stopped in front of the cabin.

"It's Braxton," Norris said. "He's just sitting there looking at his phone."

"He's checking the security cameras' recorder. Move in," Drake said.

Four figures in black tactical clothing came out of the woods with their weapons aimed at Braxton.

Drake ran to the front of the car and called out, "Braxton, I just want to talk. Put both hands on the steering wheel where we can see them."

Braxton froze with his phone held in front of his face.

"Drop the phone and put your hands on the steering wheel," Drake said.

Braxton didn't move and smiled. "You're trespassing, Drake, and you won't shoot me. I'm calling the sheriff."

"If you do, you won't be here when he arrives. Don't you want to know who tried to kill you?" I can show you who it was."

Braxton stared at Drake but didn't say anything.

Norris moved forward slowly until he was at the passenger side door of the Civic. "There's a Glock 30 on the seat. If he reaches for it, can I shoot him?"

"Braxton, get out of the car now," Drake said. "We're not here to kill you, but we will if you reach for that gun."

"How do I know it wasn't you?"

"Think about it. How would I get into your building and plant those explosives?"

"How do you know there were explosives in the building?"

"I saw the explosion," Drake said. "I saw you run to the storage shed and escape through the tunnel. And I saw the man who ran out before you and used a detonator to blow up your building."

Braxton tipped his head back and then set his phone on the dash. "I'm coming out," he said.

Sanchez moved forward as the door opened and told Braxton to put his hands on the roof of the Civic while she searched him for a weapon. When she finished, she said, "He's clean."

"Leave your things in the car, and let's go inside," Drake said. "It's cold out here."

Drake walked Braxton to the cabin's front door. Before he punched in the code to open the door, Braxton asked, "How did you know I was coming here?"

"We found the probate records and saw the cabin was still in your uncle's name. We thought you might go here."

Braxton opened the door and said, "I need to disarm the security system. I'll give you the code if you want to do it."

"And have it explode in my face because you gave me the wrong code? You go ahead, I'll watch."

Braxton walked to the entry hall closet and entered the code on a panel inside the closet door."What now?" he asked.

"We search for weapons, and then we talk," Drake said.

"The weapons are in a gun safe in the master bedroom," Braxton said.

"Except for this K-Bar I found in the kitchen," Sanchez said, holding up the knife.

"Okay, except for the K-Bar. Look, I've been driving for nine hours. I could use a drink. Would you guys like to join me?" Braxton asked.

"If that will help you relax, go ahead," Drake said.

Braxton walked to the kitchen and returned with a bottle of Jack Daniels and five glasses in his hands.

Drake watched him pour two fingers of Jack in each glass and said, "Thanks."

"So, who tried to kill me?" Braxton asked.

Chapter Sixty-Seven

WHILE MORALES GOT a fire going in the wood-burning stove in front of the brick fireplace and Norris and Sanchez searched the cabin, Drake sat on one end of a brown leather sofa across from Braxton on a matching sofa on the other side of a maple burl coffee table with the bottle of Jack Daniels sitting on it.

Drake's pistol was in his right hand, resting on the sofa beside him as he told Braxton what he knew.

"We were standing outside your security fence when the explosion occurred and saw a man come out of the building and run to the storage shed," Drake said. "When he got there, he pointed something in his hand, probably his phone, toward the building and detonated the explosives. Then you came running out with your clothes on fire."

"Why were you there?" Braxton asked.

"You have something of mine you shouldn't have. I wanted it back."

"What would that be?"

"The copy of my classified military records Senator Morris gave you."

Braxton finished off his glass of whiskey and refilled it from the bottle on the coffee table without looking at Drake.

"I don't know what you're talking about."

"Yes, you do," Drake said. "We have a recording of you talking about it with the senator on the water taxi. If you don't want to tell me what you know, that's okay. We can wait for the FBI to arrive and let you finish your bottle of whiskey. Because it will be the last bottle of whiskey you'll be drinking for a while, Marcus, I promise you."

"What's the FBI got to do with this?"

"Unauthorized possession of classified materials is a crime," Drake said. "Why did Senator Morris have them?"

"Someone asked him to get them."

"Who, Daniel Franklin?"

Braxton blinked twice before sitting back and crossing his arms across his chest. "Tell me who you think tried to kill me, and maybe I'll tell you."

Drake took his phone out and found the video from Wayne Beardon's surveillance camera. "I don't know his name, but this is the man who detonated the explosives at your place last night."

Braxton took the phone Drake handed him and held it close to his face to watch the video.

"His name is Carl Marston," Braxton said softly.

"How do you know him?"

Braxton shook his head and asked, "Why are you here, Drake? Why did you mention the FBI?"

"Because the FBI is investigating the hovering munitions drone you used in Seattle, and I want you and Senator Morris prosecuted for having my classified military records."

"Before I tell you anything, I'll need a grant of immunity for the drone and the classified materials," Braxton said.

"Why?"

"Because I know who's trying to kill me, and I need to disappear."

"Who is it?"

"Daniel Franklin and maybe the CIA," Braxton said. "Carl Marston is a CIA contract killer, and I know too much about Franklin and what he's doing."

Dan Norris came up behind Drake and whispered in his ear. "We have visitors."

Drake stood and looked at Braxton. "Are you expecting visitors?"

"No, why?"

"Men with rifles are walking down your driveway. Did you tell anyone you were coming here?"

"No, of course not."

Drake moved to the front window and looked out. Six men were walking down the long gravel driveway, wearing Woodland camo clothing and carrying assault rifles.

"What's in your gun safe?" Drake asked.

"A couple of AR-15s and a Mossberg shotgun."

"Go with Dan and get them," Drake said. "We need to get out of here."

Drake moved back to the back of the cabin and opened the blinds enough to see that no one was in the backyard.

"Carol, make sure the front door is locked," he said. "Marco, help Dan bring Braxton's guns in here. We're leaving through the woods."

Drake unlocked the sliding patio door and stepped out onto the rear deck. With his M18x pistol raised in his right hand, he edged along the wall to the right side of the deck and peeked around the corner.

He saw one man standing in front of the cabin with his rifle aimed at the front door. When he turned his head and looked, Morales was standing at the open sliding door carrying an AR-15.

Drake made a cutting motion with his left hand toward the railing at the back of the deck, signaling Morales to lead the others into the woods.

While he stayed at the corner of the deck to cover their retreat, Morales walked quickly across the deck with Braxton, Norris, and Sanchez in a single file behind him. Morris and Norris were carrying AR-15s, and Sanchez had the shotgun in her hand as she slipped over the railing and dropped to the ground.

When they reached the tree line and turned to cover him, Drake moved to the center of the deck and followed them over the railing and into the woods.

"Carol, take Braxton and follow Marco," Drake said. "If he tries to get away, shoot him. Dan and I will protect our flank in case they follow us."

"Roger that," she said, turning Braxton around to follow Morales. "Get moving."

Drake and Norris backed through the woods until they were out of sight.

The barrage of rifles firing at Braxton's cabin scattered birds into the air from the trees.

"They were carrying XM7s," Norris said, jogging behind Drake. "Military?"

"Probably CIA," Drake said. "Braxton thinks they want to kill him."

"It won't take long before they find Braxton wasn't in the cabin."

Drake gave a thumbs up over his right shoulder, sprinting after Sanchez as she dodged around the trunk of a tree fifty yards ahead of them.

Chapter Sixty-Eight

DRAKE CALLED Wayne Beardon in Maryland while they were racing back to the airport in Killington and Steve Carson was scrambling to prepare for takeoff.

"Wayne, check us out of Embassy Suites and bring Kevin. Meet us at Reagan National."

"What happened?"

"I'll explain when I get there."

"Did you find Braxton?"

"He's coming with us."

"Do you want us to move out of Bethesda?"

"Stay where you are," Drake said. "If I learn something that changes that, I'll let you know."

"Understood."

Dan Norris was at the wheel next to Drake in the passenger seat, with Braxton between Sanchez and Morales back in the second row of seats.

"Why are you going to D.C.?" Braxton asked.

"To turn you over to the government," Drake said. "You said you wanted a grant of immunity."

"Then I'm a dead man. They're all involved with Franklin."

"I have someone I trust," Drake said. "You'll be okay."

After speeding around Pierce's Corner onto Route 103, a white Gulfstream V turbojet flashed overhead to land at Rutland airport.

"That's a plane the CIA likes to use," Braxton said. "We're not going to make it out of here."

Drake watched the jet touch down and roll down the runway.

"Are you cleared for takeoff?" he asked Steve Carson.

"Yes, where are you?"

"Coming down Airport Road. That white Gulfstream that just landed might be trouble. Taxi away from it if it gets close to you. We'll come to you to board."

"Roger that," Carson said.

Drake took a hundred-dollar bill from his RFID wallet and put it in the cup holder.

"Leave the keys above the visor," he told Norris. "I'll call Enterprise when we're in the air."

The white Gulfstream reached the end of the runway and was turning to taxi to the terminal area when Norris pulled alongside the PSS G280.

"Get Braxton on the plane," Drake told Morales, opening his door.

"I'll get your gear."

Norris popped the Yukon's tailgate and hurried with Sanchez and Drake to grab their luggage and get on the plane.

Carson taxied to the runway as soon as the airstairs were up. He turned and asked Drake what had happened.

"Six men came after Braxton and shot up his place as

we left through the woods out back," Drake said. "He thinks the CIA is trying to kill him."

"Are they?" Carson asked.

"If that's a CIA Gulfstream that landed, they are."

"I've seen a Gulfstream V like that being used by the CIA for extraditions in Afghanistan," Joe Ryan, the copilot, said. "It might be."

"Just get us to D.C., gentlemen. They don't know we have Braxton."

Drake walked to the back of the cabin and relieved Morales who was guarding Braxton.

"You have an hour and a half to tell me what you know about Daniel Franklin," Drake said, sitting across from him. "If you do, I'll make sure the CIA doesn't kill you."

"I know the president's your friend, but that won't stop them. Franklin is too important to them."

"Why?"

"Two reasons," Braxton said. "Franklin does more than supply personal data to the Intelligence Community. He analyzes it and gives them a list of potential security risks for their surveillance programs. Then, the military's secret army puts them under surveillance to see if they are a threat to national security. That's sixty thousand people, in and out of uniform, carrying out assignments here and abroad without government oversight. They call it the 'signature reduction' force, and it's ten times the size of the CIA's clandestine services.

"I know what I'm talking about, Drake. They use private contractors, and I'm one of them. This thing is too big to fail. They can't let Franklin go down and expose everything."

"That's one reason, what's the other? If you're just one of the private contractors they use, you can be replaced."

"Because I do other things for Franklin," Braxton said, shrugging his shoulders.

"Like you did in Las Vegas and Seattle with the drone?"

"That was the guy in Seattle you saw running from my building. I was doing what Franklin wanted done, but Carl Marston's on loan from the CIA. He's not one of my employees."

"What else do you do for Franklin?"

Braxton rolled his shoulders and stretched his neck from side to side. "He sells personal data to people he shouldn't. Sometimes, I deliver it to them for him."

"What kind of people?"

"Cartels, Russians."

"That's not illegal, as far as I know," Drake said.

"The way he analyzes the data for them when they give him a specific target, it is."

"Explain."

"Let's say there's a company you want to hit with a ransomware attack, and you need a way to breach its IT system. Franklin will analyze the personal data of the company's employees to be compromised or blackmailed."

"Hackers do that all the time. Why is Franklin different?"

"Because he did it for a cartel, and the target was a U.S. nuclear power plant," Braxton said.

"When was this?" Drake asked.

"This week."

'Do you know which power plant it is?"

"When I have immunity, I'll tell you."

Drake laughed. "Very clever, Marcus. Why should I believe you?"

"There's no reason you should," he said, "But do you want to be the one they blame when it happens?"

Drake studied Braxton's grinning face and got up to leave.

"I'm telling you the truth."

Drake kept walking and told Morales to go back and watch Braxton.

It wasn't his job to believe Braxton, but he knew whose job it was and looked for Kate Perkins's name on his list of contacts.

"Perkins," she said after the third ring.

"Kate, I have someone who says he knows about a ransomware attack on a U.S. nuclear power plant," Drake said. "Would you like to meet him?"

"Is he credible?"

"He might be."

"Can you bring him to me?"

"Meet me at Reagan National in about an hour," Drake said. "I'll call you when we land."

Chapter Sixty-Nine

ASSISTANT DIRECTOR of the FBI Kate Perkins marched across the lounge of the Signature FBO at Reagan National at 1:30 p.m. Monday to meet Drake with two FBI agents trailing behind her.

"Where is he?" she asked.

"In our plane."

"Are you going to take me to him?"

"I will, if you agree to meet him by yourself."

"Why would I do that?"

"Because he won't talk to you if you don't," Drake said. "He doesn't want anyone else to know he's talking to you because he doesn't trust the FBI. I convinced him he could trust you because I do."

"No one trusts the government anymore," she said. "That doesn't mean I can't get him to talk to me."

"You might be able to, but not in time to prevent the attack on the power plant."

Perkins shook her head and said," I don't know why I trust you, Drake, but okay, I'll go alone."

Drake turned around and motioned for her to come with him. "He wants immunity, so be prepared."

"They always do."

The airstairs came down when they were halfway across the tarmac to the plane, with Dan Norris standing at the top to greet them. Drake stepped aside and let Perkins ascend first.

"Hello again," Norris said.

"Dan," she said as she brushed past him and waited for Drake.

"This way," Drake said and started through the galley toward the rear of the cabin.

Morales shook hands with Perkins as he stood aside and let Drake enter the rear compartment of the cabin. Two beige leather seats sat facing each other on both sides of the aisle ahead of the lavatory bulkhead. Braxton was facing forward in the rear seat on the plane's starboard side.

"Assistant Director," Braxton said to greet Perkins.

"Mr. Braxton," she said and sat across from him.

Drake sat on the other side of the aisle from Perkins.

"I didn't expect you to be the one Drake asked me to meet," she said.

Braxton nodded and said, "I didn't expect it would be either."

"How did you hear about this ransomware attack you told Drake about?"

"I want immunity before I tell you what I know," Braxton said. "Will you grant that?"

"You know I can make that happen if I believe what you tell me, and that you're not responsible."

"I might be, in a small way."

"How small a way?" she asked.

"I might have inadvertently delivered information from one responsible party to another responsible party."

"And you can identify these responsible parties?"

"I can."

Perkins tilted her head slightly to one side and searched Braxton's face for any sign of deception before standing and walking back into the main cabin.

When she turned around, Drake was standing behind her.

"What else can you tell me?" she asked.

"Braxton does work for Daniel Franklin, the data broker. He says Franklin analyzes the personal data of employees who can be compromised or blackmailed to gain access to a targeted company's IT system for a ransomware attack. He claims he delivered information to a cartel for a ransomware attack this week on a U.S. nuclear power plant."

"Did he know which power plant it is?"

"He said he'd tell us when he had immunity."

"If I can't get that approved, is there a chance he'll tell us anyway?"

"I doubt it," Drake said. "He thinks the CIA is trying to kill him. What I saw at his cabin in Vermont this morning seems to confirm that."

"Why would the CIA want to kill him?"

"That's another story."

"If he won't talk, any suggestions?"

Drake smiled and said, "Leave him with me. We'll fly out over the Atlantic and toss him out if he refuses to talk."

"I didn't hear that."

"Because I didn't say it, but I would consider it."

Perkins took a deep breath, walked back, and sat across from Braxton.

"Mr. Braxton, Mr. Drake thinks I should believe you," she said. "I need something specific before I'll consider granting you immunity."

"Like what?"

"Who are the responsible parties you mentioned, and which power plant is the target of the ransomware attack?"

"If I tell you, you will grant me immunity, correct?"

"Yes, once we agree on what crimes the immunity will cover."

"It will have to be a blanket immunity for everything?" Braxton said.

"That's not possible, sorry," Perkins said. "I don't know what else you've been doing."

Braxton crossed his arms over his chest and closed his eyes. When he opened them, he said, "Okay, for delivering the information about the ransomware attack and what I was involved with in Las Vegas, and Seattle concerning Drake."

Perkins looked over at Drake with raised eyebrows.

"I'm okay with that, Kate," Drake said, "If he agrees to tell me everything he knows about Las Vegas and Seattle."

"All right, I will," Braxton said.

"Then we have an agreement," Perkins said. "Who are the parties, and which power plant is the target?"

"Daniel Franklin and the CJNG cartel."

"Drake says you do work for Franklin, but how do you know it's the CJNG cartel?"

"Because I delivered the information to *El Jabalí*, the wild boar, the head of CJNG on the East Coast."

"Okay, I know who *Jabalí* is," Perkins said. "Which power plant?"

"I don't know which power plant."

"Braxton, you said you'd tell me which power plant it

was if you had immunity!" Drake said, leaning across and poking his finger into Braxton's chest.

"Sorry, I didn't think immunity would be on the table if I couldn't say which power plant it is," Braxton said. "All I know is that it's not far from D.C."

"How do you know that?" Perkins asked.

"Because *Jabali* said he didn't want to be here if the power company didn't pay the ransom. We were in D.C. when he said it."

"Does Franklin know?" Drake asked.

"Sure, he'd have to know which power plant to give them what they wanted."

"Do you know where Franklin is?" Perkins asked.

"No," Braxton said.

"I'll find him, Kate," Drake promised. "Just get Braxton out of my sight before I change my mind about flying him out over the Atlantic."

Chapter Seventy

KEVIN MCROBERTS MET Drake in the Hyatt Regency Crystal City Hotel lobby at Reagan National Airport carrying his laptop.

"Mr. Beardon told me you wanted to know where Daniel Franklin is," Kevin said. "He's in San Francisco."

"How did you find him?" Drake asked.

"He owns an Embraer Predator 600 business jet. It flew out of Logan International last night at seven o'clock. Its flight plan lists San Francisco as its destination."

"Do we know where he is in San Francisco?"

"Not exactly," Kevin said, "But he has a house in Mill Valley, and his sailing yacht is moored at the San Francisco Yacht Club."

Drake fist-bumped his talented IT expert and world-class hacker and told him to be ready to fly to San Franciso with the team. "If Franklin isn't at his house or on his yacht, we'll need you to find him as quickly as possible. I want you on the ground with us."

"You bet, Mr. Drake," Kevin said. "I'll keep looking and see if I can find anything else."

Norris, Morales, and Sanchez were waiting for him at the elevator.

"Kevin says Franklin's in San Francisco," Drake told them. "I'm going to shower and change my clothes, and then let's get something to eat before we leave."

"Roger that," Norris said, punching the elevator button.

"What do we do when we find Franklin?" Morales asked.

"Braxton said he sold information to the CJNG cartel for a ransomware attack on a nuclear power plant," Drake said. "Franklin knows which power plant. After he tells us which one it is, he has an appointment with the FBI."

The elevator stopped on the sixth floor, and when Drake found his room, his duffel bag was on the bed. Before stripping down to shower, he called Liz in Seattle.

"Hi beautiful," he said.

"Where are you?"

"D.C., but we're leaving for San Francisco soon. How are you?"

"I'm fine," Liz said. "Alex is too. Why are you going to San Francisco?"

"To find a man who knows which nuclear power plant a cartel has targeted for a ransomware attack?"

"Adam, that's something for the FBI or Homeland Security. Why do you have to do it?"

"I can do it faster," he said. "Don't worry, the guy we're looking for is a billionaire who went to Berkeley."

"Right, rich men are never dangerous."

"This won't take long," Drake said. "I'll be home soon."

"Just be careful," Liz said.

Drake took a quick shower and changed into jeans, a

gray crew-neck merino wool sweater, and white Nike Pegasus trainers. Before he closed his duffel bag, he pulled out a black windbreaker and left the room.

When Drake arrived, Kevin McRoberts was alone at a table in the hotel's Market restaurant with his laptop open.

"He's definitely in San Francisco," Kevin said. "He just used his American Express Centurion card at the San Francisco Yacht Club. He's hosting a private party at the club's Cove House tonight at seven."

"Good work, Kevin," Drake said. "What do we know about his place in Mill City?"

"I'll find what I can on the plane."

"Excellent," Drake said.

When the team had their to-go orders from the restaurant, Wayne Beardon drove them to the airport in the Yukon XL he rented for the surveillance team to use.

Drake sat in the passenger seat on the way to the airport when Beardon asked what he wanted the surveillance team to do.

"Follow us to San Francisco, Wayne," Drake said. "If Franklin's at home and we can talk with him, you can take everyone home to Seattle. If we have to chase him around San Francisco, I'll need you to stay with us."

"Understood," Beardon said. "We'll be on the next available flight. You might know which it is by the time we get there."

Two hours after landing at Reagan National Airport, the PSS Gulfstream G280 left Virginia with California as its destination on its flight plan.

Drake and Norris sat in the first seats behind the plane's galley, eating and deciding the best way to get Franklin to identify the nuclear power plant.

"How do you plan to get him to talk?" Norris asked.

"It won't be easy," Drake admitted. "He has powerful friends in Washington, and he's rich. He's used to having lawyers fight his battles and using money to fix problems. But we're not going there to arrest him. We're going there to make him an offer he can't refuse."

"Okay, I'll bite. What can we offer him that he can't refuse?"

"Him not dying a slow and painful death when the CJNG cartel finds out he's responsible for exposing their ransomware attack on a U.S. nuclear power plant. We can keep the cartel from finding out."

"He'll try to blame that on Braxton."

"It won't work," Drake said. "Braxton works for him."

"What if he's not afraid of the cartel?"

"We'll make sure he sees the evidence the FBI has of victims tortured and killed by the cartel."

"Do we have the evidence?"

"Not yet," Drake said. "Why don't you call Kate and tell her what we need?"

"She doesn't want to talk to me. Don't we know someone in law enforcement who can get what we need? Mark Holland has friends in the NYPD. He could get it for us."

"Kate needs to be a part of this, Dan. When we get the name of the power plant, I want the FBI to take Franklin to the cleaners, not only for this but for what he tried to do in Las Vegas and having Senator Morris get a copy of my classified records for him."

Norris closed his eyes and rubbed his forehead with his left hand. "I don't know what I did to make her mad. She won't tell me."

"Maybe calling her will give you a chance to find out."

Norris got up and walked to the rear of the cabin to call

Kate Perkins, the Assistant Director of the FBI and his former fiancé.

Kate and his wife were friends, and he knew why Kate didn't want to talk to Norris. It was the same thing he and Liz had to work out before Liz left her position as Executive Director of Homeland Security and moved to Seattle.

Perkins wanted Norris to return to Washington, and as much as he wished them both the best, he didn't want to lose Norris. Not when he was thinking of transferring some of his duties at PSS to him.

Chapter Seventy-One

A CARPET of sparkling lights burst into view when the PSS G280 broke through the clouds to land at San Francisco International Airport at 5:45 p.m. Monday.

That afternoon, crossing flyover land at forty thousand feet, Kevin McRoberts located aerial views online of Franklin's house and its floor plan from a realtor's ad from five years ago. The three-story, five-bedroom, five-bathroom luxury home had floor-to-ceiling windows on three sides and was advertised to have incredible views of the San Francisco skyline across the bay. There was a private dock on the waterfront below the house with a large motor yacht moored beside it.

Drake knew the problem would be getting Franklin alone without breaking too many laws or killing anyone to do it. He expected Franklin to have security at the house and bodyguards when he traveled. Waiting for the perfect opportunity to snatch him when he wasn't being guarded wasn't feasible because it might happen too late to prevent the ransomware attack.

Drake needed more intel before they made a move on Franklin.

To find out what Franklin would be doing that night, he was sending Norris and Sanchez to the San Fransico Yacht Club to check out the party Franklin was hosting. All they knew was that the private room at the Cove House was reserved from seven until ten o'clock. He needed to know where Franklin would be after the party ended, and he wanted to know who the people Franklin invited were.

The San Franciso Yacht Club allowed visitors, but only if they were members of another yacht club with reciprocating privileges. Fortunately, Mike Casey was a member of the Seattle Yacht Club and had added five new members' names to his corporate membership before they landed. Norris and Sanchez had a white Mercedes C 300 sedan from Hertz waiting for them to drive to the yacht club as soon as they landed.

Drake and Morales would leave in a second Mercedes C 300 to drive to Franklin's house to reconnoiter the property and identify his security. Satellite views showed the house was located near the end of East Strawberry Road, on a large lot with beach access and a private dock. Morales didn't see a problem getting close enough to the house to spot Franklin's security and locate routes of ingress and egress to Franklin's property.

The mission was to get Franklin to tell them what they wanted to know without harming him in the takedown. That didn't mean Franklin had to be handled with kid gloves, but it did mean he had to be capable of fully appreciating the consequences he faced if he didn't cooperate, Drake reminded himself.

Before they left the G280 and went their separate ways,

Drake stood in the aisle while the plane taxied to the FBO and asked if anyone had a question.

"If there's an opportunity to take Franklin at the yacht club, what do we do?" Norris asked.

"We need to take him without someone calling the police," Drake said. "If you get that opportunity, take it."

"If we do, where do we take him?"

"Take him to the FBO and get him on our plane. If you can't do it without being chased to the airport, find a place, and we'll come to you."

"Can we use Tasers on his bodyguards?" Sanchez asked.

"Tasers won't keep his bodyguards down long enough to get him out of there without them getting up and chasing you. If we use Tasers, let's wait until we can subdue and keep them down."

"If we can't get Franklin at the yacht club, do we follow him or stay there and video the people at his party when they leave?" Norris asked.

"First priority is Franklin," Drake said. "If you can take a video of his guests, take it. If not, follow Franklin unless you can find out where he's going. If we get lucky, he might go to his house, and we'll be there waiting for him."

"Is the FBI going to help us if this goes upside down?" Sanchez asked.

"It might, depending on how upside down that might be. Don't worry about that right now."

"What's our rendezvous point?" Morales asked.

"Back here," Drake said. "Steve and Joe are staying on the plane in case we need to fly Franklin to D.C. tonight."

"I know we're taking Tasers and the Bryna Launchers to deal with these guys, but it's okay to defend ourselves if they start shooting, right?" Sanchez asked.

"Absolutely, Carol. If it happens, defend yourself. We'll

always have your back and be there to deal with the consequences."

"If we don't get him tonight, are we staying here?" Morales asked.

"Wayne and the surveillance team are following us to San Francisco," Drake said. "If we don't get Franklin tonight, they'll help us find him. We're here until we get the information we came for."

Drake braced himself against the bulkhead when Carson stopped the G280 and got ready to lower the airstairs. "Let's do this. I'm ready to be home."

Chapter Seventy-Two

BY THE TIME Norris and Sanchez crossed the Golden Gate Bridge and found the San Francisco Yacht Club, it was after seven o'clock. When they located the Cove House and asked to see what spaces were available for private parties, a staff member said the main function room would be occupied until later that night. They were told they were welcome to come back tomorrow if they wanted to see it.

The dining room was closed, and they had time to kill before Franklin or his guests left the party, so Norris suggested they look for Franklin's 88-meter sailing yacht.

"Kevin said he has a classic 38-meter sailing yacht in Boston, but the one he has here is a DynaRig 88-meter yacht," Norris said. "I sailed with my dad on the Chesapeake Bay, but I haven't had a chance to inspect one of these modern sailing yachts."

"What is a DynaRig?" she asked.

"It's something they use on large, high-performance sailing yachts," Norris explained. "They have freestanding, rotating masts and are equipped with an automated sail handling system. It's amazing technology."

"Is this what Franklin uses to cruise to Cabo San Lucas each year?"

"I believe so. He calls it the *Black Falcon*."

They found it moored at the end of the 100s dock, with two men standing alongside, taking pictures.

"Is this Daniel Franklin's *Black Falcon*?" Norris asked.

"It's a beauty, isn't it?" one man said.

"Yes, it is," Norris said.

"It looks brand new. Does it sail often?" Sanchez asked.

"He takes it out a couple of times a year," the other man said.

"Here in the bay to show people around?" Norris asked.

"Are you a member here?" the first man asked.

"No, we're members of the Seattle Yacht Club," Norris said. "I thought he might be like a couple of Seattle guys who only use their boats to sail their guests around after business functions."

"No, Daniel's a real sailor," the second man said. "He'll use the motor yacht at his house to cruise around the bay. That's what he usually does if he has guests here. But he sails it to Cabo each year."

Norris used his new surveillance tool, an iPhone 16 Pro Max that PSS supplied, to walk up and down the length of the *Black Falcon*, say goodbye to the men, and leave with Sanchez.

"Let's tell Drake the party's headed his way and take some pictures of Franklin's guests," Norris said.

———

DRAKE DROVE past Franklin's home and returned to a small park a quarter of a mile away. Franklin's house was built high above Richardson Bay's waterfront, with a security gate and fencing that prevented them from getting close enough to check out his security without being seen.

Morales reached a hand back to the rear seat and brought the case forward containing his old friend, the Black Hornet nano drone.

"With all the windows that place has, it won't take long to find out what we're dealing with," Morales said, slipping on the harness with the case for the drone's controls and video screen. He opened the window, powered up the drone sitting in the palm of his hand, and held it out to send it flying toward Franklin's house.

The Teledyne Black Hornet 4 nano drone has a high-resolution thermal imager, an electro-optical 12-megapixel daytime camera with superior low-light capabilities, and a range of two kilometers. It provided the kind of covert surveillance that long-range reconnaissance soldiers like Morales couldn't begin to imagine when they were serving.

Drake leaned over toward Morales to see what the little drone's cameras were transmitting on the video screen. "After you check out the house and grounds, let's see what his seventy-foot Italian motor yacht looks like."

"This guy's really into expensive boats," Morales said.

"A billionaire's toys."

Morales flew the drone high above the house, moving it slowly from one side of the property to the other, searching for anyone in the shadows.

"I don't see anyone outside," Morales said, guiding the drone to hover outside the bank of floor-to-ceiling windows on the southern wall of the top floor of the house.

"One man's inside at the front door," he said, moving

the drone along the windows and around the windows on the other side of the rectangular structure.

Clearing the top floor, Morales moved the drone down to the windows on the second floor and started back around. Another man stood at the railing of a second-floor deck, looking at Franklin's yacht at his private dock.

Morales zoomed the drone's camera in to get a look at the weapon hanging at his chest. "That's a CZ Scorpion carbine," he said, turning the screen so Drake could see it.

"Franklin's expecting us," Drake said. "Wayne said he hasn't had security before."

"If he has them here, he'll have them at the yacht club. Getting to him isn't going to be easy."

"Check the floor below and then his yacht. I see movement there."

When Morales moved the drone out from the house and dropped it down to hover alongside the yacht, two men wearing white chef coats and black pants were loading cases from the dock onto the aft terrace off the main deck.

"Looks like Franklin's going to party after they leave the yacht club," Drake said.

"If he has security, how will we get to him?" Morales asked.

"We wait until he sends his guests home, then take out his security," Drake said.

Chapter Seventy-Three

DAN NORRIS CALLED Drake to tell him Franklin was leaving the yacht club.

"He's leaving in a black Mercedes S500, ahead of a stretch limousine with twelve people from his party," Norris said. "We think he's taking them to his house for a cruise around the bay in his yacht."

"Copy," Drake said. "Two chefs are getting his yacht ready here for something. Follow him."

"Roger that," Norris said.

"Bring the drone in. Franklin's leaving the yacht club," Drake told Morales.

Flying the drone over the houses along the waterfront when they arrived, Morales found that Franklin's neighbor was leveling the slope below his home and had a small fork-lift parked there. To access the lower area, the fence on the south side had been removed, allowing the forklift to drive down.

They quickly locked the Black Hornet 4 in the trunk of

the Mercedes and jogged along the road to Franklin's neighbor's house. Only one car passed them before they darted into the shadow of the neighbor's house and followed the access lane to the waterfront.

Morales led the way across the soft earth and raised his right fist when he saw the guard on the deck of Franklin's house looking his way. When the guard's head turned away, he moved forward.

A four-foot-tall stone wall with evergreen shrubbery on top separated Franklin's property from his neighbor. Pushing aside the branches at the bottom, Drake saw a flight of steps with outdoor lighting descending to a broad terrace of sand-colored pavers that extended out to the dock. Accent lighting on half a dozen potted palms illuminated the area.

A humming sound from the engines on Franklin's yacht confirmed their intel that Franklin was taking his guests on a late-night cruise around San Francisco Bay.

"See if we can get around the wall down at the waterfront," Drake told Morales.

"Do you want me to look for somewhere over there to wait for him?"

"It might get messy if we can't separate him from his bodyguards and guests when he returns," Drake said. "See if there's a way we can get into his house and wait for him there."

"Roger that," Morales said and moved along the wall to the waterfront.

Drake stayed where he was, waiting to see Morales, when a shadow moved across, suddenly blocking light coming from the terrace.

"There's no one down here," Morales radioed. "I'm out

of sight moving along the retaining wall. I'll see if there's a way into the house."

"Copy that," Drake said, seeing movement on the yacht. "Chefs are taking a smoke break on the aft deck. I'll keep an eye on them."

"Copy."

Drake caught a whiff of cannabis coming from the yacht. The two chefs stood side by side, looking across the bay and laughing.

At least the chefs aren't expecting trouble, he thought.

"Steps leading to the lower floor through a break in the retaining wall," Morales radioed. "I'll check it out."

"Copy that," Drake said, checking his Garmin Tactix Delta watch. If Morales found a way to get in the house, he needed to be ready to move. Franklin and his guests would be arriving soon.

"The steps end at a locked door, don't know what's on the other side," Morales radioed.

"Any other way in?"

"With your help, I can make it to the deck on the second floor."

"Where the guard is?"

"Yes."

"I'm on my way."

Drake edged down the wall, extending out into the bay another six feet as a breakwater, stopping intruders from entering the property from the waterfront. He reached his hands out along the top of the wall, dropped down, hanging by his fingers, and moved to the end of the wall and around to the other side.

When he was above a flower bed bordering the wall, he dropped to a crouch to see if the guard on the deck had seen him. The guard wasn't there.

Drake ran to the retaining wall, looked at the yacht to see if anyone was watching, and sprinted to the steps. Morales motioned for him to hurry.

"There's no one on the deck," Drake whispered and pointed above.

"When this one's down, do you want me to go after the other one?"

"No, come back for me. We'll be inside when Franklin gets here," Drake said, cupping his hands to boost Morales up to the deck.

Morales sprang up, grabbed the deck railing, and vaulted over it.

Drake crouched down and waited.

The two chefs were standing at attention at the aft cockpit when Drake heard voices coming from the other side of the house.

"Hurry," Drake heard Morris say when he got back. "They're here."

He jumped up, grabbed Morales' hands, and hoisted himself onto the deck.

"The first guard's down," Morales said. "The other one's upstairs."

"When Franklin's on the yacht with his other body-guards and guests, we'll deal with him," Drake said. "Then Norris and Sanchez can join us."

"You want me to take care of the other guard?"

"Go ahead, I'll see if Franklin is going on the cruise with his guests."

Drake ducked inside and stood at the edge of the sliding glass door. Franklin's guests were boarding the yacht and taking flutes of champagne from the chefs as they were ushered into the main cabin.

Franklin remained on the dock, holding out a helping

hand to women as they stepped onto the yacht.

Drake watched to see if Franklin was going to board with them.

Chapter Seventy-Four

FRANKLIN SHOOK hands with the last man in the line, who looked vaguely familiar to Drake, and when his guests were onboard, said something to the bodyguard on his right holding a gray briefcase.

When Franklin took the briefcase from him, the bodyguard raised the yacht's boarding steps and remained there to keep anyone else from boarding. The other bodyguard moved to Franklin's side and walked beside him across the terrace.

"Franklin didn't get on his yacht," Drake told Morales. "Take the guard upstairs down. If Franklin comes here, we'll have to move him before his guests come looking for him. I'll tell Norris to be outside when I call him."

Morales ran to the stairs at the back of the entertainment center, and Drake moved to the windows to watch Franklin marching up the steps alongside the house.

"Dan, Franklin didn't get on the yacht," Drake radioed. "Do you have eyes on his house?"

"Yes, we're across the road."

"He might come in here. If he does, we'll take him here and move him. Be waiting outside when I call you."

"The limo is still parked out front. If he gets in, what do you want us to do?"

"Don't let it leave," Drake said. "If we have to, we'll use the limo to take Franklin, his bodyguard, and the driver."

"Roger that."

Franklin was near the top of the steps, and Drake ran after Morales to be ready if he came inside. When they reached the top floor, Morales stood at one side of a massive carved wood double door holding his Taser in the ready position.

Drake moved to the other side of the door and rocked the Taser out of the cross-draw holster on his left hip.

He was straining to hear Franklin outside when the door suddenly opened inward, blocking his view.

Drake saw the gray briefcase swing forward in Franklin's hand, heard him say, "I'll just be a minute," and then heard the sparking sound of Morales' Taser.

"What the…" Franklin started to say when Drake stepped around and held his Taser against Franklin's neck.

"Don't make a sound," Drake said.

Franklin froze and asked, "What do you want?"

Drake hit the PTT button on his radio and said, "Out front, now."

"Who are you?" Franklin asked.

"You'll know soon enough."

Morales had the guard on the ground subdued with flex cuffs on his wrists and ankles and duct tape across his mouth.

Drake took the duct tape from Morales, tore a strip for Franklin, and turned him around.

Franklin glared at Drake and said, "My attorneys will eat you alive, Drake."

"After the FBI and the DOJ finish with you, they're welcome to try," Drake said, slapping the duct tape across Franklin's mouth. "Let's go."

Morales opened the door and stepped outside. "All clear."

Drake grabbed the collar of Franklin's dinner jacket and pushed him forward. Sanchez was standing at the curb, holding the rear door of a white Mercedes C300 open.

"Marco, I'll go with Franklin," Drake said. "Get the other Mercedes and meet us at the airport."

"Roger that," Morales said, starting to jog down the road to the park where they left the car.

After Drake told Norris where they were going, no one spoke again until they stopped in front of the Signature FBO at San Francisco's International Airport.

"You have a choice to make," Drake told Franklin and tore off the duct tape. "Kate Perkins, Assistant Director of the FBI, wants to know which nuclear power plant the CJNG cartel is targeting. We can discuss that in the privacy of my G280 on the tarmac or in the not-so-private lobby inside."

"Why do you think I know anything about that, or that I would tell you or the FBI anything if I did?"

"Because you're a smart man," Drake said. "When you consider your options, you'll tell us what we want to know. If you cooperate, your lawyers will have a chance to negotiate with the FBI on your behalf. If you don't, we're flying you to D.C., and letting the guy you sold your data analysis to, Jabalí, know that you sold them out. Then we'll sit back and wait for your body parts to be found in some dumpster."

"You're bluffing."

Drake leaned forward and tapped Norris on the shoulder. "Find the pictures Kate sent and hand me your phone."

Norris found the evidence of the cartel's gruesome brutality and handed him his phone.

Drake held the phone to Franklin's face and let him see the pictures.

Franklin looked away after a few seconds and said, "All right, let's go talk. But know this, Drake, when this is over, I will destroy you."

"Right," Drake said. "Be a gentleman on the way to the plane. You don't want a video of you being tasered going viral for your cartel friends to see."

Franklin walked quietly through the FBO lobby with Norris on one side and Drake on the other. Outside, the G280 was waiting with the airstairs down.

When they were on board, Drake walked behind Franklin to the rear cabin and told him to sit in the same seat Braxton had been in on the flight from Vermont to D.C.

"I have too many questions and not enough time for you to answer them," Drake said, sitting across from Franklin. "The FBI has only one question, and your answer will determine if you're indicted as a terrorist or not. Marcus Braxton is with the FBI in Washington. He admitted delivering the intel you worked up for the CJNG cartel for a ransomware attack on a nuclear power plant somewhere close to the capital. If you tell us which power plant it is in time to prevent the attack, Kate Perkins won't charge you with domestic terrorism."

"I'm not a terrorist, and you know it."

"You're not a lawyer either," Drake replied. "Acts dangerous to human life that are violations of U.S. criminal law is the definition of domestic terrorism. Aiding and abet-ting the malicious use of software to extort ransom payments from a victim is a federal crime. You're doing both when you conspire with the CJNG cartel to launch a ransomware attack on a U.S. nuclear power plant."

Franklin crossed his arms across his chest and said, "You can't prove any of this."

"We have Braxton's statement," Drake said, "With it, we already have."

Franklin stared at Drake and then looked out the window. "Let me talk to Perkins."

Chapter Seventy-Five

FRANKLIN WAS TRANSFERRED from the PSS G280 to the FBI's private jet, a Gulfstream G550, the following day wearing handcuffs. He agreed to identify the nuclear power plant following a two-hour encrypted video conference with the Assistant Director of the FBI, Kate Perkins, after she promised he would not be indicted as a terrorist. That was as far as she was willing to go, she told him, until the FBI finished its investigation of his involvement with the CJNG cartel.

Drake and his tired team left San Francisco with the sun rising in the east. They stood in line in the galley to enjoy a catered breakfast courtesy of their Director of Special Projects, Adam Drake, thanking them for a job well done.

Kevin McRoberts was ahead of Drake and turned to ask, "We forgot to give them Franklin's laptop. Do you want me to see what's on it before we hand it over?"

"We didn't forget to hand it over," Drake corrected. "I didn't tell Kate Perkins everything I know about Franklin. Look for anything relating to Senator Wayland Morris,

Marcus Braxton, the CIA, and his guests at last night's party."

"Mr. Norris has a video of them leaving the party," Kevin said. "Do you want me to use Clearview AI to identify them?"

"I'm not familiar with Clearview?"

"Clearview AI is a facial recognition service law enforcement uses to identify unknown people from their online images. It won't take long for them to do it."

"Go ahead," Drake said, "And see what you can find about them when you know who they are."

"I'm on it, Mr. Drake, as soon as I finish eating."

Norris stopped with a plate loaded with French toast and bacon and asked Drake, "Did Kate get anything out of Braxton about the drone at our headquarters?"

"She said she'd fill me in when she's done with Franklin."

"I'd like to know where he got it."

"So would I."

Drake was the last one in line. He spooned what was left of the egg and sausage casserole on his plate, picked up the last cup of fresh fruit, and returned to his seat. He was proud of what they'd been able to do by preventing a ransomware attack on a nuclear power plant, but Franklin's involvement with the Mexican drug cartel wasn't what President Ballard asked him to investigate.

The president wanted to know about the collusion between the Intelligence Community and the private sector in a conspiracy to spy on American citizens. Franklin was part of it, as a data broker selling personal data to government agencies, but so were Franklin's Big Tech friends with their social media platforms and America's legacy media. He just didn't know how to prove it.

Drake got up to refill his coffee and saw Kevin carrying Franklin's laptop coming behind him.

"You need to see this, Boss," Kevin said when they reached the galley.

"What?"

"What I found on Franklin's laptop."

"That didn't take you very long."

"He used his initials plus the year he graduated UC Berkeley for a password," Kevin said. "There's a file with your last name. Have a look."

The file was labeled "Drake/Records."

"I thought he might have those," Drake said.

"What are they?"

"Records he's not supposed to have. What else did you find?"

"Two hundred files with initials, probably the initials of people's names. Do you want me to see if I can open them?"

Drake took a moment while he filled his cup before he answered. "Let's leave them alone. Have you identified the people at his party?"

"Not yet," Kevin said. "I'm waiting to hear back from Clearview."

"All right, let me know when you have something."

It was time to talk with President Ballard.

Drake walked to the rear cabin and opened the Signal app on his phone, using its end-to-end encryption to call his commander-in-chief.

"Mr. President, do you have time to talk?"

"My chief-of-staff is waiting to see me, but go ahead," President Ballard said.

"The FBI flew Daniel Franklin to the capital this morning from San Francisco," Drake said. "Kate Perkins persuaded him to name the nuclear power plant in time to head off the ransomware attack."

"I was briefed about that thirty minutes ago. I understand you had a hand in that."

"Yes, sir. I need your advice on something. Kate Perkins has Franklin, but she doesn't have his laptop. I do. I need to know what you want me to do with it."

"Is there a reason you didn't let her take his laptop?"

"There are two reasons. Franklin has a copy of my classified army records on his laptop. If it becomes evidence, the classified records of my missions won't stay classified."

"What's the other reason?"

"Franklin has files on two hundred people on his laptop that we think he uses, like Hoover did, to coerce and blackmail people. I trust Kate Perkins, but not everyone at the FBI."

"What do you want to do with the laptop?"

"I don't know, sir. That's why I called you."

"Franklin will want to know who has his laptop," President Ballard said. "When he finds out, he'll come for it."

"I know that. If I keep it, we might find what we need to expose the extent of the Intelligence Community's domestic spying. If I turn it over to the FBI, it will disappear because they're part of the IC. You asked me to investigate and find everything I could about the government's domestic surveillance programs. Franklin's laptop will help me do that."

"All right, keep his laptop as part of your investigation. I authorized it," the president said. "We'll deal with it later if we have to."

"There is something else we'll need to deal with," Drake said. "Franklin has a copy of my classified army records. I believe he got it from Senator Wayland Morris."

"Can you prove it?"

"Yes."

"Did you discover this as part of your investigation?" the president said.

"Yes."

"Send it to me. I'll make sure he's held accountable for leaking your records."

"Thank you, Mr. President."

"Will I see your report before the new Congress is sworn in next year?"

"Yes, sir."

"Excellent," President Ballard said. "Enjoy Thanksgiving with your family."

"I will. Thank you, Mr. President."

Chapter Seventy-Six

WHEN THEY LANDED IN SEATTLE, Drake returned to PSS headquarters with the team and called Liz.

"Hello, beautiful. We just got in," he said. "I have a couple of things to do before I come home. Do you need me to stop for anything?"

"No," Liz said. "Did you get him to tell you which power plant it was?"

"He did when Kate said she wouldn't charge him with domestic terrorism. She's opening an investigation, I expect she'll charge him with other crimes."

"Are you okay?"

"We're all okay, Liz. I'll tell you everything when I get home."

"Hurry then, Alex missed his father."

Drake opened his laptop and scanned his mail, looking for anything that needed attention before he left for home. Mike Casey's message said he'd be out of the office all day. Stop by tomorrow to tell him what he missed out on by staying in Seattle. Paul Benning's message said to let him know when he had time to approve some changes to the plan for the new PSS training facility in Hood River.

The rest of his mail didn't need attention. Drake picked up his travel duffel from the floor to return his gear to the armorer when Kevin McRoberts knocked on his door.

"Here's the report from Clearview AI on Franklin's party guests," he said. "You'll recognize them. They're all heavy hitters, CEOs, billionaires, and they're on the board of that non-profit with Franklin, The Collective. I haven't had time to do the deep dive on them you wanted."

Drake set his duffel bag down, glanced at the list, and whistled. "America's ruling class, all board members with Franklin. I'd like to know why."

"I'll find out," Kevin said.

"Not today. Take the day off with the rest of the team, Kevin. These people aren't going anywhere."

He wondered what Franklin and his twelve guests were up to. He knew Franklin was a campus radical at Berkeley. Judging by the video he'd seen, the other board members appeared to be about the same age as Franklin. Several were also Silicon Valley tech billionaires. He would leave it to Kevin to find out what they had in common, but he knew it was more than being board members of a non-profit organization with a mission to preserve poster art from the 1970s Free Speech Movement.

If Daniel Franklin was doing business with one of the deadliest Mexican drug cartels, a transnational criminal organization like the CJNG, and the members of The Collective were his friends, they were all dangerous.

Exposing The Collective wouldn't be easy, but he would find a way.

The Story Continues...

vinci-books.com/adamdrakeseries

His fight is far from over.

Adam Drake dismantled the Collective, but now his victory comes with a deadly price: a five million dollar hit on his head. Pursued by lethal hit men, Drake must rely on his Special Forces training to protect his family, and eliminate the threat before it's too late.

Get ready for the next unmissable chapter in the Adam Drake series.

Coming soon…

About the Author

Scott Matthews lives in Oregon, where he met his wife, attended the University of Oregon, and earned degrees in Journalism and Law. He served in the Oregon National Guard for nine years, first as a CBR Specialist and later as a JAG officer.

That's the bare bones of his Bio. The rest of the story is that he got hooked reading Ian Fleming's James Bond novels at an early age and read thrillers in that genre since then. He outlined stories he intended to write for years before he finally sat down and wrote THE ASSASSIN'S LIST, the start of the Adam Drake Thriller series.

He likes wine from Oregon's wine country, Oregon football, fishing and hunting, and following Formula One racing. And, of course, reading thrillers.

If you want to learn more about Scott Matthews and his Adam Drake series, go to www.scottmatthews-books.com and subscribe to his newsletter. It provides information about new releases, bonuses and contests, and other things he thinks might interest his readers. He will never spam you, and you can unsubscribe at any time.

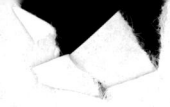